PACIFIC
FIRE

OTHER BOOKS BY GREG VAN EEKHOUT

Norse Code

Kid vs. Squid

The Boy at the End of the World

California Bones

PACIFIC FIRE

Greg van Eekhout

A TOM DOHERTY ASSOCIATES BOOK

NEW YORK

PACIFIC FIRE

Copyright © 2015 by Greg van Eekhout

A Tor Book
Published by Tom Doherty Associates, LLC
175 Fifth Avenue
New York, NY 10010

www.tor-forge.com

Tor® is a registered trademark of Tom Doherty Associates, LLC.

The Library of Congress Cataloging-in-Publication Data is available upon request.

ISBN 978-0-7653-2856-4 (hardcover)
ISBN 978-1-4299-4569-1 (e-book)

Tor books may be purchased for educational, business, or promotional use. For information on bulk purchases, please contact the Macmillan Corporate and Premium Sales Department at 1-800-221-7945, extension 5442, or write to specialmarkets@macmillan.com.

First Edition: January 2015

Printed in the United States of America

0 9 8 7 6 5 4 3 2 1

To Sarah Prineas and her vicious goat, Nutcracker

PACIFIC
FIRE

The golem sat on the motel bed, watching TV with the sound turned off. It was a commercial from Los Angeles, and a man in a cowboy hat was selling used boats. Even without sound, the golem could tell he was shouting. That was his memory of Los Angeles: a lot of shouting and earthquakes and landslides and things burning all around him.

When the TV went back to a news show, he picked up one of the books he'd arranged in a protective circle around him. The wizard had bought it from a thrift shop once the golem told him he knew how to read.

The wizard stood at the window, now, peering out through a crack in the avocado-green curtains. His name was Daniel Blackland, and he was always afraid. Afraid of being followed, afraid of people sneaking up. Afraid of people stealing the golem. Afraid of things he wouldn't talk about.

Outside were a bean-shaped hotel swimming pool, the parking lot, the highway, and the endless black-night desert.

The parking lot only had three cars in it, including the wizard's. Not much traffic came down the road. Still, the wizard said it was too crowded here.

The pool glowed turquoise with lights hidden beneath the water.

"Can I go swimming?" the golem asked. He'd never gone swimming, though he felt at home in water. Most of the motels since they'd fled Los Angeles a week ago didn't have tubs, just showers. But the place where they'd stayed last night did, and he filled it all the way up to the over-flow drain and pushed his hands against the sides to keep himself below the surface. He'd been born in a tank of osteomantic fluid, just a few days before leaving LA, and he missed the way sounds seemed distant and the earth's weight, less harsh.

This was the first motel they'd stayed at that had a pool.

Daniel turned away from the window.

"It's nighttime," he said. "Kids can't swim in motel pools at night."

"Why not?"

"Because the world is arbitrary and capricious. It's a rule."

Daniel had a lot of rules:

Eat when you can.

Use the bathroom when you can.

Sleep when you can.

If someone tries to take you, scream and stab them with your little pocketknife.

And now, no swimming at night.

The golem didn't like the rules, but he liked Daniel.

Daniel had saved his life, and he'd also bought him books and drawing paper and markers. And he was teaching him magic.

Daniel took another glance out the window before letting the curtain go. "Let's try an animal," he said.

The golem put down his book.

Daniel removed a scarred leather wallet from his duffel bag—his osteomancer's kit. He took out a copper lighter, a small bowl made of bone, and a long, glinting needle.

"Ready?" Daniel asked.

The golem nodded.

Daniel stuck the needle deep into the tip of his own right thumb. His face didn't change, but it must have hurt, because he took a small, quick breath. Five red drops splashed in the white bowl.

"What do you smell?" he asked.

The golem closed his eyes and tried to concentrate. He smelled stale cigarette smoke and disinfectant and mildew from the bathroom. He smelled diesel fumes from the highway and chlorine from the pool and the metallic tinge of Daniel's blood. Wizards like Daniel gained magic by consuming the remains of magical creatures, and the golem knew Daniel had eaten kraken and sint holo and griffin and Colombian dragon and the essences of dozens of other creatures. He was brimming with their osteomantic power.

But the golem was full of even more power. That's what Daniel told him, anyway. He'd been grown from the cells of the most powerful wizard in California, the century-old Hierarch, who'd eaten entire banquets of magic. Except the golem didn't feel that power in himself. Daniel said he had to learn to find it first. He had to learn what magic smelled like, what it felt like, so he'd come to recognize it in his own blood and bones and marrow.

Daniel worked some of the dials on the lighter. They sold cigarette lighters in the gas stations, but Daniel's was more complicated than those, with all sorts of little controls. The flame changed color from orange, to red, to green, and then the light faded, even though the heat was still strong enough to warm the golem's face. In the bowl, Daniel's blood thickened and turned black as tar.

The golem shut his eyes and tried to smell magic, and when he could no longer bear to concentrate on what he smelled, he began to pay attention to the slick texture of the blanket, the hum of the alarm clock on the bedside table, the way his ear itched. All the things he was supposed to ignore.

"Okay," Daniel said. "What's in the crucible?"

"I don't know."

Daniel didn't seem upset. He seemed a little bit relieved. "You can't expect to learn this stuff overnight. We'll try again tomorrow."

The golem was relieved, too. Maybe the magic inside him should stay inside.

The golem uncapped his black marker and started working on a drawing. He made an eagle's head attached to a lion's body. He gave it wings and he somehow knew this creature was called a griffin. He wasn't sure exactly what a griffin was, but he understood its essence was speed and flight and rending with beak and claw. He wondered if

Daniel had bled griffin osteomancy in the bowl, or if he'd drawn a griffin because there was griffin in his own body. For some reason, he didn't want to tell Daniel about it.

"Can I go swimming tomorrow?"

Daniel went back to the window. "Sorry, buddy. We're getting an early start. I want to be in the Sierras by sundown. But we might end up camping near a lake, so maybe there'll be some splashing. No promises."

There was only one thing Daniel had promised him, when they were heading away from the city. He promised the golem he'd protect him to his last breath.

That's what the magic lessons were about. Daniel was a thief, and he'd stolen the golem, and people from Los Angeles would come for him, to take him back. They might not take him back alive, but instead they'd cut him into pieces and press his body to get all the osteomantic oils out and remove his bones and grind them to powder. Daniel promised to protect him, but in case he couldn't, the golem had to learn how to protect himself.

"Do you want to see my drawing?" He got up to show Daniel.

"No," Daniel said. He didn't shout, but his tone was sharp, and the golem felt as if he'd been shoved back into the pillows. "Stay away from the windows. Lock yourself in the bathroom. Don't come out unless I tell you to."

"Why?"

"Visitors," Daniel said.

The golem backed toward the bathroom, and Daniel went out to meet whoever was there.

As soon as the flimsy door shut, the little motel room closed in on him like a jail cell.

The golem went to the window.

A single lamp from the motel office cast a yellow glow over the parking lot. At the edge of the light, three men came charging out of the back of a white van. The driver remained behind the wheel with the motor idling.

There wasn't anything remarkable about the way the men looked. One was maybe a little bit tall. Another, a little bit fat. But the way they sped across the parking lot wasn't human. They took long, bounding strides, and they curled their fingers into claws, and their scents pushed through the thin windows. The golem smelled things that reminded him of his drawing. He smelled their speed and their ability to rip flesh with their fingernails. He smelled cold air rushing past sleek fur in flight.

Daniel headed them off before they reached the door.

The golem knew he should do what Daniel told him. He should run into the bathroom, lock the door, hide. But his feet were glued to the floor, and he couldn't remove his hand from the curtain. He didn't want to take his eyes off Daniel, because he was afraid for him, and he was afraid to be without him.

That was only part of the reason.

He also wanted to see wizards fight.

New and more powerful smells washed away the griffin scents as if they were just a few drops of milk in the ocean. There was a deep, muddy, rotten odor of the sea floor. The smell of darkness and crushing pressure. The smell of lightning lacerating the sky. The golem recognized the smells. They were kraken.

Daniel extended his hand. Blinding forks of electricity shot out and struck the three men in their hearts. The men collapsed, twists of smoke rising from charred and bloody flesh.

Another smell blended into the others, but this one wasn't osteomantic. It was just burning meat.

With a squeal of rubber, the van backed onto the highway. Daniel ran after it, but by the time he reached the edge of the parking lot, it was too late, and the van was too far gone. He spent a long time staring after it.

He returned to the dead men and bent over them, smelling them and nudging their pockets with the toe of his boot.

The golem came out to see.

Daniel turned on him. "I told you to hide." From the window, he'd seemed calm, even with lightning crackling over his body. But his face was red and shiny with sweat. His chest heaved.

"I wanted to see," the golem said. It was an honest answer.

Daniel rubbed his face and pushed damp hair off his forehead. Scanning the road, he regained control of his breathing.

"I guess it's for the best," he said after a while. "You should know what you're facing."

The men still smelled of griffin, and the golem had a thought. "Are you going to eat them?" he asked Daniel.

Daniel didn't answer. He knelt before the golem and stared into his eyes, searching for something.

"Do you want to eat them?"

"Yes," the golem said.

"How old are you?"

"I don't know."

He'd become alive inside a tank in the attic of a sprawling house on the side of a hill. He didn't know how long he'd spent in that tank. He didn't know how long it had taken to become him.

"Seven or eight, I'd guess," Daniel said. "I don't know. I'm not really experienced with kids. But you're old enough to hear this." He paused, as if he were about to leap and wasn't sure about the landing. "You're the creation of the worst man I ever met. Maybe one of the worst people who ever was. The Hierarch was powerful, and he got that way by consuming power. He ate the remains of more osteomantic creatures than anyone I've ever heard of. He ate mammoths and dragons and griffins and eocorns. He ate basilisks and seps serpents and hydras. And he ate people. He ate other sorcerers. He ate my own father."

"And then you killed the Hierarch and ate his heart," the golem said.

Daniel seemed very tired. The golem knew he'd barely slept for a week.

"I've had to do things that I wish I didn't," he said. "I'll probably have to do more things like that, to keep you safe. But I don't want to be like the Hierarch. And you don't have to be. You can be your own person. You can be whatever you want to be."

"I don't even have a name," the golem said.

Daniel smiled. He did so rarely, and it looked painful, like he was wincing into harsh sunlight.

"You should have a name, shouldn't you? How about Jehosephat?"

"That's not a name."

"Sure it is. But maybe not for you. How about Binky?"

The golem laughed. "I know that's not a name."

"You're sharp. I can't get one past you. Maybe something from your books?"

The golem liked that idea. "Sam I am," he said.

"Sam you are." He ruffled the boy's hair, and something inside Sam's chest loosened, and he was glad to be with Daniel and hoped to be with him for a long time, wherever they went.

Daniel rose to his feet. "Pack your things and get in the car, Sam. Before anything else from Los Angeles catches up to us."

ONE

Ten years later

The Grand Central Market was the largest floating bazaar in Los Angeles, and for Gabriel Argent, it was enemy territory. With the Hierarch gone, slain by Daniel Blackland, the realm was split up like a ten-slice pizza at a twenty-person party, and Gabriel wasn't friends with the man who claimed the Central Market slice.

Max inched Gabriel's motor gondola around piers, barges, boats, and suspended catwalks, past stalls fringed with looped sausages and hanging barbecued ducks. Merchants on rafts offered every kind of white and brown and speckled egg. Neon signs buzzed with fantasy Chinese scrolls, advertising chow mein and chop suey and cartoon pigs at the Pork Kitchen. The scents of onions and grilled meat and chili peppers made Gabriel wish he had time to stop for lunch.

"You should have a security detail," Max said, maneuvering around a vendor in a flat-bottom calling out a song for boat noodles. In profile, Max's face looked like a scientific instrument, his silver hair trimmed for aerodynamics, his brow providing a protective hood over sharp gray eyes. His nose led the way like the prow of an ice cutter.

Gabriel shot him an encouraging smile. "I have a security detail. I have you."

Max slowed to let a duck and three brown ducklings paddle past the bow. "Everyone else will have a security detail," he said. "Otis will bring his thugs, and Sister Tooth will have her . . . things. I'm not even carrying a gun."

"Bodyguards are a sign of weakness," Gabriel said. "The fact that I'm coming here with only you demonstrates how confident I am. It makes me look bigger."

"That's a lot of pressure to put on me."

"Max, if the people I'm meeting want to kill me, you having a gun won't help. Neither will a security detail. They'll just kill me."

"And this makes you feel powerful somehow?"

"Power is a complicated thing, my friend."

"It must be." Max turned under the arch of a six-story redbrick warehouse and steered the gondola into the waters of Otis Roth's stronghold.

Beneath whirring ceiling fans, dockworkers unloaded goods for distribution across the realm: vegetables and spices, boxed bird's nests for medicinal soup, crates and barrels of osteomantic preparations.

Max's nose twitched. He'd been raised and transformed to sniff out contraband magic, and he still grew excited in the presence of osteomancy.

"Good stuff here?" Gabriel asked.

"Not here. Deeper in the building. Sure you won't change your mind about bodyguards?"

"You seriously think I should?"

Max thought about it for a few seconds. "No, you're right. Security won't save your life. I'd be happy if you told me to turn the boat around."

"Park the boat, Max."

Max killed the engine and guided the gondola into a slip, where they were greeted by one of Otis's muscle guys. He looked like a solid piece of masonry.

"Lord Argent," he said, lowering a ladder to help Gabriel and Max up to the concrete pier. "If you'd allow me to take you—"

Max cut him off. "Who's going to guard the boat?"

"Your gondola will be perfectly safe, sir," the thug said, addressing Gabriel, not Max. "But if you're concerned, I'll be happy to summon someone to watch over it."

"That's not necessary," Gabriel said. But Max wasn't satisfied. He waved over a girl loading an aluminum dinghy with boxes of radio alarm clocks.

She came over, more curious than cautious.

"Do you have a knife?" Max asked her.

She nodded.

"Show me."

She reached into her jacket and produced a butcher knife the length of her forearm.

Max slipped her a twenty. "Anyone comes near the boat, you cut off their thumbs for me, okay? If my boat's still here when I get back, you get another twenty."

She snatched the twenty and made it disappear. "And another twenty if you're more than an hour."

"Good kid," Max said.

The thug squared his architecturally impressive shoulders and looked down at the top of Max's head. "You are guests of Otis Roth. Nothing is going to happen to your boat."

"Max has a fondness for orphans," Gabriel said.

The thug took them deeper into the building, through warrens of wooden crates stuffed with clucking chickens and quacking ducks. Otis's office was a modest room, small, drab, outfitted with a steel desk and battered office chair, upon which sat one of the most influential power brokers in the two Californias. Otis's hair was still the bright orange of a campfire; his eyes, bug-zapper blue. He'd been a TV pitchman and a minor character actor in his youth, and even though he was the biggest importer of osteomantic materiel in the kingdom, he was still an actor who could play your jolly uncle or your executioner without changing costumes.

Blazing and happy, he stood and offered Gabriel a rough, freckled hand.

"Lord Argent, thank you for accepting my invitation."

Gabriel didn't offer his hand in return, because he didn't want to find it hacked off and pickled for sale in one of the market stalls.

"I'm not a lord. I'm director of the Department of Water and Power."

"Ah, just a humble public servant who oversees a vast network of dams, reservoirs, aqueducts, canals, locks, pump stations, and pipes threading into the tiniest capillaries, all laid out in a thrumming mandala of magical energy. You're not some clerk, Gabriel. You're the chief water mage."

"You know Max," said Gabriel.

"Your hound, of course."

"Max is my assistant director, assigned to special projects," Gabriel corrected.

Otis gave Max a nod. "No disrespect intended. I admire men of ability, and Assistant Director Max—no last name?—Assistant Director Max still has the reputation for the best nose in the kingdom."

Hounds didn't have last names. They were recruited as children, imprisoned, osteomantically altered, and trained. Whatever they were before was irrelevant. Max could have chosen a last name after Gabriel freed him, but it would have been arbitrarily chosen, and Max was not an arbitrary sort of man.

Otis's eyes twinkled. "What do you smell now, Assistant Director Max?"

Gabriel was about to put a stop to this, but Max obligingly took in a deep, noisy sniff.

"I smell smarmy."

Otis laughed and nodded, as if he'd plotted the course of this small talk to land exactly here, on this note, at this moment. "Would you like to see my most recent acquisition?"

"I don't see how I can say no," Gabriel said, resigned.

Otis escorted them past the well-tailored henchmen stationed just outside his door, down a hallway lined with more henchmen, and then into a cavernous space of bare concrete floor and concrete pillars soaring to a thirty-foot ceiling. The walls were massive stone blocks, and spelled out on them in black ceramic tile were things like TRACKS

1 AND 2 and old canal names. At the far end of the room was an arched tunnel opening.

"This was the old subway," Otis said. "The cars were so red and shiny they could light up the tunnels, even in the dark. I think Los Angeles lost something when she let the water mages take over the transportation system."

"I don't know," Gabriel said. "You should see the underground waterfalls beneath Pasadena."

Otis took them into the tunnel, their footsteps echoing off the walls. The distance was lit with new fixtures and wiring that did little to dispel the sensation of entering the belly of an ancient, calcified whale. There were no henchmen along the route, which meant Otis didn't fear attack here. More pointedly, he didn't fear Gabriel here.

From the tunnel, they emerged into another station. Gleaming brass chandeliers cast warm light, and in what was no doubt a nontrivial bit of retrofitting, a palatial fireplace crackled where the next tunnel opening ought to have been. Above the fire were mounted the twelve-foot-wide antlers of a *Megaloceros californis,* the extinct giant elk. Most osteomantic bone in Los Angeles had been dug up from the earth and from the La Brea Tar Pits and broken into fragments, ground into powder, heated or cooled and mixed and messed with by osteomancers to leech out their magical essences, and then consumed to transfer those magical essences to whoever ate or smoked them. But these antlers were perfectly intact. Gabriel estimated their value as enough to buy two or three Beverly Hills mansions.

Otis hung them as decoration.

Behind a massive redwood banquet table stood Sister Tooth in full armor and regalia. Twin incisors from a griffin rimmed her helmet of polished bone, which revealed only cold stone eyes and glimpses of white cheeks. Her breastplate came from the single scale of a Colombian dragon. At her hip, she wore a dragon-tooth sword. The rest of her armor came from hundreds of linked teeth, from osteomantic fossils and from the mouths of living osteomancers. She bowed slightly in greeting and chimed with tones that made Gabriel's spine tingle.

Sister Tooth's bodyguards, her *praesidentum,* remained standing in a row behind her as she took a thronelike chair at the table.

Gabriel knew Max well enough to see how all the magic in the room was driving his senses mad. He pulled out a chair for him, but Max shook his head no. He'd look stronger standing. It would also make it easier to run away.

"A bone sorcerer, a merchant master, and a water mage walk into a bar," said Gabriel, claiming a chair. "But aren't we missing a few players?"

There were none of Sister Tooth's rival osteomancers here. No Mother Cauldron. No glamour mages. No representatives from the triads or cartels.

"We're at war," Otis began, as if that explained the absence of others. "And we have been for ten years, since Daniel Blackland killed the Hierarch. No one's in charge, and the kingdom suffers."

"The Hierarch's rule wasn't short on suffering," Sister Tooth said.

Gabriel laughed at the understatement, but Otis pushed on.

"There are no big people left in LA. The big people are dead or moved on. And what's left isn't power. It's not control. It's just people like us now, medium-sized and insecure."

"And fewer of us every day," Gabriel observed. "Your war with the Council of Osteomancers is getting bloody."

Sister Tooth narrowed her eyes at Gabriel. "It's not all due to Otis. The Alejandro drowned in his swimming pool last month. Which wouldn't be so remarkable if the same thing hadn't happened to my head of security."

Gabriel shrugged. "Swimming is dangerous."

Otis folded his hands on the table. "And in retaliation, the Council obliterated La Ballona Dam. How many people died in the flood? And wasn't your Ivanhoe Reservoir turned to sand last month? And your hydroelectric plant at Pyramid Lake burned to a crisp by salamander resin? You don't have to call it a war. Maybe it's just squabbling. Maybe it's just sport. But whatever's going on between our organizations, it's nasty, and it's costing lives and resources. And while we rip ourselves apart with our internal problems, the outside world is noticing. Our borders used to stretch from Bakersfield to San Diego. We've lost territory in the north to Northern California, and in the south to Mexico. We used to consider Japan and China our trading partners. In another few years, we may be their spoils. I'm even hearing of incursions over the Nevada border. However cruel the Hierarch may have been, he was our open paw. Stick a finger too far inside, and he'd tear it off. We need something like that now."

Gabriel poured himself a glass of water, and everyone watched him as if he were playing with a grenade. He was only thirsty. "Otis, if you think I'll accept you as the new Hierarch . . . Don't take this the wrong way, but of all the horrible people I've met, and believe me, I've met a bunch of them, you have to be the fourth worst. I'd elevate you to third worst, but you're relatively easy to kill. And you, Sister Tooth, as Hierarch? You're too hard to kill. No. Not either of you, nor any other individual, nor a new formation of the Council of Osteomancy, and unless you're serious about supporting my proposal for a republic, what am I even doing here today?" He drank. "No disrespect intended."

Otis continued smoothly. No doubt he'd expected the nature of Gabriel's objection, along with its length and pitch. "I'm not proposing a new Hierarch. I'm proposing a triumvirate. The three of us, allied against other rivals, united in mutual interest, and numbered for balance."

Sister Tooth seemed unmoved. "We three are powerful, but even if we joined our resources, we'd still be outnumbered. Our rivals will form their own alliances, and they'll have the power to gore us."

Otis leaned back in his chair. The corners of his mouth quirked in amusement. He'd delivered his patter. Now, for his inevitable trick. "Boys," he called out to the air, "bring in the bone."

It took two forklifts to bring the "bone" from the tunnel.

It was a skull, sleek and streamlined and at least thirty feet long. A high, bony ridge bisected the brow like a sail. The eye sockets were caves big enough for Gabriel to shelter in. It lacked a lower jaw, but the teeth of the upper were fearsome scimitars, built for cutting through griffin hide.

Max put a hand on the back of Gabriel's chair to steady himself. His eyelids fluttered. From his reaction, Gabriel knew the skull was authentic, and richly, deeply osteomantic.

Sister Tooth's white cheeks flushed pink. "Is that . . . a Pacific firedrake?"

"Mm-hmm," Otis purred.

The species had been identified by a single tooth said to exist in the Hierarch's Ossuary. The records that came with it indicated it was a spoil of war, taken from Northern California in the Conflict of 1934. Just one tooth, and the Hierarch's possession of it was the cause of the War of 1935.

Except for the lower jaw, Otis had a complete skull.

"Bribe or threat?" Gabriel asked.

"Neither," Otis said, standing with a flourish. "A proposal. A project. A collaboration. One that will give us the strength we need to overcome any hint, any shadow, any whisper of a threat from Northern California or Mexico or South America or the United States or China or anyone else. A weapon. A tool. A power. All the power we need."

Now it was Gabriel's turn to lean back in his chair, though not with Otis's affected humor. He was genuinely confused. "That's a very, very fine piece of bone, Otis. It's honestly the best I've ever seen. And I'd love it if someone could get Max some saltines, because it's clearly potent enough to make him queasy."

"I'm fine," Max said, his voice rough.

"But even with all the osteomancy packed in this skull, it's not equal to the power of the Northern Kingdom, not when combined with everyone else who might have a problem with us declaring ourselves the three-headed king of Southern California."

Sister Tooth composed herself. "Lord Argent is right."

And now Otis allowed a little of his real smile to break through. It was a cold smile, and, Gabriel had to admit, a very winning smile.

"It is, indeed, a very good bone. And it cost me dearly in treasure and blood. But it's not my only bone. I have in my stores the makings of a complete Pacific firedrake skeleton. As well as bits of tissue. Armor. Even hide. And what I don't have, I can make."

"More confused now," Gabriel said.

"I'll make it plain, then. I can make a living dragon."

"Impossible," Sister Tooth said.

But Gabriel didn't think so. Otis wasn't the kind of man who'd gather the realm's most powerful osteomancer and chief hydromancer in a room and unload an avalanche of bunk on them. He must believe he could make a living dragon.

His need for Sister Tooth was clear enough. She had skill, and she had alliances with other osteomancers, even ones outside Southern California. But what else would it take to build a patchwork dragon? What did Gabriel have that Otis would need?

The answer was, of course, prosaic.

"You need electricity."

"A lot of it," Otis affirmed. "Your wave generators can provide it."

"Bone, magic, and power, and we make Los Angeles strong enough to control this part of the world. I like it. Audacious yet simple."

"So," Otis said, pleased. "We have an agreement."

"The beginnings of one, maybe," Gabriel allowed.

"And Sister Tooth?"

"How can I pass up the opportunity to work with such exquisite magic?"

Otis called for champagne to toast their new partnership. It arrived on a smart silver trolley that had been readied just outside the room. A white-suited henchman was there with a saber to slice off the top of the bottle. There had been very little risk that the bottle would have to be sent back, unopened, or that the henchman would never get to use his sword. There was no chance that the ice in the bucket might melt because the meeting took longer than Otis calculated. Otis knew what he was selling, and he knew his buyers.

The henchman struck the bottle with his blade and celebratory foam gushed out. Otis filled the glasses and raised his own.

"We have a lot of work to do, but before we get too ahead of ourselves, there's a critical resource we'll need." He paused, and Gabriel counted out the beats. "To Daniel Blackland," Otis said. "And the treasure he stole."

D aniel pricked his finger with a copper needle and squeezed two fat drops of blood into the Salton Sea. He gazed across the water and waited for the feeble waves to carry his blood away. The water shimmered blue in the distance, all the way to the craggy desert hills on the far shore, but closer up, it was oily brown, like thinned gravy. It stank of chemical fertilizer and bacterial decay. This was not a pleasant place. Few people came here. Which made it perfect for Daniel and Sam.

His shoes crunched along the white-sand beach, which wasn't actually sand, but the pulverized skeletons of millions of dead fish. Once, this had been a resort for aristocracy, a Palm Springs with water, an oasis in the middle of the Mojave Desert. Marvelous palaces used to line the shores. Luxury barges plied the waters. Barons and baronesses sipped martinis while being fanned with palm fronds like pharaohs. Now, the sea was a slow-motion disaster.

The water splashed as the fish fed on his blood. When

he arrived here a few weeks ago, the fish were just descendants of the tilapia and corvina tanked in for sport fishing, but over the course of days he'd fed them small bits of osteomancy and transformed them into grakes. The predatory fish had a taste for magic and provided a decent alarm system if anyone came across the sea for him. And if he stayed here long enough, someone surely would. There'd be bounty hunters and leeches and hounds and duelists and assassins and kidnap specialists. There'd been enough of them in the ten years since he'd fled Los Angeles that he considered them inevitable. Their corpses littered roadside ditches and parking lots all across the land. Much preferable to know they were coming and move on before they got too close.

He was just about to turn from the shore when the whine of a boat engine drifted across the water. He spotted a small craft several hundred yards out. Nothing unusual about that—morning anglers still set out from the trailer parks scattered along the shore. But this boat was surrounded by a glimmer of copper-amber sunlight winking off disturbed water and churning fish. The grakes smelled magic.

As the boat drew closer, Daniel made it out to be an open inflatable of the sort commandos used for amphibious assaults. The man steering it wore a blue windbreaker, and his single passenger wore a tan suit. Clearly, not out for tilapia.

Daniel decided to kill them before they reached shore. Blue sparks snapped beneath his fingernails.

The man in the tan suit stood in the boat and waved both arms over his head.

It was Gabriel Argent.

Daniel kept the kraken electricity in his hands.

As the boat approached, he noticed that Argent's hair had thinned a little over the last ten years, and the lines in his face deepened, but he looked healthy and prosperous. Power seemed to agree with him.

The man steering the boat was his hound.

Daniel allowed them to fetch up on the beach, and the hound, Max, tossed over a barbell weight to anchor the boat while Argent walked carefully along the hull and leaped to the beach, managing not to get his expensive loafers wet.

"It's been a while," Argent said, offering a handshake.

"You don't want to do that with me," Daniel said.

Gabriel looked to Max.

"He's charged with kraken storm," said the hound.

Daniel let some tiny blue arcs of electricity dance between his fingers.

Gabriel pointed to his DWP lapel pin. "It's a bad idea to attack the director of the Department of Water and Power while he's standing next to seven and a half million acres of water. Besides, if I meant you harm, I wouldn't have dumped three ounces of hippogriff-infused tea in the water to warn your fish."

"Let's not be the kind of people who talk to each other more than necessary, Gabriel. What do you want?"

"Where's the treasure?"

"Safe, and none of your business."

Argent gazed up at the sky, uneasy. "Can we talk indoors? Some of the LA osteomancers have been working on crows for aerial surveillance."

Daniel hadn't been aware of that. It was a disturbing but useful thing to know.

"Thanks for that," Daniel said. "We can talk in my trailer."

He took Argent and Max through the dead neighborhood of Bombay Beach. Other than the occasional rusted soda can or discarded television, the timber frames and crumbling foundations of destroyed homes were all that was left of the housing development. Grim faced, Argent took in one of his department's most conspicuous failures. The desert was never meant to have a permanent, inland sea, despite his predecessor's engineering and magic.

The raked earth around Daniel's trailer was undisturbed, as were Daniel's osteomantic wards. It had taken Daniel weeks of effort and pain to draw enough fire magic from his bones to craft them, but he'd done good work, and any sorcerer or magic-charged lackey who crossed a ward would die in a swirling inferno.

The trailer was a 250-square-foot box. The only furniture was a pair of camp chairs, inflatable mattresses, and sleeping bags. Duffel bags sat near the door for a quick escape.

Max took in quick, short sniffs, analyzing residue magic in the walls and fibers.

"Home sweet home," Argent said.

"Just for the last few weeks."

"That's a long time for you."

"My truck broke down. The lady who runs the café down the road took me on as a cook and I stuck around long enough to rebuild the engine. I was about ready to head out again. Now it'll be sooner, since you found me and I don't want you knowing where I live."

Argent looked a little sad. "I'm not your enemy, Daniel. My mother was an osteomancer, like your father. She was killed in the Hierarch's purge, like your father. Her magic and her body were consumed by the Hierarch, like your father's. I successfully acquired power, and so did you."

"And you used yours to become one of the great dark powers of Los Angeles, and I take occasional work as a short-order cook. What do you want, Gabriel?"

Argent fingered the brocade curtain. He seemed nervous. He'd taken a risk coming here.

"I met with Otis a few weeks ago."

"Was he alive at the end of the meeting?"

"I'm afraid so."

Daniel sat in one of the camp chairs. "Then it wasn't a good meeting."

"He's building a Pacific firedrake. A living one."

Daniel laughed. "Shut up."

"A living dragon out of patchwork pieces. I've seen the skull, and part of a wing he acquired from a dig in Siberia, and a sample of pyromantic essence. Max analyzed it and declared it authentic."

"I don't care what Max smelled; you can't make a living creature out of old parts. It's called osteomantic revitalization. It's the highest expression of the art. The absolute pinnacle. But it's a dream. My dad spent years on it, and he didn't even make a dent."

"Otis partnered with Sister Tooth," Argent said, undiscouraged, "and a number of Northern California osteomancers, some defected, some abducted. I'm sure he also has some shadow partners I don't know about. I'm providing him with power for a facility on Catalina Island where they're building this thing."

"That's sweet of you. What do you get out of it?"

"Ostensibly, I get to rule Southern California with Otis and Sister Tooth as one third of a new Hierarchy."

"Then when you come up dead, Max will only have to narrow down the suspects to two."

The hound, who had been busying himself by sniffing the perimeter of the carpet, seemed to find this funny. His grim visage broke into the beginnings of something that, with work, might be developed into a smile.

"You know I don't want to be the Hierarch," Gabriel said. "The only reason I'm still in charge of Water and Power is because I haven't figured out a way to give it up that won't leave the kingdom dry, drowned, and dark."

Daniel could have become the new Hierarch himself, if he'd wanted it. But like Argent, his ambitions didn't run that way.

"Then what *do* you get out of it?"

"I get inside position on the project. I get to help make sure Otis never gets possession of a weapon of mass destruction."

Daniel stood up. "Well, that's a relief. Obviously, Otis

shouldn't be running around with his own firedrake. Looks like you've got your work cut out for you."

"Show him the papers," Gabriel said.

Max handed Daniel a diplomatic pouch. He wouldn't have opened it, but it weighed more than papers should, and he liked to know what strange things had been brought into Sam's general vicinity. He unclasped the pouch and tried to cram his eyes back in their sockets. There were stacks of paper currency and rolls of gold and silver coins.

"A bribe?"

"Don't get hung up on the cash," Argent said. "Have a look at the documents."

"There's got to be at least twenty-five thousand bucks here, and you're telling me not to get hung up on the cash? Have you seen how I live? I'm not exactly bathing in doilies and caviar candles."

As Daniel continued to mutter about the squalid state of his life, he leafed through the rest of the materials. "Plans, diagrams, sentry posts, schedules . . . You must have some very efficient spies."

Gabriel said nothing.

"So you're providing electricity. That seems like an underutilization of a great water mage."

"The power is just Otis-style pretense. My involvement is merely a tacit agreement that I won't sink Catalina with a tidal wave."

Daniel eyed him skeptically. "You can't make tidal waves."

"No, I can't. But there was a storm three years ago. It destroyed half the Port of Long Beach."

"Yeah, saw it on the news. That was you?"

"No, but I took credit for it, and now Otis thinks I can make tidal waves."

"God, I miss Los Angeles like I miss chicken pox." He tried to hand the pouch back to Argent, but Argent left it hanging between them.

"Listen, Gabriel, I'm not kidding, my dad tried to make a living griffin. The Hierarch gave him the best tools and materials, no expense spared. My dad spent fourteen years of his life and a thousand times more money than you've got in this pouch. You can sew together all the bones and skin you want, and you can kettle-brew some semblance of dragon blood, but all you're going to have at the end is an impressive piece of taxidermy. You need a vitalizing force. You need a source of coherent osteomantic energy equal to the creature you're trying to bring to life. In the case of a Pacific firedrake, it'd take a power equivalent to the Hierarch himself."

Argent only arched his eyebrows and waited until Daniel got it.

"The treasure?"

Argent nodded. "A source of coherent osteomantic energy equal to the Hierarch. Exactly equal. If you think you were hunted before, that was nothing. You're not just facing the usual nuisances anymore. Now Otis and Sister Tooth are united against you. You've got a whole new concerted effort to find you, kill you, and take the treasure."

Daniel looked out the window, across the road, across the ruins of Bombay Beach, out to the sea. The waters were calm and empty, broken only by a squadron of pelicans soaring low in search of prey.

"Okay, Gabriel, thanks for the heads-up. Good luck with Otis and the firedrake."

"Daniel—"

"That was your cue to get back in your boat and putter home."

"You know I didn't come all this way so you could bury your head in a hole. The firedrake is your problem."

"Keeping the treasure safe is my problem."

Argent rubbed the bridge of his nose, as if he were developing a sinus headache. The chief water mage wasn't used to having to persuade people. Usually, he could get what he needed by turning a valve.

"Do you have people you love in Los Angeles?"

Daniel didn't think he meant that as a threat, but he didn't answer.

"If Otis and Sister Tooth get the dragon online, they'll use it to make war. They'll make war on Northern California. They'll make war on Mexico. Maybe even on the United States. And they'll make war against their own rivals in Los Angeles. You know the bombs the U.S. has? Imagine them in Otis's hands. Thousands will die. Maybe millions. You ate half the Hierarch's heart, and you have at least half the responsibility to keep the kingdom from burning to ash. If you won't do it for the kingdom, do it for your friends. They'll die in the same flames and earthquakes."

Argent set the pouch on one of the camp chairs. Daniel stared at it, not sure why he wasn't picking it up and throwing it at Argent's head.

"The dragon goes online in fourteen days. Fourteen days to keep Otis from having his very own apocalypse engine. You've got all my intel. The cash is for supplies and operating expenses. Don't try to contact me. Don't visit my office. If you need to get my attention, just over-water your lawn and I'll be all over your ass."

"That's not funny."

"Max thought it was."

"No, I didn't," said Max.

Daniel kept looking at the pouch, even after the water mage and the hound crossed the road and picked their way back to the beach, and their boat was just a thin white wake dissolving into the sea.

S am was in a lot of trouble. He was supposed to be in Bombay Beach, washing dishes at the café, but he'd ditched the job, ditched the wreck of a town, and ditched Daniel.

Taking off from the job wasn't such a huge violation, since he'd gotten permission from Faith, the owner. She'd even let him borrow her pickup truck, which, unlike Daniel's, was capable of moving backward and forward and stopping without sounding like a horse giving birth to a sack of gravel.

From the passenger seat, Valerie pointed into a field. "Park there."

Sam did as he was told. He would probably do anything he was told, as long as Valerie was the one telling him.

She got out and Sam followed. Mounds of lumpy gray mud rose from the earth, some as high as five or six feet. Steam vented from craters, and every several seconds a mound would erupt, sending rivulets of mud down the sides.

"Well, what do you think?" she asked.

"I've never seen an actual, active volcano."

Pretending to give the surroundings a 360-degree appreciation, he performed a quick threat assessment: no other people, no other vehicles in sight. To his back, a few hundred yards of low scrub brush. Not much place for anyone to hide.

On the opposite side of the field sprawled a shut-down geothermal plant. This, Sam didn't like. Anyone or anything could be lurking in the maze of rusted pipes and tanks. But to get close to him, they'd have to come over the high chain-link fence surrounding the plant, or come through the gate, which was shut with heavy chains and a padlock. Sam would have plenty of warning.

He took a deep sniff and smelled no magic.

The place was safe enough for a first date.

"Okay, technically, these aren't volcanoes," Valerie said. "I might have lied a little when I said I was going to show you volcanoes. These are just mud pots. Telling someone you're going to show them mud pots isn't as impressive as telling them you're going to show them volcanoes."

"You don't have to worry about impressing me. You're impressive enough."

Was that flirty or just lascivious? Sam worried. He didn't talk to girls much. He didn't talk to anybody much. And when he did, most of the conversations consisted of things like "Coffee, black, to go" or "Is there a public restroom?"

Up until this point, Sam had thought the date was going well. Not that he had experience upon which to judge. He wasn't sure where people his age went on dates or what they did. But there were no theaters, malls, clubs, or restaurants other than Faith's café around the Salton Sea, so not having a baseline for normal might not be too much of a handicap in these parts.

And so far, Valerie seemed as happy and interesting as she'd been when he met her yesterday. He saw her coming out of the grocery with a bag of bread and dry pasta and eggs, just as he was going in to buy a little bag of donuts. The first thing that struck him were the freckles on her nose, and then her blue eyes, and then all her nice contours. In a desperate bid to start a conversation, he asked her for the time.

There was some fumbling with her grocery bags that he skillfully helped her resolve as she checked her wristwatch. After five minutes they knew each other's names, and Sam knew that, like him, she was new in town, living in Niland with her mom, and that she and Sam shared a hatred of this remote, desolate place.

A day later, here they were, out on their first date.

It probably wasn't a date. But Sam chose to think of it as one so, if he should die today, he wouldn't have gone through his entire life without ever having gone on a date.

"Come on."

Valerie led Sam into the field. Cracks ran through the dried, putty-gray mud. It got gloopier as they came close to the mounds, splattering his shoes and the cuffs of his jeans.

"It comes out in the wash," Valerie assured him, her own shoes sinking in mud over the laces.

That was good news. He could do laundry when he got back to Bombay Beach while Daniel was working at the café. He'd be in enough trouble for taking off without telling Daniel; he didn't also want to explain how he'd gotten volcanic mud all over himself, because then he'd have to talk about Valerie, how he met her, who she was, and everything he'd revealed to her. Sam didn't want to hear another stranger-danger lecture. In Daniel's mind, the only safe person was a dead person, and he even had suspicions about some of the dead.

"Watch your step," she said, climbing the slope of a mound. He followed her to the top, more mud slopping over him. A crater the breadth of a laundry basket vented steam and gurgled. Globes of mud inflated and burst.

This was one of those places where the thin skin of the earth broke open to reveal secrets from below: long-buried creatures, fossils, essences of magic, osteomancy. Daniel would always tell Sam when he smelled magic. He would suck it in through those thin nostrils of his, tilt his head back in his smug and superior way, and say, "Colombian dragon, remarkable for its armor plating. Its essence imparts imperviousness." Or "Monocerus, for speed and brute force."

Sam didn't have his nose. He snuck a deep sniff and smelled only sulfur and Valerie's shampoo. It was enough.

She wiped her palms on her thighs. "So where are you from? I mean, originally."

He automatically began to recite the current version of the cover story Daniel had devised. "San Diego. My dad took off when I was a baby and I never knew him. My mom died two years ago. Ovarian cancer." He'd learned that if you blurted out blunt details, people would have questions, but they'd usually be the ones you were prepared to lie about.

"I'm sorry," Valerie said, with such apparent sincerity that Sam felt like a complete heel for giving her nothing but fictions.

"Thanks. It sucks, but, you know."

She nodded, as though she did.

"So I'm just traveling around with my uncle. He's kind of a tramp, but he's okay. We don't stay anywhere very long."

She was gazing down into the crater and he couldn't see her face.

"What about you?" he asked. "Studying volcanology, or just really into mud?"

She was from LA, she told him, the San Fernando Valley, mom and dad divorced, dad a shit who stopped sending money, mom out of work, friend had a house she wasn't using in Niland, ergo, living there now.

"What about school?" he said.

Sam had never attended a regular school. For him, school was books scavenged from wherever, and lessons from Daniel. The idea of school seemed exotic and scary and attractive.

"There's a high school down in Brawley," she said. "It'll probably suck, but it's got to be better than mud and dead fish. I kind of figured that's where you'd be going. We could be the new kids together, bonded by our outsider status, reviled for not being cool while secretly being cooler than everyone. Maybe there'd be some deep, dark secret being covered up by the community, and we'd be the ones to solve it."

She smiled sadly, and Sam's heart felt like it was swimming in his chest. Were her lips extraordinarily beautiful? Maybe they were just regular, unexceptional lips. Maybe every girl standing so close and crafting a future that included him had those lips.

He was in love with her, which did not surprise him, because she was pretty and verbal and because he'd been in her presence for over half an hour. Half an hour was not even close to his falling-in-love speed record. There was the girl he'd made out with for two minutes behind the truck stop in Lebec. And the one who'd waved at him through the window of her family's car outside Bakersfield. He didn't know her name, but he thought of her as Darlene when he closed his eyes.

"Maybe me and my uncle will stay longer," he said. "Maybe I can enroll. I've never solved a mystery before, but I'm a fast learner."

Sometimes a wish spoken aloud could be a lie, and this was one of those times.

"You got some mud on your face." She brushed her fingertips over his cheek, and her lips parted, just slightly. He was crazy to have ever wondered if her lips weren't the most beautiful lips he'd ever seen. He planted his feet to make sure he wouldn't slip down the side of the mud pot, closed his eyes, tilted his head, and moved his face closer to hers.

"Sam!"

The familiar voice came from the roadside, where Daniel stood next to the sad pickup. There'd been no engine noise, no crunch of tires rolling up to park, no door slam. Maybe Sam had been too distracted to hear it. Or maybe Daniel had expended some meretseger magic to dampen the sounds of approach.

The expression on his face was calm, but that meant nothing. Daniel could keep any amount of sorrow or fury from showing when he wanted to.

"Your uncle?" Valerie asked.

Sam grunted. "Let me go see what he wants." He half climbed, half slid down the mud pot.

"I didn't mean to get you in trouble," Valerie said.

He stopped and turned to look at her, standing at the top of a runny, muddy mound like some triumphant explorer. He knew almost nothing about her, really. Maybe they didn't have enough in common to sustain a friendship. Maybe they'd get bored of being school chums and they'd drift apart and things would trickle into awkward waves and nods as they passed each other in the hallways.

And even that would be okay, because it was better than nothing.

Sam crossed the field over to Daniel, and Sam saw the way Daniel looked him over, assessing him to see if he was okay, if he was injured.

"I'm fine," Sam said, waiting for Daniel's anger to flare. He'd gone off without telling Daniel where he was going or who he was with. He'd put himself in danger of attack and abduction from leech gangs and worse.

"I'll be home in a couple of hours," Sam said.

"We're leaving."

"Just like that. Again."

"Afraid so."

"Give me two hours."

Daniel shook his head sharply. "Now. Treasure hunters are coming, and not the usual sort. Your bag's already in the truck."

So, back to measuring life by the rotating digits of an odometer.

Daniel wasn't just interrupting a kiss. He was slamming the door on a life that Sam could almost touch, one that promised more than coin-op showers at truck stops and hoping the motel had a swimming pool. A life that included the alien but attractive concept of friends.

What made Sam most bitter was knowing that Daniel was right to do so.

Valerie came down from the mound and began picking her way across the field toward them.

"Who's your friend?" Daniel asked.

"Her name's Valerie. Met her at the grocery. Didn't tell her anything she shouldn't know."

"I have to fog her with lamassu."

"No, you don't," Sam whispered, sad and angry and a little desperate. "I said I didn't tell her anything."

"I believe you. But I don't want her to be able to tell anyone what kind of car we drove off in, or which direction we were headed. And the less she can say about you, the better."

The lamassu was an extinct winged lion from the Fertile Crescent. Its fossils carried psionic properties, and if Daniel exuded it from his pores and touched Valerie, her memories would become confused. She wouldn't remember Daniel. She might not remember anything about this morning, or about Sam.

All Daniel needed to do was touch her.

Arriving at Sam's side, she stood close, a maddeningly intimate distance, and took his hand. Her grip on him was cool and firm, and she directed a frank, challenging gaze at Daniel.

No, there would not have been awkward passings in the hallway. She would have been a good friend. She would have been an ally.

"Aren't you going to introduce me?" Daniel said.

"Valerie, meet my uncle," Sam said, becoming an accessory to poison.

Valerie let go of Sam's hand and offered it to Daniel, and Sam said nothing when Daniel gripped her hand and shook it.

THREE

Sam watched sun-bleached houses and stunted palms blur past as Daniel sped through the town of Thermal in the stolen pickup. The truck belonged to Faith, the café owner. She'd given Daniel and Sam jobs and a good bargain on the trailer and had generally been kind and decent to them, and Daniel stole her truck because they needed a more reliable vehicle than their own limping junker. He'd left three thousand crowns in the café's till from Gabriel Argent's funds and insisted it was not theft, but merely an involuntary trade.

This was Daniel, in his own way, acknowledging he'd done something awful. But not apologizing for it.

And Sam saw it was necessary. This was definitely a bug-out situation—the visit from the water mage, the news about Otis and his collaborators and the patchwork dragon, and their intention to use Sam as the osteomantic engine to drive it. Obviously, they needed to flee their home on the Salton Sea, such as it was. Obviously, they needed a new truck. Obviously, Daniel had to wipe Valerie's memories of Sam, before she acquired too many.

But Sam was still furious with him. And he hated being angry at Daniel, because it always left him feeling teen-angsty and sullen.

To keep himself from brooding, he went about the business of taking inventory of the truck's glove compartment, standard operating procedure whenever they acquired a new vehicle.

"Sunglasses. Pack of mints. Map of Imperial County. Fishing license. Tire gauge. Flashlight. Tampon. First-aid kit with nothing we don't already have. Three dimes, a nickel, six pennies, a stray aspirin."

Daniel checked his mirrors for signs of anyone following them. He peered up to the sky for spying birds, which seemed paranoid to Sam until Daniel told him about the possibility of osteomantically altered crows.

"We'll mail Faith's junk back to her first chance we get."

"And we're going to mail her more money, right? A lot more?"

"No. We'll need the money." Daniel's tone didn't invite question.

"What for? Twenty-five thousand is a windfall."

Daniel checked his mirrors again. Another skyward glance. "Operating expenses and supplies."

It took Sam a few seconds to understand what Daniel meant. He wasn't talking about gasoline and motor oil and cheap loaves of white bread from gas stations. He wasn't talking about splurging on a motel with a working hot-water heater.

"You're taking a job from Gabriel Argent?" Sam's heart pumped at the very thought. When he was younger, he'd begged Daniel for stories about his days as a thief, sneaking through osteomancers' strongholds and stealing magic with his little band of accomplices. Daniel always growled disclaimers that these weren't meant to be fun stories, that most of the time he'd been scared, and sometimes he'd gotten hurt, and sometimes he'd lost people he loved, and that he'd been tricked and manipulated into pulling these heists. But by the time he got to the end of the tales, he'd made them sound exciting and wonderful. They became Sam's bedtime stories.

"I'm not doing it for Argent," Daniel said. "It's just something that's got to be done. For a lot of reasons."

The reasons were clear enough. The firedrake sounded scary and important. Deleting it from the world was fine with Sam.

"You have a scheme?"

"The start of one. I've got some old friends with an airplane, and I think I can get a nighttime flight to Catalina without paying them all of Argent's money. And I'll need some bone to destroy the firedrake."

"Okay, then. Where's our first stop?"

Daniel didn't answer. And then it struck him. Sam wasn't going to be a part of this. He wasn't going with Daniel. He was going to be shunted off to hide somewhere while people did things and the world spun around and around.

He was mad at himself for the few seconds in which he allowed himself to believe he could be alive.

"I'm leaving you at one of the Emmas' safe houses, and—"

"No."

"—you'll be safer with them than you are with me right now—"

"No."

Daniel sighed. "Listen, I'm really not trying to be a jerk about this. I know you're strong. I know what's in your bones. And you've been training. Your skills are coming along. Don't think I haven't noticed. You're on your way to becoming one of the most powerful osteomancers in the country. Which is no gift. I'd rather you be a regular kid. I'd rather you'd gotten to go to the prom with Valerie, and college, and did something nice and fulfilling with your life."

"You'd like me to be a nobody," Sam said, loathing the whine in his voice.

"I'm not going to keep you on the road forever. There'll be a time when we can settle somewhere. Not LA, but maybe somewhere like Tahoe, someplace where the border gets kind of squiggly and nobody's really in charge. I know it seems like forever. But if I engineer this right, I can reduce forever to weeks. I can wipe the biggest threats to you off the face of the earth. That's Otis and the Los Angeles osteomancers. They think a firedrake is going to be their weapon. But what they're building on Catalina is a bomb, and they're sitting on it."

"And you're going to do all this alone." *Without me,* is what Sam meant.

"I'll bring a small team," Daniel said. "Moth. Maybe Cassandra. Maybe Jo Alverado."

"Getting the old band back together." Sam loathed himself even more. He was being a kid.

"We need to fuel up," Daniel said, ending the conversation. A gas station shimmered in the heat mirage a half mile down the road. Open or closed, they'd get gas, and if there was a store, they'd get some water and anything else they needed. Maybe they'd even leave some money, though Daniel might decide to keep every remaining cent for his grand dragon-slaying adventure.

As they approached, Daniel opened the air vents and cracked his window to smell for magic. Sam did his part, taking note of anything along the roadside that seemed weird or out of place—motorcycle tracks leading behind a boulder, uprooted bushes placed together for cover. But the gas station was on a desolate stretch of highway cutting through sandy soil, peppered with knee-high creosote and rocks no larger than bowling balls. The gas station itself was just a stucco hut, a portico, and two pumps. Between the gas station and the tan ridge of cliffs paralleling the road was about two miles of nothing.

"No stranger danger," Sam said.

"Smells okay, too."

The tires crunched on gravel and onto tarmac as Daniel pulled up to one of the pumps. A heavy chain and padlock secured the building's only door. Sam reached behind the seat for the bolt cutters in his bag.

"I'll do this," Daniel said.

Sometimes, when Daniel didn't smell osteomancy and

was certain there were no villainous types lurking about, Sam would be permitted to pick a lock or cut a chain or make a contribution beyond trying to find a clear radio station in the desert wasteland.

"May I at least pump the gas?"

"No. Leave the engine running and stay in the truck until I say otherwise."

"Holy shit, Daniel. At least let me take a leak."

Daniel grabbed the bolt cutters. "When I come back."

Sam wasted a string of profanity that used most of his vocabulary and all the parts of speech as Daniel went to break into the gas station and switch on the pumps.

Sam was grown from the osteomantic cells of a man who'd stood at the top of a mountain with a sword and blasted U.S. bombers from the air. A man whose magic enabled him to rule a kingdom for almost an entire century. And yet Sam needed permission to take a leak?

He stepped out of the truck just as Daniel placed the parrot-beak blades of the bolt cutters around the lock hasp. Then Daniel paused. He sniffed the air, and his eyes widened. "Get back in the truck," he shouted, just as the gas station windows burst outward.

Glass fragments struck the gas pumps and the truck with the sounds of pebbles and marbles. Through the broken windows scrabbled three people, thin as sticks, dressed in clothes that fit like loose bags. Their flesh was dust-gray, hair like broom bristles, and they converged on Daniel.

If it had been Sam in Daniel's place, he might have swung the bolt cutters as a weapon. He might have lashed out with a kick or tried to run away. Daniel was not physically impressive. He was shorter than Sam, and scrawny, and sometimes Sam forgot he was magnificent. As the people or things or whatever they were surrounded him, Daniel stood still, relaxed, his shoulders slumped, a slight belly pushing out his T-shirt. Sam could sense the power building in him, bristling off his skin as he reached into sense memories for the magic his father fed him. There was a blinding flash of white light and a thunderclap so loud it punched Sam in the heart.

While the thunder rolled over the sky into the far distance, the three attackers lay sprawled on their backs, bloody and charred. Smoke rose from the melting rubber soles of their boots. The air stank of brine and dark mud and ozone and crackling osteomancy: kraken storm.

"In the truck," Daniel said, leaping over the bodies.

Sam ducked back into the truck. He shut his own door and reached across the seat to open Daniel's.

Daniel made it several steps before pitching forward and falling on his face. A slender shaft jutted from his back, dead center between the shoulder blades. Two more gray men came out of the dark store through the shattered window. They barely took notice of Daniel's motionless form and came for Sam. Each carried a speargun.

Daniel's instructions were explicit on what to do if Sam were threatened and Daniel incapacitated or dead: *Escape is your first priority*. He was supposed to run away, even if it meant leaving Daniel behind.

Sam slid into the driver's seat. He threw the truck into gear and slammed the gas pedal to the floor. The pickup launched forward with a scream of tires. When he reached the end of the tarmac, he jerked the wheel left and yanked the hand brake. Rear tires kicking gravel, the truck did a 180-degree spin—a perfect bootleg turn, just as Daniel taught him.

There was barely a truck-width's distance between the gas pumps and Daniel's motionless body. The two gray men obligingly stood in the middle. Screaming and trying to keep his head below the dashboard to avoid getting shot with a spear, Sam threaded the needle. The thud of the truck's front end struck the gray men with a sound both sickening and satisfying.

One of the men went flying. He landed a few dozen feet away, resting on his knees with his face on the ground, ass pointing in the air. The other was on the pickup's hood, his head making a bowl-shaped dent in the windshield.

If you can't escape, reduce the enemy's ability to do damage.

Sam hurried out of the pickup. Before attending to the gray men, or even to Daniel, he collected the two spearguns and tossed them in the truck bed. Then he went around to the front of the truck. He grabbed the man sprawled over the hood and threw him to the ground. He was lighter than Sam expected, as if his bones were made of balsa wood. He landed with his head cocked aside, his ear touching his shoulder. Sam was pretty sure he was dead, because it would take a lot of magic to keep him alive with an obviously broken neck.

Before approaching the other gray man, Sam took a calming breath, hoping to bring kraken energy to his own hands. It was hard enough for him during his lessons with

Daniel, when he had time, and with Daniel's patient coaching. He gave up and retrieved one of the spearguns.

The spear tip was a glossy black corkscrew with an iridescent sheen. Not a bone Sam recognized by sight or smell.

Creeping up to the man, speargun raised, he curled his finger around the trigger. He aimed the spear at the man's ass.

"Tell me who and why or you're getting a spear enema."

Sam liked that line. It was a good line. It was the kind of thing Daniel would say, and Sam liked that his voice didn't quaver when he delivered it, even though he felt as if he might collapse into shakes at any moment. And it turned out to be a wasted line. He was just as dead as the other.

Sam ran back to Daniel and dropped to his side.

The spear shaft had fallen out of Daniel's back. With his knife, Sam sliced through Daniel's T-shirt and examined the wound. The only sign of the spear tip was charred skin around the puncture wound. It must have dissolved into Daniel's body, which was bad news, because it meant the entirety of whatever osteomancy it contained was now fully absorbed by Daniel's system.

Sam turned him over. His eyes were open and distant, as though he were staring at something beyond the sky.

"Daniel?"

No response.

"Daniel!" Sam slapped him across the face, hard enough to make his hand sting.

Nothing. His flesh looked like ash.

He pressed two fingers against his throat, certain he'd find a pulse, because he didn't know what to do if there wasn't any. Daniel's skin was dry and cool. There was no hint of a heartbeat.

They had protocols for what Sam was supposed to do if Daniel was killed. He was supposed to leave Daniel behind. Even in a burning house. Even in the middle of a crowded parking lot. Or in a gas station on a desolate highway. He was supposed to get as much distance from the threat as he could, whether that meant driving away in their car or carjacking a passing motorist. He was not supposed to look back.

There was a different protocol if Daniel died in a manner such that Sam had time to deal with his corpse. He was supposed to dine on him and add Daniel's magic to his own.

A grasshopper alighted on Daniel's ear, crawling with its sharp feet across the soft skin of his earlobe. There would be insects and crows, and they would make a meal of Daniel's corpse and be transformed by his magic into things more wondrous.

Sam took in a long, slow breath. When he released it, it came out as a sob.

He snatched the grasshopper off Daniel's ear and crushed it in his palm.

He would heal Daniel.

The Hierarch had eocorn and hydra in his blood, and that meant Sam did, too. The hydra was a polycephalic serpent with such potent regenerative magic that it could lose its head and regrow a new one. And the eocorn, a Pleistocene-era unicorn, was the very essence of renewal.

Sam held up his hand to his face and inhaled. He smelled the road, and he smelled the sour stink of his own panic. He knew there was more than that in him.

Any osteomancer could craft mixtures of bone. A good osteomancer could consume magic and use their body to increase the power of what they consumed. But a great osteomancer could find in themselves the barest trace of magic and bring it to the surface.

Sam imagined green, fungal scents. Mushrooms. Earth. An almost sickening, gelatinous flesh smell. Things that reminded him of starfish and salamanders and a basic, fundamental sense of life. Things that Daniel tried to teach him to dig out from his own cells.

"I am Daniel Blackland's student and the Hierarch's heir," said Sam.

He pried out the largest blade of his pocketknife and drew it across his palm, letting it dig deep. Blood and pain welled up from the cut, and he let it fall into Daniel's parted lips.

Daniel's eyelids fluttered and opened.

He took a shallow breath.

His eyes closed again, like a fading light.

Sam had to drive twenty-five miles until he found another gas station with a phone. In the backseat, Daniel dangled from his shoulder harness. Every several seconds, he would take a ragged breath that sounded like radio static. An awful sound, but good, because it meant he was still alive.

Sam left him in the truck.

A pay phone was mounted on the wall next to a humming ice machine. Sam grabbed the receiver, smearing blood from his palm on the sun-heated plastic. He put it to his ear. Several jabs of the switch hook produced no dial tone.

He barged into the gas station's snack shop, jangling the tin bell tied to the door handle with string. Behind the counter, a bored-looking guy in his late teens slumped on a stool, sipping from a bottle of Mexican Coke. His name tag said CHAS.

"I need your phone."

Chas peered at Sam through long bangs hanging over his eyes.

"There's a pay phone outside."

"It's broken. This is an emergency."

Chas regarded Sam. Then he regarded his Coke. Then he regarded the phone behind the counter.

"Is it long distance?"

Sam vaulted over the counter, sending Chas teetering back on his stool.

"I don't have a key to the safe, man, just what's in the drawer, seriously, just take it."

Sam lifted the receiver. "I'm not going to rob . . . Oh, whatever. Yeah, give me what's in the drawer." Sam might need more cash on the road.

While Chas scrambled to gather up the contents of the cash drawer, Sam dialed a number.

From here, he could only see the top of Daniel's head in the truck.

"Do you want an envelope or a bag or what?" Chas said, showing Sam a meager stack of bills.

"You got a rubber band?"

Chas searched around a bucket of lollipops on the counter. "I got a paper clip. Is a paper clip okay?"

"Sure, fine."

After seven rings, someone finally picked up the line.

"I want to order a pizza," Sam said before the person on the other end could speak.

There was a long pause. Then, a woman's voice: "What's your address?"

That was not a question Sam ever expected to answer over the phone, to a stranger.

"I'm at a gas station about forty miles north of Thermal."

"Toppings?"

That meant *Are you being pursued?*

"Meatballs," he said. "Sliced."

Yes. But current pursuers dead.

"We can't deliver," the woman said. "It'll have to be carry-out."

"Okay. Where's your store?"

"You know I can't give you an address."

"We've ordered pizza from you before."

"No addresses over the phone. But if you can find us,

there's a twenty-five percent discount. Plus double ancho-
vies and chicken."

Twenty-five percent. Double that, and it meant Sam
would be looking for a place about fifty miles away. An-
chovies meant look for a river. Around here, there was no
such thing as flowing water, so he was probably looking
for a dry gulch. And something to do with chicken.

"This is urgent. Can you please just tell me where you
are?"

"Good-bye." A click, and the phone went dead.

Sam put down the receiver.

"Oh, god," Chas said. "You're going to keep me as a hostage."

"What? No I'm not. Why do you think . . . ?"

"Because that's what hostage-takers do. They make de-
mands, and one of them is always a pizza."

Sam plucked the wad of cash from his hand. "You're in
luck, Chas. The pizza place doesn't do deliveries."

An hour of driving with Faith's map as a guide brought
Sam to a cracked-earth wash. Stacked boulders
loomed over sparse scrub. He came to a granite slab with
water-eroded hollows, forming the eye sockets and nasal
cavity of a skull. Half a mile past that, he found a track
cutting through fan palms and scrub oak. With only
some darting roadrunners for company, he drove on until
coming to a weathered rail fence, crowned in coiled razor
wire.

Three low buildings on the other side of the fence stretched in parallel lines the length of a city block. The chicken farm was no longer in operation, but the smell of chicken shit and slaughter clung to the earth. The odor wasn't too strong, but thinking about its source made Sam uneasy. He didn't eat meat, and especially not eggs. The sight of a golden, gelatinous yolk made him think of his own origins, a little nub of a person suspended in an electrified flask deep within one of the Hierarch's workshops.

"You take me to the best places," said Sam.

Daniel moaned softly and took a thin, wheezing breath.

"Hang on a little longer, Daniel. Okay?"

Daniel's head wobbled.

Tucked away from the chicken barns in a stand of piñon pines was a sprawling log house. One of the trees had a tree house in the upper branches. A sniper's nest. Someone was probably up there now, looking at Sam through crosshairs.

Sam got out of the truck.

A copper bell mottled with green patina was bolted to one of the gateposts. He jiggled the string hanging from it, making some rude-sounding clangs.

A woman came down the path from the house and up to the gate.

"Who are you?" she said from the other side of the fence.

She was maybe in her early twenties. Sam took in her frank, gray eyes. Her long nose. The pale skin of her face and her prominent cheekbones.

Sam recognized her. Or thought he did. Like him, she was a golem, in her case grown from the cells of the osteomancer who developed the art of golem-making, Emmaline Walker. How many Emmas were running around in the world, Sam didn't know, but he and Daniel had stayed with Emmas in the past. They ran a sort of underground railroad with safe houses all across the kingdom, dedicated to helping as many other golems as they could.

"I'm the guy who ordered the pizza. I'm Sam."

"And in the backseat?"

"It's Daniel."

Her eyes narrowed.

"You brought his body?"

"He's still alive. He needs help. Hydra and eocorn and someone who knows how to use them."

She did some business on the other side of the gate with bolts and latches and swung the fence open.

"Drive up to the house," she said.

Sam parked in the shade of some trees. Four women came out with a litter and took Daniel inside. They differed in age, hair color and style, sun exposure, musculature, and clothing, but otherwise resembled each other. Feeling helpless, he followed them inside.

Sam had never been in a nicer safe house. In fact, he'd never been in any kind of house this nice. The rugs gave a little squish when he walked on them. The log furniture was draped with blankets and throw pillows, and while the curtains were shut to prevent anyone on the outside from snooping or targeting, lamps cast a warm glow. This didn't feel like a temporary place. It felt like a home.

They took Daniel into a room and eased him onto a bed. A fifth Emma was already waiting there. This one had steel-gray hair and a keener face than the rest, softness hewn away by wear. She leaned over Daniel and pried open his eyelids to examine his pupils. She felt his pulse, smelled his breath.

"We were attacked by some kind of osteomantics," Sam said, handing her one of the bone-tipped spears.

She smelled it and held it up to the light. Feeling Daniel's forehead with ropy, calloused hands, she told one of the other Emmas—the young one who'd met him at the gate—to go fetch her red box.

"I gave him some eocorn and hydra," Sam said. "It seemed to help a little."

"You fed him raw, I suppose? From your own body?" The corner of her mouth rose in a half smile. Every Emma Sam had met wore some version of that smile. There was always something superior about it.

"It's all I had. It's not like we go around carrying a pharmacy."

"You and Daniel can't sneeze without spreading a cloud of osteomancy for miles. You especially, little Hierarch."

Sam ignored the taunt.

"Can you help him?"

The Emma's expression grew kind, which scared Sam.

The Emma she'd sent out returned with the box, and the old Emma dug out several tiny glass vials full of oils and powders. She arrayed them on a tray, and then, from the box, took a stainless-steel syringe the size of a road flare.

"Let her work," the younger Emma said, taking Sam by the arm.

"No, I'll stay with him."

"Do that and you risk being poisoned yourself," the old Emma said. "This room's sealed for fumes. You'll wait outside."

The young Emma gently but insistently pulled Sam to the door. "She'll do everything she can."

Reluctantly, Sam let himself be led away.

FOUR

The Venice Boardwalk was alive and festive on a warm Friday afternoon. Shoppers drifted in and out of the stalls, buying cheap sunglasses and gimmick T-shirts and bongs. Skateboarders slalomed around pedestrians. It was a day for getting henna tattoos on sun-browned legs and for dropping coins into buskers' guitar cases. Gabriel wished he could park himself at a café patio and order a fluffy iced drink and watch the sun set over the blue lifeguard towers. Instead, he and Max crossed the beach to a storm drain outlet exposed by the low tide.

Gabriel showed his identification to a group of LAPD officers milling around a yellow tape barrier. The cops stood up a little straighter and lifted the tape for him and Max to duck under. There were no cops on the other side of the tape, only Gabriel's Department of Water and Power people and a corpse.

Gabriel went to the senior DWP officer, a woman named Tate, who'd worked for him for almost a decade. She wasn't intimidated by him, but she was clearly perplexed that he was here.

"Our chief is a poor delegator," Max volunteered by way of explanation.

"Any trouble from the police?" Gabriel asked Tate.

"A little territorial pissing, but we straightened it out."

Homicide investigation wasn't part of Gabriel's portfolio, but this morning, a red light showed up on his mandala map, and a phone call revealed that lifeguards had found a corpse in the Venice Beach storm drain. Not in itself a completely unusual occurrence, but there were enough circumstances about this one that Gabriel decided to have a look, even if it put law enforcement's noses out of joint. After the Hierarch's fall, the LAPD reorganized themselves as an independent operation. Street-gang warfare and organized crime had declined, but only because the police supplanted them. And the cops weren't reckless enough to declare war on the Department of Water and Power.

Gabriel approached his workers, busy waving sand fleas away from the sheet-covered body. He knelt and peeled back the sheet himself.

The powerfully built man lay on his back, blue eyes open, lips only slightly chewed by fish and bugs. His face was white, washed clean by the sea. A red, dime-sized hole in his forehead looked like a third eye. An execution shot.

He took the man's cold, white hand in his own and spread two of his fingers. A membrane of shark skin stretched between them.

The man's face wasn't relevant to Gabriel's interests, but he found himself lingering over it. He didn't know this man, and few people did. He had no wife or known lover, no children, no living parents. His body would be incinerated and the ashes dumped in a landfill, ugly tasks that were merely small parts of an ugly business. He would never enjoy spending the very large sum of money Gabriel had paid him.

He tucked the sheet back over him.

"You know what to do?" he said to Tate.

She nodded. "Yes, sir."

"Thank you."

Max waited until they were halfway back across the broad beach before he spoke.

"How bad is this?"

So many ways to answer, but Gabriel chose to respond to the practical matters embedded in the question. "It's not bad at all," he said.

"But now Otis knows you sent a spy."

"He already knew. This just confirmed it for him."

"You don't seem worried, either that Otis is on to you, or that you lost an asset."

Gabriel didn't answer. Max was his most loyal servant, and the closest thing he had to a friend, and sometimes Gabriel just wished he'd shut his face.

Asset? He meant a person.

"I guess he didn't have a family," Max said.

"He did. A sister. She's a sophomore at Loyola Mary-mount. Thinks her brother is a commercial diver. Scraping barnacles off boat hulls. That kind of thing."

"Should I have someone arrange a payment?"

"No," Gabriel said. "I'll take care of it."

It was a little ridiculous that the LA's chief hydromancer handle a clerical task, but Max knew better than to argue with Gabriel about it.

Gabriel would type out the check himself. He'd put it in an envelope, and he would address it himself. He would lick the stamp.

It would be a very large check. Because that would solve everything, wouldn't it? It would make it okay that the girl lost her brother. It would assuage all of Gabriel's guilt.

And, yes, of course Otis would be suspicious of him. But he'd be even more suspicious if Gabriel hadn't sent a spy to Catalina.

And when Daniel Blackland got to Catalina Island, he'd need updated, current intel.

Which was why Gabriel had sent two spies.

Yy ou'll sleep here tonight." The young Emma chaperoned Sam to a second-floor bedroom containing an oaken monstrosity with a mattress the size of a storm cloud and four towering posts that Sam imagined might be useful for hanging clothes or perhaps supporting a roof. There was a writing desk, a chair in the corner that served only to make sure the corner wasn't too lonely, and a four-drawer dresser. Sam dropped his duffel on the bed next to Daniel's.

"Here's your intel and money back," the Emma said, handing him Gabriel's diplomatic pouch. "Snuck a peek when you weren't looking."

Sam checked the pouch. Everything seemed intact.

"What name do you go by? Emma?" Most of the Emmas called themselves Emma, which Sam found hopelessly confusing.

"We don't need names among ourselves, but you can call me Em if that helps you."

"Em."

Strange how just giving her a semblance of a distinct name impelled him to look at her more closely, as an individual, not just as a variation on a theme. He may have overestimated her age before, fooled by something in her carriage. He revised her down to maybe a year or two older than him, eighteen or nineteen on the outside. Her hair was dyed blond, with typical-Emma chestnut at the roots. An effort to distinguish herself from the others? Or maybe something to do with one of their paramilitary operations. A very thin scar ran from her temple, along her sharp cheek, and down her neck.

"When you're ready, come down to the dining room and we'll put some food in you," she said.

She left, and Sam stowed the pouch in his safe box, where he kept his papers for various identities. The box was lined with the vertebrae of a sint holo serpent, for the creature's properties of visual confusion. Open it, and it would appear to be empty.

After washing up, he took a circuitous route to the dining room. He counted the doors on the second floor, noted the locations of the covered windows.

Footsteps thudded overhead. Attic space, probably.

Downstairs, as he passed from room to room, Emmas gave him furtive glances. They knew he was the Hierarch's golem.

The Emmas were an industrious bunch, loading first-aid supplies into backpacks, examining maps spread over tables, cleaning rifles.

"Looks like you guys are getting ready for war," he said to an Emma replacing a radio's batteries.

"Just a little raid in Palm Springs. There's a baron trafficking golems across the border."

"Routine stuff for you?"

"Pretty much."

He found Em in the dining room, behind a massive, scarred oak table. The doctor was with her. Sam's tongue stuck to the roof of his mouth when he asked about Daniel.

"He's still alive," the doctor said.

Not "He's going to make it." Just "He's still alive."

She was a shade paler than her sisters and stooped, as if she'd endured years of hard labor. Knowing the fate of most golems, Sam wouldn't have been surprised if she had.

"I've never seen the kind of osteomancy that was used on him," the doctor said. "It's a toxin with elements of tsuchigumo. That's a shape-shifting magic, and it's been altered to make it even more complex. As soon as Daniel's defenses key in on it, it changes shape and begins a new attack." The doctor took a sip of tea. "Now, don't lose hope. He was born strong and raised strong. He's the man who ate half the Hierarch's heart. He has a chance."

A chance of life meant also a chance of death. Sam felt all the blood in his arms and legs drain, a fear response to a world that didn't have Daniel in it. He would gladly surrender his own heart to avoid that.

"Can I see him?"

"Not for a few hours. I want to be certain he's not venting poison before anyone else comes near him."

"Think you can eat?" Em asked.

Eat when you can, Daniel always said.

"Sure."

Bowls of chili were brought from the kitchen. The smells made him salivate, but he raked his fork through his bowl, cautious.

"It's vegetarian," Em said. "No meat here, no eggs."

Sam took a spicy, succulent forkful and closed his eyes in bliss.

They were joined by a couple more Emmas, one in her midthirties and obviously pregnant, and a slightly younger one with, of all things, an eye patch. Sam liked the eye patch, a considerate piece of equipment to help tell them apart. The doctor asked that the door be closed, and Sam understood this wasn't lunch. This was a meeting. Maybe an interrogation.

The questions bypassed the general and went straight for detail, in fine enough grain that it was clear Em had done a thorough reading from her little "peek" inside the diplomatic pouch.

Sam told them everything he knew.

The dragon was being built on Catalina Island, twenty-two miles off the coast of Los Angeles. Previously, the island had been used for ranching, smuggling, and tourism. And, for a time, it had been the Hierarch's island fortress.

The plan, as worked out by Gabriel Argent, called for a small team to take out the facility's power transfer station to create confusion and shut down the pumps delivering osteomantic fluids to the dragon. The team would then travel through the large pipes to the dragon-assembly hangar, neutralize the guards, and destroy the dragon.

"I imagine Daniel's team would be Moth, Cassandra Morales, perhaps Josephine Alverado and the Bautistas," the doctor said.

"He didn't mention any Bautistas," Sam said.

"They're alfalfa farmers, not too far from here. They have a plane they can use for water landings. Mostly they're smugglers working the Baja circuit, but they've done some work with us, too. Lovely couple."

Sam would have to take her word for it.

"Where was Daniel going to acquire munitions?" she asked him.

Again, Sam was at a loss.

"Firedrake scales are nearly indestructible," the pregnant Emma said. "Pacific firedrake scales will be even more so."

Sam wanted to become more of a participant in his own interrogation. "Do you think it's feasible? To sabotage the firedrake?"

Eye-patch Emma took this one up, addressing her answer to the old doctor. "Blackland has the skill set for it. He knows how to break into secure complexes. He's the only person to ever breach the Hierarch's Ossuary and come out alive."

Barely alive, thought Sam.

"And his crew is experienced and skilled, individually and as a team. There's a good chance Blackland might have been able to do it."

Might have. Past tense. Because Daniel might die. And if he lived, he'd be in no shape for adventure.

The pregnant Emma took a thoughtful bite of chili. "I think we should move up the Palm Springs operation. We need transportation infrastructure intact, and who knows what Otis Roth and his collaborators will do if they deploy their firedrake."

The conversation switched to various contingencies and alterations of strategies, all predicated on the idea that the power structure of the kingdom was about to take a major shift, and that instability and possible widespread destruction might result. This all had to do with rescuing golems from various places. No one was talking about a mission to Catalina. No one was talking about sabotaging the firedrake.

"Excuse me," Sam said. "About the dragon?"

The doctor gave Sam a nod of assurance. "As long as you are in our care, no matter who or what Otis sends for you, we will not let you get within three hundred miles of Catalina. You have our word."

"I'm not worried about me. I'm worried about the *dragon*. Who's going to take over for Daniel?"

The doctor poured some more tea for herself. Her movements were deliberate and precise, a wordless lesson in control, in contrast to the disorder Sam had brought to her house. He felt rebuked. The old Emma could *really* pour tea.

"Even with Daniel's background and skills, his chances of succeeding were never more than dismal. If he were caught, they would drill holes in him and drain his blood and lymph and bile. They would strip off his skin and carve away his fat and muscle. They'd wring out all his organs and grind his bones to fine dust. He's a treasure chest of magic. And if you were caught, they'd do the same to you, only they wouldn't let you die. You are exactly what they need for their project, Sam. And as much as I'd hate for that to happen to you, I'd hate it even more if they used you to bring the firedrake to life."

"I'm their best source of magic," Sam said. "But if it's not me, they'll find another."

Her eyes fixed on his over the rim of her cup. "Don't go to Catalina. You'll fail, and you'll die. That's not a prediction."

It felt cowardly to admit it, but she was right. He wasn't the Hierarch, or Daniel Blackland, or even a competent osteomancer. He was just a resource.

"If it's not going to be Daniel or me, then the ball's in your court."

"Daniel's mission is outside the scope of our interests," the doctor Emma said flatly.

"There are golems in Los Angeles. They're as much at risk as anyone if Otis gets a firedrake."

"We'll step up our efforts to liberate as many of them as we can. We'll contact our other cells to do the same. And then we'll evacuate our safe houses in high-population and high-value target areas. This one as well."

"We'd have to do that anyway," Em explained. "You and Daniel being here puts us at risk."

Sam was having a hard time caring very much about the Emmas and their problems.

The doctor Emma finished her tea. "We'll be relocating to the Sierras. It's not as comfortable as this, but it's secure, and we'll be able to take care of you and Daniel there."

Assuming Daniel survived.

Em patted him lightly on the shoulder, like a big sister. "It's really the best option, Sam."

"Sure, thanks," Sam said. "I'm sure that's what Daniel would want."

Sam went back to his room. He took an inventory of his duffel, as well as Daniel's, and transferred things of use from Daniel's bag to his own. He took Daniel's osteomancer's kit, a leather wallet containing a bone crucible, a few envelopes and vials of magic, and Daniel's mechanical torch, a gift from his father. He took Daniel's knife, which was keener than his own. And he checked his sint holo box.

It looked empty, as it was supposed to. But when he reached inside, his fingers landed on nothing. Because it actually *was* empty.

"Okay," he said. "So it's going to be like that."

He spent the next several hours volunteering around the house doing laundry, sweeping, peeling potatoes. While he did, he tried to notice everything. Which doors required keys. Which rooms made people nervous when he neared them. How postures and expressions changed when he spent a long time in a particular corner, pretending to examine a painting, or looking at the ceiling, sniffing. For the most part, nobody seemed to care very much where he poked his nose. The house was secure to the outside, but it wasn't a prison or a bank. The Emmas all trusted one another. They also seemed to have a good relationship with Daniel, which was useful.

After sundown, the old doctor told Sam he could see Daniel.

Part of him thought he'd find Daniel sitting up in bed, sipping chicken soup. He'd constructed a hope that the doctor was just being overly cautious, trying not to inflate Sam's expectations. He'd thought that, when he left tonight, he'd do so knowing that Daniel would be all right.

Instead, he found Daniel lying flat, his skin like wet limestone.

"I guess we're counting on good luck," Sam said to the doctor, lingering in the doorway.

"Good or bad, luck is shorthand for what happens when intention meets chaos. I intend to cure him, and I think Daniel intends to live. Sometimes I forget what this boy's already been through. And how well his father prepared him for it. So, I'd say our side is better armed."

"I tried to heal him with my own magic at the gas station. No luck."

"Don't blame yourself. You're a strong osteomancer."

"I'm not an osteomancer," Sam said. "I don't have the magic."

"You have the Hierarch's magic. You have all the magic."

"Well, yeah, I'm a big fizzy bottle of pop, but shake me up and I pour out flat."

"Better that than the bottle explodes."

The doctor left him alone with Daniel.

Daniel wasn't a big man. Sam had outgrown him by the age of fifteen. He'd seen Daniel tired from long drives, and he'd seen him worn from his burdens. But he'd never seen Daniel weak. The first time Sam ever laid eyes on him was at the Magic Castle. Daniel had been only a few years older than Sam was now, and he'd just brought down a ceiling on the Hierarch. He'd bristled with electricity and exuded waves of redolent osteomancy. He was strong then, and he was strong when he took Sam's hand and led him away from the burning wreckage of that battle. He was strong when he said good-bye to his friends and left his life behind to protect a boy he barely even knew. He was strong when he finished a sixteen-hour drive by building a campfire and cooking Sam an amazing meal out of salt, pepper, water, and whatever vegetables he could scrounge from remote desert grocery stores.

Sam touched Daniel's hand. It was damp and cold.

"Thank you," he said.

Valuable things were kept in the attic. Sam determined this by noticing when people came and went with guns, ammunition, osteomantic materials for first-aid kits, and when he heard squeaking floorboards above his head.

He went back to his room after midnight and took a pee. *Use the bathroom when you can,* Daniel always said. Then he slung his duffel over his shoulder and slid the window open. There were some dizzy moments as he climbed onto the eave, out into the chill desert air.

Sam wasn't much of a climber, but the house's log construction gave him good hand- and footholds. He managed to get himself perched on the attic windowsill, but his feet didn't quite fit, and the weight of his duffel bag threw off his balance. If there was a point at which he was going to fall to his death, it would be now. He gripped the window frame and wished he'd done more finger pushups, or any, ever.

He decided that Daniel had lied about all the second-story jobs and roof entries he'd bragged about. This was *difficult*.

Praying to gods he didn't believe in moments ago—and, if he was honest, wouldn't believe in moments from now—he asked for strength and agility and skill before prying the window open with Daniel's knife. He tumbled through the window to the attic floor and lay there, marveling that he hadn't pancaked in the dirt and pine needles two stories below. *Thank you,* he thought to the gods who'd responded during his brief and now expired interval of faith.

The beam of his pencil flashlight revealed a low, sloping ceiling, duct work, and insulation. Two wooden chairs faced each other in the middle of the floor. Nearby, a bucket. The arrangement suggested unpleasant conversation.

Up against the wall stood three metal cabinets—gun lockers, Sam presumed. And beside them was a smallish safe.

He examined it with his flashlight and scratched the dial with his knife. Smelling the blade, he picked up some sphinx-riddle oil, but nothing very complicated. On heists, Daniel had never been the box man. That job fell to his ex, Cassandra Morales. But Daniel had some rudimentary safe-cracking skills, and he'd taught them to Sam.

Ten minutes later, he had the box open. Easier than falling through a window.

He shined his flashlight in the box. It looked empty, but he wasn't too disappointed. With a safe this easy to bust, the Emmas might have dusted the interior with sint holo. He felt around, hoping not to put his fingers into a hidden mousetrap, but felt nothing.

"Looking for this?"

With a sigh, he rose to his feet and swung his flashlight around.

It was Em, with the pouch.

"As a matter of fact, yes, I am."

"What for?"

"Because it's mine." This argument did not appear to move her. "May I have it, please?"

"Depends. What are you going to do with it?"

Sam hiked his duffel bag higher up on his shoulders. "What do you think?"

"An ill-advised and probably suicidal mission to Catalina Island to destroy Otis Roth's Pacific firedrake."

"Gosh, you're sharp," Sam said. "Can I have my pouch back?"

"I have some more questions." She lowered herself to

one of the chairs. He didn't know if it was the torturer's chair or the victim's. He remained standing.

"Any black-ops experience?" she began.

"What's black ops?"

"Have you broken into a secure facility? Have you ever dealt with armed sentries? Have you ever been in a firefight? Have you ever blown shit up? Have you ever killed someone?" Her eyes gleamed like flint in the shadows. These were all fair questions, Sam had to admit.

"I'm woefully inadequate to the task. But the guy who was supposed to do it is laid up right now, and the network of golems with all kinds of black-ops experience passed on the job. Two weeks. The dragon goes online in two weeks."

"I know," she said. "I argued with my sisters after chili. Actually, both me and Emma—sorry, the Emma with the eye patch—but Emma won't be persuaded. I mean our doctor, Emma. She's the leader of the cell, and she has our loyalty, because she's never wrong."

"She's wrong about this," Sam said.

Em took a breath, signaling another barrage of rapid-fire questions.

"Are you trying to prove something to someone? To Daniel? To yourself? Do you feel that you were created with the Hierarch's power and were cheated out of your destiny? Do you just want to do something dramatic to prove that you're worthy of your magic?"

"Em, may I pretty please have my pouch back?"

She stood and took a few steps over to him. In the harsh beam of his flashlight, her scar looked like a red thread. She handed over the pouch. "Here."

Sam looked inside. It was all there: the hand-drawn diagrams of the Catalina facility, a map of the island with surveillance posts marked, the cash.

"Thank you," he said. "You want to come with me?"

"As if I'd give you a choice."

SIX

Leaving the house was easy, thanks to Em. There was an Emma on watch in the garage, where Daniel's—or, rather, Faith the café owner's—truck was parked. But Em told the Emma that she had insomnia and figured she might as well do something useful instead of staring at her ceiling all night and would be happy to take a sentry shift.

Em told another Emma guarding the gate that the doctor had instructed her to take Sam to Bermuda Dunes for transfer to another safe house.

The Emmas were a family, and they trusted their own. If Em had misgivings about betraying that trust, she kept them to herself.

Half an hour later, they were speeding down open highway with Sam behind the wheel and the headlights off and every star in the sky looking down on them.

Em had Gabriel Argent's intel documents on her lap and was reading them by flashlight. Her kit was packed tighter than Sam's, but it was like a bottomless bag from which she'd pulled not just the flashlight, but a warm hoodie, a thermos of coffee, a spare aluminum cup, and two tomato, lettuce, and mushroom sandwiches. Sam also caught sight of a bowie knife, a coiled rope, and the grip of a handgun emerging from a canvas holster.

"How's your stealth osteomancy?" she asked.

The same sint holo that concealed objects in his bone-lined box was in his cells. A skilled osteomancer like Daniel could summon it and make himself vanish, or least make himself hard to spot.

"Not great," he said.

"How impenetrable are you?"

"You mean like to bullets and things?"

"Yeah."

"I am utterly penetrable," Sam admitted.

"How about offensive magic? Kraken energy, fire breathing?"

"Not so much."

Em shined her light on him, as if searching for some defect. "You *are* the Hierarch's golem, aren't you?"

"I don't live up to my potential."

She kept the light on him, concluded an unspoken observation with a "Hmm," and went back to the documents.

"I can manifest magic," he said, trying not to sound too defensive. "But I'm not nimble at it yet. Daniel's been training me ever since he got me out of LA, but it still takes a lot of effort."

"Maybe you need a better tutor."

"Daniel's the best osteomancer I've ever met," Sam said, a little too forcefully.

"Those who can do can't necessarily teach. Anyway, what about when you were attacked? Emma—the *doctor* Emma—said you may have saved his life."

At the gas station, the hydra and eocorn had flowed out of him, like sweat under a hot sun. He barely remembered what he'd been thinking and feeling, other than desperate fear that Daniel would die right there on the asphalt. "I don't know. I don't know how I did that."

"What if you draw on freshly ingested osteomancy? Like if you ate some fresh griffin bone. Can you manifest magic then?"

That's what Daniel called surface osteomancy, as opposed to deep osteomancy. "Sure, that's easy."

The dim silhouettes of Joshua trees along the road looked like twisted sentries. Em neatly folded the documents and returned them to the pouch.

"Changed your mind about doing this with me yet?" Sam asked.

Em took her time answering. She was thinking about it.

"No," she said, after a while. "But we'll have to score some magic."

"That's where we're headed," Sam said. "I know a guy."

"Someone we can trust?"

"Yeah. But not someone you'll like. In fact, I'm sure you're going to hate his guts."

"I can't wait," she murmured.

Em tilted her seat back and closed her eyes.

Sleep when you can.

Damnation Mountain revealed itself at the end of a dirt road, a two-hundred-foot-wide, adobe-slathered cliff face painted in a dizzying palette, like a quilt assembled by a deranged grandmother. A yellow trail from the foot of the cliff to the top was surrounded by swirling stripes like the whorls of God's fingerprints. Biblical passages painted in crude brushstrokes crawled over the mountain. Dead center on the mountain's face was a painted red heart the size of a garage door, and written on the heart was *Matthew 10:34 I did not come to bring peace, but a sword.*

"What a sweet sentiment," said Em as they pulled into the dirt field before the mountain.

"If you want cheerful, Salvation Mountain's down the road."

They got out and approached a broken-down truck parked in the field. Its old-timey rounded fenders were like something out of a cartoon. A handmade plywood camper shell perched uncertainly on the truck's bed. Like the mountain, the truck and shell were scrawled with Biblical passages. *John 1:18 No one has ever seen God* was painted across the windows.

"Are the Emmas religious?"

"Some."

"You mean you have some religion, or some of you are religious?"

"Both."

Her answer seemed more complicated than evasive.

"Mason?" Sam called out. "Mason, I need to talk to you."

There was no answer.

"He's probably working. Follow me."

An artificial cave of concrete and adobe grew from the cliff like a fungal growth. Inside, dead trees blended into the walls and ceiling, limbs spreading like veins and arteries. Shafts of sunlight came in through gaps in the ceiling. The bright pastels lent an atmosphere of whimsy, even when the candy-colored walls were scrawled with messages like *His rage blazes forth like fire and the mountains crumble to dust in his presence.*

"Careful. Paint's wet."

Mason King emerged from a pink alcove carrying a stiff-bristled brush and a gallon of paint. His face was red, his eyes bloodshot, his wispy white hair splattered with paint.

He looked at Sam with distaste, and then his gaze lingered over Em. He nodded approvingly.

"It is better to plant your seed in the belly of a whore than to let it spill on the ground. I've got work to do, Blackland. Don't smear my walls on your way out."

Em blinked. "What did you just call me?"

"Mason, I need your help," Sam said with haste before a fight broke out.

"Well, I don't need yours, Blackland. You're an antenna, and the only thing you pick up is radio station pain-in-my-ass. You and your dad both."

"He's not my dad."

"I keep forgetting. Happy shall he be, that taketh and dasheth the little ones against the stones."

"I'll dasheth his little stones," Em muttered.

"Mason, I have money."

Sam ostentatiously unfolded a five-tusk note. Mason snatched it from him and held it to the light. A war of disgust and desire played on his face, his eyes burning with rage and liquor. Sam knew he'd take the money. Paint wasn't free.

"My office."

Sam and Em followed him into another adobe chamber. An entire palo verde tree hung from the ceiling, the upper branches plastered in place, the root ball hanging down and spreading across the floor. The room was furnished with a few barstools, a bathroom sink and medicine cabinet, and paint cans containing light bulbs, washers and bolts, baby-doll heads, cotton swabs, paintbrushes, and actual paint. Everything, the tree included, was done in canary yellow and mint green. Sam felt like he'd been swallowed by an Easter egg.

Mason picked up one of the cans of paint strewn about the floor and dabbed at flaws on the wall apparently only he could see. "What are you in the market for?"

Em ticked off items on her fingers. "Sint holo, salamander fire, and something that can penetrate substances harder than steel."

"Oh, is that all? What about flight? What about griffin?" He waggled his hairy, old-man eyebrows with sarcasm.

"Sure, if you have it," Em said.

There probably wasn't an osteomantic weapon on earth

capable of destroying a Pacific firedrake. Once on Catalina, their best hope would be to foul the machinery the project depended on. They already had osteomancy from Daniel's kit, and all Sam wanted from Mason was a little more to handle anything that got in their way.

"We just need some defense and offense, Mason."

Mason sorted through some more buckets of empty toothpaste tubes and cotton swabs and yet more paintbrushes. He uncovered a bucket full of small bones. Some still had bits of earth clinging to them.

Daniel was meticulous in the way he handled and stored bone. Mason's paint cans would have given him fits.

The old man picked out a white pebble of something, held it up, and sniffed. "Not him," he said, dropping the bone back in the bucket. He picked up another, performed the same hasty analysis, rejected it. "Ah, here she is," he said after some more sorting. Pinched between his thumb and forefinger was a yellowish bone the size of a pencil eraser.

Sam moved in closer to sniff it.

"Well?" Em asked.

"Some essences of salamander and diluted seps serpent. Very diluted. Maybe a few other useful things, I'm not sure."

"Her name was Dolores Shenandoah," Mason said. "Lovely woman. Very powerful."

"Mason's a grave robber," Sam explained.

"Oh, great."

"How much you want for her?" Sam asked Mason.

"Wait," Em said, astonished. "You won't eat chicken eggs, but you're okay with eating human remains?"

"It's not like I had her custom-killed for me. Mason, when did she die?"

Mason peered at the bone with his moist, red eyes. "It was 1956. Natural causes. I mean, she got hit by a tomato truck. But in a natural way. She wasn't murdered for her bones."

"See?" Sam said. "Eating her isn't morally suspect."

Em pondered that for a while, while Mason looked on in anxious silence. He really did need to make a sale.

"How do we know he's not lying?" Em said.

"I'm an honest businessman." He dug under some boxes and produced a newspaper clipping, preserved in a plastic sheet. He handed the clipping to Em. It was an obituary.

"Dolores Shenandoah, prominent osteomancer," Em read. "Struck and killed by a tomato truck . . . Bakersfield . . . served in Ministry security forces . . . yeah."

Mason snatched the obituary back.

"Okay?" Sam said.

Em relented, and Mason betrayed a relieved breath.

He wanted five thousand tusks.

Em talked him down to six hundred.

Steam billowed from the engine.

A mile outside Mecca, the truck's temperature needle had swept into the red faster than the second hand on a wristwatch. They caught some luck by breaking down less than a mile from a travel center on an otherwise lonely stretch of highway, and Sam had managed to limp into the gas station parking lot without the engine seizing up.

Sam joined Em, peering into the dissipating steam under the hood.

"Radiator hose," Em said. "If we can't fix it in ten minutes, we steal another car, yes?"

"Right. You get things started here. I'll see if I can buy a hose inside."

Em nodded and went around to the back of the truck to fetch the tool kit.

Sam liked the way they worked together even having known each other just a few hours. There was something about Em that made him think of high school hallways and solving mysteries. Also, he liked her nose. It was graceful. Was it weird to like a nose? Em had a sexy nose.

Inside the shop, Sam found the auto-supply aisle. No hoses for sale, but he scooped up a patch kit, a roll of black tape, and two gallons of coolant. He considered stealing all of it. The more cash they saved for the job, the better. He located the antitheft fish-eye mirrors up near the ceiling and assessed the vigilance of the middle-aged woman behind the counter. From where Sam stood, the cashier seemed friendly and distracted. She chatted with customers buying road snacks and cigarettes, complimented a girl on her cute haircut, and never once did she lift her gaze to the mirrors.

Sam decided not to steal the items. He might start having to make people pay for their friendliness later in the journey, but not yet.

He was about to head to the register when a woman entered the store. She stopped all conversation at the counter, and Sam hunched down and watched her in the mirror. Her head was bald, with pharaoh eyes tattooed in glossy black ink on her temples. Built tall and thin, like a greyhound, she turned her head slowly from side to side, as if detecting odors with her tattooed eyes.

Hound.

Sam left the patch kit and tape and coolant where they were and moved to the beverage cases at the back of the store, as far away from the hound as he could get.

He reached into his osteomantic cells for sense memories, for the dark brine of kraken, for the crushing pressure of magma and the heavy, pungent smell of griffin. Without more time and preparation, he couldn't use those essences to defend himself, but he just needed a hint of electric tingle in his fingers. Some heat rising from his lungs. A nervous energy in his legs, just the barest suggestion that he could spring across open savannah and take flight. He just needed a little magic from the vast wells buried deep and inaccessible in his bones.

In full view of a mom trying to convince her kid he wanted orange juice instead of cola, Sam coughed up a magically redolent wad of mucus and hacked it to the floor.

The kid gaped bewilderment, and the mom gaped in disgust, and Sam winked at them both.

He looked up to the fish-eye mirror. The hound stiffened and started making her way down the jerky aisle toward the drink cases.

Sam hurried to the front of the store down an aisle parallel to the hound. Waving at the cashier, he gave a glance over his shoulder before exiting. The last thing he saw was the hound closing in on his spit wad.

He sprinted over to Em and the truck.

"You're empty handed," she observed.

"Hound's on our trail," Sam said, breathless. "How fast can you hotwire a car?"

"My record's two minutes ten seconds."

"I'm faster. That white van by the air compressor. Go."

"No need." She pointed at an empty blue La Jolla sedan at the pumps with the nozzle in the tank. "That guy left his keys in the car."

Em snatched their bags out of the pickup while Sam went to the La Jolla. He yanked out the nozzle and let himself into the driver's seat. Em threw herself in after him. An air freshener in the shape of a marijuana leaf hung from the rearview mirror. *Gas, ass, or grass. No one rides for free*, read the jaunty cursive printed on it. The seats and floor mats smelled much more of grass than gas or ass. The odor could be a problem, making it harder for Sam to detect and conjure osteomancy. But that was a worry for another time.

The hound rushed out of the store, scanning the air with her tattooed eyes. Her head snapped toward the gas pumps.

Sam turned the key. He shoved the shifter to reverse, just as a hatchback pulled up to the pump behind him.

"Hold on to your paint," he said, shifting to drive. He hit the gas, squeezing through the seam between the SUV in front of him and the cars pumping gas at the next island.

The hound broke into a full-speed run.

Sam steered toward the driveway and within seconds was back on the road, accelerating away. He didn't look back.

"I was going to buy snacks," he said. "Do we have any more snacks?"

Em looked around. "Afraid not. Is the hound with the same crew that took down Daniel?"

"Could be. I didn't see her then. There's probably more than one crew after me."

"What makes you think that?"

"Because there's always more than one crew after me. I'm the treasure of Los Angeles, remember?"

And now he didn't have Daniel protecting him.

"So you don't recognize the hound?"

"No. But I almost never see a hound more than once. One chance is usually all they get before Daniel kills them."

"Well, this one lives another day."

Sam drove with his eyes on the rearview and side mirrors more than on the road ahead. They were nearing populated ground and sharing the road with more cars. Since they didn't know what the hound was driving, all vehicles were suspect. There was also the matter of cops looking for their freshly stolen car.

After speeding down the road for a few more dozen miles, Sam slowed and pulled to a stop at the side of the road.

"Really terrible time for a pee break, Sam."

Ignoring her, he reached into the backseat and dug out Daniel's osteomancy kit, then opened his door.

Em followed him out of the car.

Clutching one of the vials from Daniel's kit, Sam cocked back his arm and let the vial fly into the desert. The glass barely made a tinkle when it shattered against a rock.

"You just shot a rock with five thousand tusks' worth of osteomancy," Em said.

"It's kolowisi essence. From a sea serpent. We can spare it."

"Catalina Island is twenty-two miles off the coast. You don't think sea serpent essence might be useful if we have to swim?"

"It's not enough to last us twenty-two miles. Anyway, we have to sacrifice something if we're going to shake off that hound."

He chucked three more bottles of magic, then ran across the highway and shot another three in the opposite direction.

"Can we go now?" Em said, impatient. The highway traffic was sparse, but a few cars whizzed past, enough to make them both nervous.

"I need to try something first."

He knelt by the rear bumper.

It was a small thing, something Daniel was able to do when he was only twelve, under circumstances even worse than having a hound on his trail. If Sam couldn't manage this now, then he'd never be able to do it. And if he couldn't actually use his osteomancy, then the Emmas were right: he had no business going to Catalina.

He thought of visual distortions, of funhouse mirrors and frosted glass. He thought of confusion and photons refusing to ride orderly waves. The smell of sint holo serpent rose from his hand, a creature whose essence granted properties of invisibility.

He smeared his palm over the license plate.

"Come here and read the plate," he told Em.

She stared at it for a few seconds, frowning.

"LEF439. No, wait. PEF . . . wait . . . LE . . . Huh."

"What color's the car?"

She stared intently at the car, shut her eyes, blinked a few times. "Okay, you're good. I have no idea."

"Just a little sint holo magic."

"Sexy," she said. She smiled at him and got back inside the car.

Sam's brain felt like it had become untethered and was swimming around inside his skull. His face felt hot. He didn't think it was an effect of his own magic.

Sexy?

Trying not to smile too much, he returned to the driver's seat and sped down the highway.

SEVEN

The Bautistas lived in a white clapboard house among fields of alfalfa. A tire swing hung from a single oak tree surrounded by a scattering of toy trucks, a wagon, a faded red tricycle, and some partially clothed dolls.

"I didn't know the Bautistas had kids," Sam said.

Em went to the front door by way of a tidy path bordered by gladiolas.

"They're good kids. They don't blab."

Responding to Em's knock, a woman opened the door and stood behind the screen. Midthirties, a bit worn and harried, she kept one hand in the pocket of her apron. Her posture relaxed when she recognized Em.

"You and your friend by yourselves? Where are your sisters?"

"Not here. Just me and Sam. He's Daniel Blackland's . . . He travels with Daniel Blackland."

The wooden grip of a handgun peeked from her apron pocket.

She opened the screen door. "Dinner first, then we can talk business."

Dinner was spaghetti and green beans with the whole family—Sofía Bautista, her husband, Fernando, and their son and two daughters. Sam supposed they were as cute as any children. The table conversation focused on chores to be done around the farm and house, and drilling the older daughter, eight, on her multiplication tables. The house was small and cluttered with the detritus of small children, and there were crayon drawings stuck to the refrigerator with magnets, and the smell of tomato sauce lingering in the kitchen, and Sam loved it here and wished the meal would never end.

After dinner, there was coffee, and then dishes, and then the kids were put to bed, which took both parents another hour.

Finally, the Bautistas returned to the table. Fernando, a pudgy man with a quiet manner, a soft face, and calloused hands, unfolded a map of the Southern California realm.

"Where is it you need to get to?"

Em tapped Catalina Island with her finger. "Here."

"That's far." Sofía pressed her lips together.

Fernando nodded. "What's the cargo?"

"Us," Sam said, indicating himself and Em.

Sofía gave them an appraising look, as if she were estimating their weight and value. "So this isn't for-profit. What kind of trouble are you kids in?"

Sam gave her an honest answer. "I don't want to say too specifically, but it could be a lot of trouble."

"If Sofía's going up, you will have to be very specific,"

Fernando said. "That's the way it works. You make a pro-posal, you tell us everything, and then we decide if it's worth it." There was a bit of gentle admonishment in his tone, as if Sam were one of his kids and was getting a lec-ture on the importance of brushing his teeth. Sam didn't mind. He found it oddly comforting.

"The Emmas trust the Bautistas," Em said to Sam. "Daniel did, too. He would have told them everything."

Sam didn't know if that was true, but then, how much choice did he have? They needed a flight to the island, and the Bautistas had a plane.

So Sam told them things. But not everything. He told them why he needed to get to Catalina, and what Daniel had intended to do once he got there. He told them he was an osteomancer, but not how rare he was. No need for them to know how much money they could get by selling him to a rich Angelino.

When Sam was done talking, Fernando stroked his mustache and looked over the map. "That explains what you need us for. Hounds aren't much of a threat when you're a couple thousand feet up. And we can get you from the desert to the island without ever having to touch ground. You'll need a pickup, too?"

"Once we're on the beach, you'll take off again," Em said. "When we're done, we'll signal you."

Nobody needed to say that this arrangement doubled the risk. One undetected landing was optimistic enough. Two would be pushing it. And while Sam and Em were running around the facility, Sofía would be circling in en-emy airspace.

Sam looked up at the drawings on the refrigerator. They were nonsense scribbles, nothing recognizable in them, but they moved him all the same. He'd never drawn a picture that ended up on a refrigerator.

Fernando brought up the subject of money.

Sam opened the diplomatic pouch and placed all their remaining cash on the table. "This is 24,400. It's all we have."

Em gave him a look, but he ignored it. He wasn't just paying for a round-trip flight. He was paying for the chance to orphan three kids.

The tire swing swayed from the oak branch, the ropes creaking softly against the sounds of crickets and frogs in the irrigation ditches. Alone in the yard, Sam sat on the swing and looked up beyond the sharp edge of the roofline. The black sky was punctured with stars. He wanted to go back in the house and tell the Bautistas he'd changed his mind. Better yet, just grab Em and drive away, be miles distant before anyone noticed they'd left.

The screen door banged, and Fernando came over and joined him at the tree.

"How can you be okay with your wife doing this?"

Fernando looked tired, and the smile he gave Sam was one he probably never revealed to his children.

"Sofía is a good woman. She's a good wife and a great mother. I love her very much. But if Los Angeles ever decides they need our water for something else, the farm's done, and so are we. Flying brings in twice as much as farming, and we won't see our children impoverished and sold off seven times a week as day slaves. We won't see them digging a rich man's ditch, or doing unspeakable things for some pornographer."

"If you lose your wife, it'll turn out a bad bet." It sounded cold, but math was cold, and life was measured on balance sheets. What didn't show up on the bottom line was the pain of living with those calculations.

"Did they ever tell you in school that you could be anything you wanted to be?"

"I didn't go to school," Sam said.

"Well, that's what I learned. From school, from my parents, from the air. All I had to do was set my mind on a goal, work very hard, and I could be anything at all."

"And what did you want to be?"

"For me it wasn't a what. It was a where. I wanted to be anywhere outside the Southern realm. Somewhere without the Ministry of Justice Dispensation. Somewhere without cartels. Somewhere without a Hierarch."

"Everywhere has a Hierarch," Sam said. "They may call it something else, and it may not be one man or one woman, but wherever you go, there's always someone who gets to eat more magic than everyone else, or pile up more money than everyone else."

Fernando nodded. "I figured that out. I worked for many of those people, the little Hierarchs. I couldn't get away from them. But Sofía and I could build this." He waved his hand at his house and fields. "It's a tiny fortress. Or an island. We're not untouchable here. We track our shoes through the kingdom's dirt all the time. But a flimsy fence is better than none at all."

And that's what Daniel wanted for Sam. Escaping to Tahoe, or Mexico, or to the shaded creases between the Sierra mountains . . . It would never be more than a flimsy barrier between Sam and some kind of Hierarch. But Daniel considered it worth striving for. And to risk dying for.

"Come back inside," Fernando said. "Get a few hours of sleep. We'll want to be in the air before dawn."

The stars were still out when Sam and Em helped Sofía push her four-seat prop plane out of a corrugated metal barn. It was an awkward contraption, with a pair of amphibious floats below the wings and three-wheeled landing gear attached to each float.

"Isn't this a little big for crop dusting?" Em asked.

Sofía stroked the fuselage like a cowboy in love with his horse. "She's more than just a crop duster. This is an AM-Garuda 1015. She belonged to the Ministry of Fire, back when they still operated this far from the capital. I can skim across a lake and fill the floats with water, or use them to store contraband. I've even smuggled people in there. Fernando swapped in engine and cockpit armor, put in self-sealing fuel tanks and a bulletproof windshield. He's a crack mechanic, and I'm a crack pilot, and she's the best bird in the Mojave. She'll get you to Catalina."

Sam couldn't help but grin at her pride.

Fernando came over from the house, where he'd been watching the kids. He handed Sofía a shotgun and box of shells and kissed her passionately enough that Sam felt it proper to look away.

While Sofía walked around the plane for a preflight inspection, Fernando came up close to Sam.

"You're a powerful osteomancer?" he asked.

Daniel had prepared Sam to answer this question, whether asked by a stranger, a friend, or a cop, whether asked out of idle curiosity or from someone making a business proposal or interrogating him or beating him or begging him for magic to heal a wound. The answer was always supposed to be the same: No.

He glanced toward the house. The children were standing on the back steps in their pajamas.

"I'm more of an ingredient than a proper osteomancer."

"How powerful?"

"Very," Sam said. "A high-value ingredient for any soup."

Fernando nodded. "If there's a problem, if there's trouble, if you can help my wife but you decide not to, because it'll compromise your own safety, because it'll cost you something . . . if my wife comes to harm and you didn't do everything you could to help her, osteomancer or not . . ."

He didn't finish the sentence, nor did he need to.

"I will," Sam said.

Fernando gave Sofía a final look, even more intimate than the kiss, and he returned to the house to stand with the children.

Sam took the front passenger seat while Em buckled herself into the back. When Sofía was done with her pre-flight routine, she waved toward the house, at Fernando and her children. They all waved back, as though she were just heading off for work. The engine coughed into life and the five-bladed propeller became a blur.

Sofía taxied onto a strip of flattened dirt between rows of alfalfa, and without ceremony she commenced a rumbling sprint. Sam hadn't anticipated things would be so loud. Every creak and squeak from the plane no doubt signaled a vital screw coming loose or a spar cracking. He'd seen planes in flight, of course, but he'd never actually been in one. Clearly, the whole enterprise was a hoax.

Sam didn't imagine Sofía would run them into the irrigation ditch at the end of the air strip, at least not for the first several seconds of takeoff. Then he began to suspect it was a possibility. And then it became a certainty. Only his unwillingness to humiliate himself in front of Em kept him from emitting a panicked little squeal.

When the ride smoothed out and Sam looked down to find they were several feet off the ground, he let out a quiet breath of relief. All was forgiven.

Minutes later, they were in deep sky. The stars twinkled above, and lights from water projects and lonely desert settlements twinkled below.

Sofía motioned for Sam to put on the bulky headphones dangling in front of him. Em already had her set on.

"You kids ever fly before?"

"Yeah," Em said, without elaborating. No doubt she'd

participated in some kind of avian black ops, probably involving parachuting and maybe some wing walking.

"Not me," said Sam.

"Well, make yourself comfortable. Sick bags are under your seats. We'll be heading south a while, and then a right turn over the San Andreas Abyss. Most pilots hate flying over it, so I don't expect company. But if you see a moving light out there, anything that looks like it could, might, maybe be a plane, don't assume I see it, too. Tell me."

The Abyss had about the same reputation as the Bermuda Triangle, but Sofía sounded chipper. She liked flying her plane. And once Sam got used to the noises and jolts and vibrations, he was surprised to find he liked it, too. Loved it, actually. If he closed his eyes, he was no longer inside a flying machine with a fuel-combustion engine. It was him flying, not the airplane. He wanted to open his door and step out and spread his arms and race beside the airplane. He wanted to soar up beyond the thin gauze of clouds. The Hierarch had eaten garuda raptor and other flying creatures. Maybe flight was in Sam's bones.

A little while later, the plane banked a sharp right turn. Sam looked over the dials arrayed before Sofía and found the compass. They were going west now, toward Los Angeles and Catalina. Since leaving the capital, Daniel had dragged Sam up and down the desert and along winding paths in sequoia forests and through mountain passes. But never into Los Angeles. The weight of their undertaking settled in his gut, and at the same time, he experienced a thrill of liberation.

"I wish it was daylight so you guys could see," Sofía said over the intercom. "We're coming up on the Abyss. It's beautiful from this high up."

Perfect black spread out below, the lights of human settlement and engineering long behind them. No canals or roads came near here.

Sam was about to say he was sad over missing the splendor when the windshield shattered. Glass and deafening wind roared through the cockpit and cabin, cutting Sam's cheeks. Papers whipped through the air—maps and Gabriel Argent's Catalina intel. There was a harsh beep that must be the stall alarm, and also an unsettling absence of engine noise. The plane flexed under stress with horrific groans and creaks, and the left wing dipped. They were falling.

Sam hunched in the crash position, icy air rushing through his ears. Bits of bulletproof glass struck his scalp as more pieces cracked loose from the windshield.

He lifted his head. Blood drizzled down Sofía's chin. She yanked on the stick with both hands, and her wail of effort penetrated through the rest of the noise, but she couldn't budge it. She was screaming something, Sam couldn't hear what. His headphones had come off and jiggled at the end of their coiled cord.

He was not frightened. He felt remorse for getting Em and Sofía entangled in his problems. He felt bad for never getting to know Valerie in Bombay Beach, and he was sorry Faith the café owner would never get her pickup truck back. He was sorry he'd never see Daniel again.

Lowering himself back into the crash position, he was

struck by an impression, or an essence, of gliding. Even with his arms wrapped around his knees, he felt as if they were spread wide. Membranes broad as yacht sales stretched out, rippling in the wind. The air was cold, but inside, he burned, hot as lava. He saw the plane from outside, contours and edges bright and clear and sharp. The plane plummeted toward a deep earthen scar below.

He was hallucinating. Stress. Fear. Maybe a concussion. Yet he knew it was none of these things.

Flames wavered outside, a bright halo streaming past the windows like water, and Sam knew the engine hadn't caught fire, just as he knew the sense of personal flight and subterranean heat was no illusion. It was osteomancy, and he was doing it.

There was a sense of slowing, of lifting, right before the plane struck the ground with a tooth-loosening impact and chewed through dirt and rock, fine dust swirling in clouds, pebbles striking the metal skin as if being shot from a machine gun. The landing gear fractured and crumpled and the propeller blades chopped into the earth.

Then, silence.

Sam twisted around in his seat. Bits of glass glittered in Em's hair. Her cheeks and the bridge of her nose were freckled with blood. A deep red line about half an inch long over her left eyebrow streamed blood, soaking her eyelashes and falling in droplets down her face, but she seemed to move fine as she unbuckled her harness. She wrestled with her door and managed to kick it open. After slinging Sofía's rifle over her shoulder, she tossed out their bags and climbed down bent wing struts and crumpled float tanks to the ground.

Sofía still gripped the stick with white fingers. Blood streamed from a red splash on her forehead.

"We crashed," she said groggily, looking at Sam as if in a state of mild surprise. "Where's Fernando? Is he okay?"

"Fernando's back home. You're hurt."

"I'm fine. Get out. We might be leaking fuel."

"Wait for help," Sam said. He jumped to the ground and came around the front of the plane to meet her on her side. A black object was flattened against the windshield. It looked about the size of a cat, and it had wings.

"Help Sofía," he called out to Em.

The plane had landed on her belly, pitched forward, the nose settled into a ditch dug by the propeller. Sam climbed the engine cowling and crawled up to the windshield. He smelled iron and shit and the scents of pursuit and of hunger and single-minded intent. These were the smells of an osteomantic hound.

He put his fingers into sticky fur and pried the creature away from the shards of cockpit glass impaling it. Its pinched, apple-doll human face was the dark brown of tobacco spit, of bones soaked in La Brea tar for ten thousand years.

This was a person. It had once been a man or a woman or a boy or a girl, and whatever kind of life it led—an unpleasant one, probably a horrific one—got canceled out when someone decided it was needed for some monstrous service. Sam set it down gently on the engine cowling.

He looked around for Argent's pouch, but the documents were lost, probably blown out of the plane hundreds of feet in the air. All the plans and diagrams of the Catalina facility, gone.

He climbed down to join Em on the ground, and they half pulled and half carried Sofía away from the wreck.

"Good enough," Sofía said, laboring. "Good enough. Let me sit."

Em got a pack of gauze from her first-aid kit and put pressure on Sofía's bleeding forehead.

"You're bleeding, too," Sam observed.

Em wiped blood off her face with her sleeve and waved him off.

"If I'm not crying, I'm okay."

"Check me for signs of a concussion," Sofía said. "Is my speech slurred?"

It wasn't.

She continued to give Em directions until Em threatened to set bones that weren't yet broken if she kept trying to be in charge.

Sofía relented. "We were in a straight dive. I had no control. How did we end up on our belly?"

"You must have done something at the last minute," Sam said. It sounded reasonable.

"We were on *fire*."

"Maybe the airstream put it out."

"No. It didn't. What happened?"

"We struck a bat. I found one splattered on the windshield. Maybe another hit the prop."

Sofía shook her head, then let out a soft, queasy moan.

"That's impossible. We were at 2,100 feet when we got hit. Bats don't fly that high."

"Trust me," Sam said. "It was a bat."

Em shined her penlight into Sofía's eyes. "Bats. So what does that mean?"

Sam looked up at the night sky. "It means someone was looking for me in the air."

"I guess it's lucky I killed it with my beautiful airplane," Sofía said mournfully.

The San Andreas Abyss was a fissure in the earth where the Pacific and the North American seismic plates met in combat. It snaked northwest from the Salton Sea to the San Gabriel Mountains outside Los Angeles before continuing north, beyond the borders of the Southern Californian realm. The Hierarchs of the Southern and Northern kingdoms both conducted osteomantic experiments on it, trying to control it, to bend it to their will, to use it as a weapon. In doing so, they'd ripped it wider and carved it deeper, and gouged a laceration in the earth almost as deep as the Grand Canyon.

The place was feared. It was said to be redolent with osteomantic essences.

Sam and Em and Sofía spent the night shivering and cowering in a nest of boulders. At first light, Em returned to the plane to see if she could bring the radio back to life, but it was too badly damaged by the crash. There was no emergency beacon to summon help, because if Sofía ever crashed during a job, the last thing she'd ever want was to let people know where she was.

In a different set of circumstances, they might have remained here a day to rest Sofía, who was suffering headaches and nausea and sometimes seemed confused. But Sam didn't like the way the earth around them rumbled. Grains of sand popped from the ground like droplets in a freshly poured glass of soda pop. Larger rocks cascaded down the canyon walls. Sam had been through earthquakes before, but these tremors felt different.

"Let's get moving," he said. "Maybe we can find somewhere to climb out."

They discussed the idea of fashioning a litter from the wreck, but Sofía was adamant that she could walk. Slowly, painfully, they trudged miles west, where eventually the canyon walls would be lower. Strata in the vertical faces twisted like layers in a swirl cake. Only a narrow seam of blue sky was visible between the walls.

After an hour, they forced Sofía to sit on a rock. She was white as newsprint and shivering.

Em took Sam aside, out of the pilot's earshot.

"She's really not doing well. She needs a doctor." Em unfolded her map on the shaded ground. "This is just an estimate, but I figure we're about here." She touched a spot that put them around forty miles outside Desert Hot Springs. "Not exactly a bustling metropolis," she said, "but they might have a clinic."

Sam puffed out air. "That'd be a long walk even if we were all healthy. And I don't like the smell of this place."

Em refolded the map. "What are you smelling?"

"I don't know . . . something deep. Like, something climbing up through pressure zones. Something that's not happy to be awake."

"Something unhappy is not a smell."

"I mean . . . not a *smell* smell. An osteomantic impression."

Em cocked her head and regarded him clinically. "I didn't think you had that kind of nose."

"I don't. But, well, that's what I'm smelling now."

He began to walk back to Sofía, but Em put a hand on his arm to stop him.

"What happened to you during the crash?"

"Same as you. I was in the plane. We all fell down."

"I was watching you, Sam." She made it sound like an accusation. "There were flames outside."

"Yeah. Something caught on fire. So?"

"There were flames inside, too. Faint, more like a glow. They were coming off you."

Sam didn't quite remember it that way. But he remembered feeling like he was flying, even as the plane dropped. He remembered feeling something in his bones, a heat hotter than fire, but one that didn't burn.

"Maybe I did have something to do with the flames," he admitted. For some reason, he felt sheepish about it, as if she'd caught him naked. "For a few seconds there, it felt like I was doing something. I don't know what, but like I was powerful and doing something. Never felt that way before."

"Daniel's osteomancy is very deep, isn't it?"

The abrupt change of subject left Sam momentarily confused. "Yes," he said, recovering.

"He doesn't just work magic from freshly consumed bone, but also magic deep in his system, from things he ate long ago?"

"That's right."

"And it's not only the magic he deliberately consumes, is it? He can draw up osteomantic essences from the ground, and from the air. It's like osmosis with him."

"His father brought him up to do that. So?"

She hesitated, her face grave, as if she were breaking some bad news to him. "Sam, you should be one of the most powerful osteomancers on earth. Maybe stronger than Daniel. But you never really have been."

Sam didn't like where she was going.

"Did it ever occur to you," she continued, drawing it out slowly, as if she was still deciding whether or not to say what was on her mind, "that Daniel's been draining your magic?"

"No," he said. "It never has."

Which was a lie.

Daniel kept telling him how stuffed with osteomantic power he should be. He was grown from the Hierarch's cells. So why wasn't he as strong as the Hierarch? Why wasn't he as strong as Daniel? And why was Daniel able to retain so much osteomancy when he'd eaten so little magic since leaving Los Angeles?

Daniel was a sponge. He'd told Sam so himself. When fighting the Hierarch, he'd drawn magic from the air the people of Los Angeles exhaled, and from the water vapor, and from the earth.

What if he'd been drawing magic from Sam?

Sam didn't want to believe it. But now that the thought was out in the open, he knew he'd never be free of it.

"That's bullshit," he said.

The ground shivered. A dim moan rose up from great depths.

S ofía seemed to gain some strength as their long march in the Abyss wore on. It took more and more work to convince her to rest, and she asked Em for her shotgun back. Sam hung behind, indulging himself in angst and worry.

The canyon walls were still oppressively high. With the ground's every jerk and shudder, he felt as if he'd stepped on a squeaky board and drawn attention.

Em kept up a steady conversation with Sofía, maybe to pass the time, but more likely to see how she was dealing with the effects of her head injury.

"He was a foot soldier in the Alejandro's operation," Sofía was saying. "Not high up. He never even met the man himself. But it was steady work, tax free."

Em had asked how she met Fernando.

"I was a pilot for the Department of Water and Power. This was before Gabriel Argent, back when William Mulholland was running it. Mostly I just took up DWP engineers for inspections. Dams, aqueducts, the mandala, that kind of thing. One day I'm on the airstrip in Santa Monica, about to fly solo to Pyramid Lake, when I see a bunch of clowns in commando gear raiding the airport. They're throwing grenades and shooting things up and all that sort of crap. The Alejandro was making a strike against the chief water mage, and how stupid is that, right? So, there I am, in my plane, and I figure my best bet is to buzz off and get in the air and ignore all the bullshit on the ground and just make my pickup in Pyramid Lake. Save my life, earn my paycheck."

"Makes sense," Em said.

"So I'm revving up, and then there's this guy standing a couple yards in front of my nose. He's all dressed up, helmet, goggles, body armor, and a gun bigger than he is, aimed right at my head. I figure, screw this idiot, I'm going to push my propeller at him and put him in the wood chipper. But just before I release the brake, he pulls down his goggles. He's got a baby face, and a ridiculous mustache, and his eyes . . . He's looking at me like I'm the most beautiful thing he's ever seen. I swear, it was just like that. And he puts his gun on the ground. And he walks over to my passenger side and knocks on the door. Shave and a haircut."

Sofía shook her head and laughed, a little sunlight in the valley.

"And I let him in. He says it was love at first sight. I say it was love at first year and a half. But, anyway, I haven't been able to get rid of him since."

Sam had heard enough to knock him out of his sullen funk. He jogged a few steps to catch up to Em and Sofía, and something below cracked like a redwood tree snapping in two. The ground jolted hard and threw him into the sand.

Fissures snaked up the canyon walls, dislodging huge slabs of rock that crashed down like bombs. Loose dirt boiled up through new scars in the earth. Sam struggled to his feet, blinded and choked by billowing clouds of dust. Blunt pillars of stone emerged from the earth, wide as oil barrels, orange as ingots in a furnace. Sam only glimpsed them before they were lost behind the dust, but they looked like colossal fingers, digging their way from a grave. The fingers broke though entirely in an explosion of dirt and rocks and uprooted creosote. An entire hand rose on a treelike wrist, soaring ten feet in the air. The fingers closed with the sound of stone grating against stone.

"Run," Sam coughed.

Sam and Em and Sofía lurched and stumbled over the shaking, shifting terrain. Tremendous booms sounded behind them, maybe just boulders impacting the ground, but too much like the footfalls of some enormous creature.

Despite knowing better, Sam turned and looked behind him.

Swirling grit abraded his eyes, but through his tears, he saw towers of boulders and clots of earth, entwined in plant roots, and a skin of rock that crackled and steamed, and magmatic crust cooling in air. At the summit of the formation was a great potato-shaped lump of stone the size of a garden shed, with asymmetrical fissures where eyes might have been. It was only a glimpse before it faded behind the storming dust, but Sam knew what he'd seen.

He dropped to one knee and pawed through his duffel for Daniel's osteomancy kit. Inside, he found the bone of the dead osteomancer Dolores Shenandoah. It was bitter as charcoal and crumbled easily between his teeth. He chased it with vials of oils and pinches of acrid powder, not even bothering to look at or smell what he was consuming. He was dimly aware of Em and Sofía calling his name, but he didn't turn around. He stood and faced the thing from the abyss, even as its thundering footsteps came closer.

The magic he'd eaten wouldn't be enough. He would have to combine it with the magic that lived submerged in his bones, that he'd never truly been able to draw out. But now, he better, because Daniel wasn't around to fight his battles for him.

And neither was Daniel here to drain his magic.

He reached for sense memories, the smells and tastes and tactile sensations of the magic he knew was in him, deep in his cells and raging fresh from the magic he'd just eaten. But he felt no ancient energies flowing through his blood, no lightning crackling over his hands.

He should run.

Time slowed, shifting from biological to geological pace, and everything blurred with motion. Every stone and swirl of dust and sound blended into a high-pitched buzz, as if the world were constructed of hummingbirds.

Sam hurt. His skin felt agonizingly raw, exposed to thin, frigid air. The sunlight sneaking through the top of the Abyss burned. He was no longer a creature of the surface world. He belonged deep down, in the crushing, molten realm of the king of the center of the world: the axis mundi dragon.

"Fall," he said.

The creature was undone. Its stone fingers plummeted to the ground, tossing up plumes of earth. A leg caved in, and its entire body tilted. The great head slid off its shoulders, slowly at first, hampered by friction and teetering on a nodule of stone, then breaking free and crashing to earth.

A mournful groan shook the ground, sending up storms of birds and insects.

When the dust settled, there was no creature, only the aftermath of an avalanche. Whatever it was, Sam had reduced it to split rocks and gravel. He stood in the center of his handiwork, truly an osteomancer.

If only Daniel could see him now.

And then his sense of triumph dampened. What if Em was right? What if this moment couldn't have happened with Daniel present?

"Sam?"

Em's voice. It was barely more than a squeak.

She was among a scattering of stones, some the size of bowling balls, some merely pebbles. Her skin and clothes were coated in the light brown of desert earth. Tears traced muddy paths down her face.

She was disassembling a pile of rocks. At first, Sam didn't understand what she was doing. Then he saw a bloody, mangled hand emerging from the rubble.

"Help me," Em croaked.

Together, they excavated Sofía. Her face looked as if it had been slapped with a bloody rag mop. Her nose was smashed flat. Scents of blood and stress hormones and the last tinges of adrenaline wafted from her body. Sam blocked those scents out. Sofía didn't need medicine, she needed magic. She needed him. Osteomancy meant forcing one's will over nature, and what mattered was not the patient, but the osteomancer.

Sam dug for odors of healing, of renewal. He reached for green smells, starfish and newts and regeneration. The sense memories broke through like a flood-shattered dam and surged from the deepest places and filled his hands.

He sliced his wrist open and bled into Sofía's open mouth, into her pores.

Em straddled Sofía's motionless form and started CPR.

Sam lost track of time. He bled until a gray film covered his vision, and everything grew distant, until Em dragged him away and he was too weak to stop her. She bandaged his wrist and made him sit in the sand.

"We lost her," she said.

Impossible. He'd performed a great feat of magic. He'd found the power in his bones. He'd found the connection between his cells and the center of the earth. It was magic worthy of Daniel. Worthy of the Hierarch.

And yet there Sofía lay.

He'd lost her.

Fernando had lost his wife. Mayra and Ana and Miguel had lost their mother.

Sam had performed a great feat of magic and lost.

EIGHT

Daniel was a boy of twelve, sitting in the passenger seat of a stolen car while his mother drove down a ribbon of asphalt. The dusty farm fields of Central California stretched into the distance. In the east, the hint of the cold Sierra mountains loomed behind clouds.

He watched his mother drive in silence for a while, the muscles in her forearms tensing as she gripped the wheel. Her squinting stare made a circuit of the rearview mirror, driver's-side mirror, passenger-side mirror, view to the sides, view to the horizon. It never seemed to land on Daniel.

He wanted to put his head in her lap, like he used to do when he was small, and sleep away horrors. Only hours ago, the Hierarch's men stormed into the house he shared with his father and murdered him on the living room floor. They cut him apart with their long knives, and then the Hierarch himself arrived to eat him. He brought his own fork.

"How much longer?" Daniel asked.

A truck passed them, towing an open trailer of toma-toes, and she kept her hand on the gun between the seats until the truck was half a mile away.

"Just a few more hours," she said.

"No, I mean until I see you again."

"Oh. We won't see each other for another twenty years, Daniel."

He understood he was sick and in pain and dreaming, and they passed the next several miles in silence.

"I still don't understand why you didn't take me with you to San Francisco."

Now she did look at Daniel, and her face wasn't as he remembered it, but older. Time had hardened her features, made her jaw stronger, ground away the softness of her youth to leave truer stone behind.

"Otis told you why," she said.

"But Otis lies."

"The border crossing was too dangerous. And I wasn't sure my friends in the Northern Kingdom were still my friends. I knew you'd be safer with him."

"But you took my brother."

"As a decoy. If our enemies thought I'd left Los Angeles with you, they wouldn't look for you as hard in LA. Doesn't that make sense?"

Daniel didn't have to think about it, because he'd al-ready spent twenty years thinking about it. "Yes," he said. "My brother . . . my golem . . . he died. He was shot at the border. He died in a strawberry field."

He watched the way her throat moved when she swallowed, and when she spoke again, he heard a roughness that most people would have missed. Messalina Sigilo was good at hiding her emotions from most people, but not Daniel.

"He didn't die," she said. "I saved him. I helped make him great."

"Why didn't you save me?"

She didn't answer, and he put his head in her lap. She took her hand off the gun and ran her fingers through his hair, and he closed his eyes and awoke.

He was in a strange place with a familiar face looking down on him.

He tried to speak, but his throat and mouth produced only a sound like air leaking from a hose.

He needed to know if Sam was okay.

"Sam brought you to our safe house outside Thermal after you were poisoned with tsuchigumo toxins. Which, of course, meant we had to discontinue that safe house. We're in the Funeral Mountains now. You've been here for two days, mostly perspiring all over our sheets. I did a pretty good job knitting you back up, and your own osteomantic defenses helped, but you're not recovered yet. A few more days, I think."

He brought her face into focus. She was silver haired, with the gray eyes and long, graceful nose of an Emma. This one was the doctor, the leader of the Mojave cell.

He tried to sit up, but the old Emma gently pushed him back down, and he didn't have the strength to resist her. She smelled his breath and hair and took his hands and smelled his fingernails. His hands seemed far off, like things that belonged to someone else.

"You almost didn't make it this time," the Emma said. "But there's always tomorrow."

Daniel licked his lips. They felt like fish scales.

"Where's Sam?"

She hesitated, just a beat, long enough for Daniel to nurture a sense of dread.

"Where's Sam?" he said again.

"Gone to slay a dragon."

Daniel propped himself up on his elbows and saw dark spots. He took a breath and closed his eyes until the spots cleared, then swung his aching legs over the side of the bed and put his feet down on the hardwood floor. The floor was deliciously warm. Lying down and resting his cheek against it would feel great, he imagined.

"You really are in no shape for this," Emma said.

"Better shape than Sam. If he makes it to Catalina, they'll vivisect him." He shot her an accusing glare. "Dammit, Emma, Otis is running Catalina. You know how badly he wants Sam. How could you let him go?"

"We did try to keep him. We locked away the documents you got from Gabriel Argent and posted guards at the motorpool and gate. But he had an accomplice. One of our own. The good news is at least he's not alone."

Daniel forced himself upright. He felt like he was standing on the ceiling and about to come crashing down. Emma put a steadying hand on his shoulder. After a moment, his gravity normalized. He found his clothes neatly folded on a chest of drawers.

"Who's with him? Someone experienced?"

"She goes by Em."

"Em. I've met her, right? She's only . . ."

"She's eighteen now."

"Sam ran off with a girl. Great. Guess I have to give the kid points for style." He stepped into his blue jeans.

"Em is a girl who is personally responsible for the liberation of three captive golems and has participated in the liberation of at least a dozen more. She's had sniper training, experience with munitions, and has been shot three times. I don't know why she went with Sam, but it's lucky for him she did."

"I need a car," Daniel said. "And gas. And food and supplies."

"You'll have it. We know how to outfit a mission."

"Will I have your help? A team of Emmas would—"

"As I told Sam, your firedrake is outside our interests."

"Even though one of your own is with Sam?"

"Even so," the Emma said.

Daniel expected nothing different from her. As a network, the Emmas were brave, principled, generous, and self-sacrificing. The Emma he'd known best had sacrificed her life for him. But they were single-minded in their purpose, and that was something Daniel could understand.

He buttoned up his old chambray shirt. It comforted him and made him feel a tiny bit stronger, like cotton armor. "Where's my jacket?"

"Try the coat closet," Emma said. "What's your plan?"

Daniel shrugged on his jacket. "My plan is hoping all the things I'm scared of haven't happened yet."

He entered the ranger station, fairly certain the cabin's half-collapsed roof would elect to finish itself off when he was under a beam. Small things scurried in a wet mulch of pine needles and fallen shingles, and the odors of shit and piss and mildew contributed to the sense that the entire house-sized structure was a dark, humid forest.

He went over to a peeling desk. Ministry of Wilderness brochures and various papers formed a sodden pile amid more pine needles and splintered shingles. The Ministry was one of many institutions in the Hierarchy that faded into unfunded deaths after Daniel killed the Hierarch. He supposed the world was a better place without the bastard old wizard, but not as good as it ought to be.

He brushed mouse droppings aside with a wad of decomposing paper and picked up the receiver of the desk phone without much optimism. The Emmas didn't have phone service in their new safe house yet, but they said they'd restored the phone line here. It seemed impossible that anything in the ranger station could withstand decay and rodent teeth for more than a few days. But, to his surprise, he got a dial tone. He punched a number and listened to rings, and was surprised for a second time when someone picked up.

"Hello?" said a male voice. It was Fernando Bautista.

"This is Daniel. You know me. We've worked together."

"Is this a secure line?"

If the Emmas had set it up, it was a very secure line. Probably.

"Can't be sure. I'm looking for my boy."

"He's not here."

That meant Sam wasn't there at present, but had been. Otherwise, Fernando would have said that he hadn't seen him.

"Any word on when he might return?"

"No word."

This didn't sound good.

"None?" Daniel said, to make sure he wasn't misunderstanding him, or that they'd got their phone protocol mixed up.

"No word," Fernando repeated.

This was bad. That meant that not only had his wife not returned from the flight, but that he'd gotten no word from her that she'd delivered her cargo and was on her way back. Daniel's mind ran through all the implications of her silence, and none finished in happy conclusion.

"I need to take off," Daniel said. "Any tips?"

He wanted to fly out and trace the route Sofía would have taken and search for wreckage. If he found none, he'd continue to Catalina in hopes of heading Sam off.

"Goddamnit, Blackland, if I could get my hands on another plane you think I'd help you get a flight? Maybe everything's fine but she can't communicate for some reason. Maybe she made her destination and got into trouble. Maybe she's lost somewhere out there. If I could get another plane, I'd be in the air right now looking for her."

Even on a reasonably secure line, it wasn't like Fernando

to completely disregard protocol. Bautista was a careful man, rational and measured. But Daniel knew how much he loved his family. In the background, he could make out children's voices.

"I'll find them," Daniel said.

He set down the receiver, already feeling like he'd just made a broken promise.

He picked up the phone again and dialed the downtown Los Angeles headquarters of the Department of Water and Power. It only rang once before someone picked up. If he'd called the Ministry of Osteomancy or Labor or Justice, he would have been shocked at the quick response. But Gabriel Argent was a monster of efficiency.

"Department of Water and Power, how may I direct your call?"

"What a spectacularly good question," Daniel said.

Hi, this is the regicidal maniac Daniel Blackland, and I'd like to speak to the realm's chief water mage regarding the location of the Hierarch's golem, whom I misplaced on my way to sabotage the weapons project of LA's most dangerous powers. Can you connect me, please?

He hung up.

The cabin was equipped with a kitchenette. There were probably raccoons in the cupboards and possums in the stove, but the sink was clear of standing water. Daniel had an idea. He opened the faucet. At first there was nothing but a choked hiss, but after a few seconds, a stuttering trickle of brown water coughed out. It gradually gained strength, if not clarity. From the osteomancy kit the Emmas lent him to replace the one Sam absconded with, he took out the torch, bone crucible, and copper needle. He pierced the pad of his index finger deep enough to bring water to his eyes and let three fat ruby drops plunk into the crucible. Dialing the torch to burn indigo, he heated his blood until it darkened to match the flame. He tipped the crucible and let his blood slide down the sink, heavy as mercury. He packed away the kit and let the water run.

The vermin sensed something happening before Daniel did. The floor skittered and squeaked with insects and rodents, and a jay he hadn't noticed took flight from the rafters and shot out of a gap in the roof. Pipes in the walls rattled before dropping to a low, humming frequency that Daniel felt in his chest and belly.

Gabriel Argent played the role of humble bureaucrat, but it was a mask behind which lurked a great, emergent power. Water magic was a different kingdom than osteomancy, and Daniel barely understood its workings, its mechanisms of flow and circulation and mandalas. Gabriel Argent, however, knew both water and bone. His mother was an osteomancer, and he'd gotten his start working in the Ministry of Osteomancy. Daniel had eaten half the Hierarch's heart, and he'd given the other half to Argent in payment for a favor.

On the Salton Sea, Daniel turned the fish into magic-detecting grakes. He'd always suspected Argent was seeding his water network with his own microscopic grakes. As the pipes breathed and moaned, he knew he was right. The water detected his magic.

"Argent, can you hear me?"

The water in the cabin hummed, as did the water in

Daniel's body, and in the saturated leaves and pine needles, and in the muddy ground, and in the air.

Yes.

"Sam took my place. I don't know where he is."

A long delay before Argent's answer. *Uncertain.*

"Did he make it to Catalina?"

The water hummed, *No.*

"What does that mean, Argent? He hasn't made it *yet*? His plane crashed? Do you know where he is now? Is he alive?"

No answer. Either Argent didn't know, couldn't better communicate through oracular manifestation, or wasn't telling Daniel for reasons unfathomable.

"Argent, if you don't care about Sam as a person, care about the fact that the treasure is unaccounted for. Tell me something useful."

Hurry, the pipes sighed.

After that, the water fell silent and Gabriel Argent said no more.

Moth didn't give out his phone number. He didn't share his postal address. To locate him, you needed to consult the Musicians Wanted section of the *Los Angeles Times* classifieds. The major flaw in this system was finding a copy of the *Times*. They published only now and then, when the presses were running, and it was rare for them to deliver out on the edges of the realm. Daniel burned fuel and nerves trying the gas stations and markets on the desert valley floor, but finally his search paid off at a bar and grill in an unincorporated settlement on the rim of the Inyo wilderness. They were using a week-old paper to wrap fried fish.

It took some cash and an order of fish and chips to negotiate release of all the newspapers they had. Surrounded by the smell of fried haddock in his parked 4x4, he rifled through the grease-stained pages until he found the classifieds.

Here it was: *Band seeks guitarist with mastery of Norwegian-style metal.*

Last time, it had been Nashville-style country. The time before that, New Orleans–style jazz. The *N* signaled northern latitude. This part of the code always struck Daniel as unnecessary, as Moth had never been south of the equator. But there was just no reasoning with Moth about this kind of thing.

> *We have 35 years of combined experience and a repertoire of 37 songs. Avg. 21 gigs per month. No waste cases.*

"Busy band you got there, buddy."

North, 35 degrees, 37 feet, 21 inches.

In the past, Moth's special-code band had excluded wimps, wusses, whiners, walruses, and wallabies. He had never excluded women, because he didn't want to be that kind of musician, even in a pretend band. The *W* stood for western longitude.

A nonexistent PO box and a nonexistent phone number completed the coordinates.

Daniel retrieved the road map considerately tucked in the glove compartment by the Emmas and munched fried fish.

Downtown Crumville was a two-traffic-light stretch of highway with a sparse scattering of sun-faded stucco buildings: a used car lot, a video store with posters in the window for six-year-old movies, and a place called Desert Tom's #17 Burgers.

The smell of chili and orange grease assailed Daniel when he pushed through Desert Tom's front door. Half the tables were occupied by parties of one or two, working on chili burgers and chili fries. A ceiling fan whirred frantically, either trying to dispel the odors or distribute them for the benefit of those who enjoyed that sort of thing. Towering behind the counter like a granite monument was Moth, all six and a half feet of him, his muscled torso barely contained in a black T-shirt. His gaze fell upon Daniel, and his grin was so radiant with genuine delight that Daniel choked up.

Moth rushed out from behind the counter, spread his arms, and charged Daniel like a freight train. He wrapped Daniel in an embrace and lifted him four feet off the ground.

"You came to visit," he said in his deep bass. Then he abruptly dropped Daniel and barked out, "We're closed!"

Customers looked up in confusion.

"Closed?" one man said, a chili-slathered fry dangling between his fingers. "It's not even two o'clock."

Moth fetched a stack of takeout boxes and frisbeed them at the customers. "I found a rat in the kitchen. You all gotta fuck off."

Meekly, his customers packed their in-progress meals and emptied out. When the last one shuffled away, Moth locked the door and flipped the CLOSED sign around. His smile returned, and he subjected Daniel to a somewhat gentler hug. "Everything okay?"

Despite an overwhelming sense of relief at being in the presence of his best friend, everything felt heavy and dark. Daniel's eyes itched.

"Moth, I lost Sam."

Moth's dark face paled. "What happened, D?"

He gave Moth a brief of the last few days' events, including Gabriel Argent, the Pacific firedrake, the tsuchigumo attack, and the Emmas, and the Bautistas.

Moth shook his head, reproachful. "Argent is a fucking drip. You should have never gotten involved with him. See what happens when you don't have ready access to my magnificent mind?"

Daniel's world started to tilt. He slumped into a booth seat.

"Still working through the poison?"

"Yeah," Daniel said. He was sure that was it. Though he feared it might be something else. There wasn't much ambient osteomancy in a place like this. Not many osteomantic fossils in the ground. And this wasn't Los Angeles, with millions of people breathing and excreting the magic they consumed into the air. Daniel hadn't eaten raw magic in a long time. And he hadn't been in Los Angeles for even longer. But he'd been near one of the most remarkable products of Los Angeles: Sam.

He wasn't ready to face the ramifications of that.

"Let's get some food in you," Moth said.

"Already ate," Daniel said, regretting the fish and chips. "But I wouldn't say no to a soda."

"Orange Crush, heavy on the ice, coming up."

Daniel just needed a few minutes. He'd sit here with Moth, rehydrate, then get back on the road.

Moth dropped a bucket-sized cup of cold soda in front of Daniel and squeezed himself into the seat across the table. "So, a search and rescue, then?"

Daniel shook his head. "I'm not convinced his plane went down. And even if it did, that's not the worst-case scenario. Him actually reaching Catalina is the worst-case scenario."

"Wow. When a plane crash is the happy option . . ."

"Yeah. It's pretty much like that." Daniel sucked sweet soda through his straw. The bubbles felt good going down his throat.

"Have you wondered why Argent tipped you off about what Otis is planning for Sam? This wouldn't be the first time you got played like a dumb trombone. The Ossuary job—"

"Thanks. I remember the Ossuary job. Of course Argent could be playing me. I blow up the dragon and Argent lands a knockout punch on his competition without bruising his knuckles. But Otis can't have a dragon." Daniel reached bottom of the soda and annoyed Moth with the noise of slurping ice. Moth snatched his cup and refilled it.

"So there's no chance, zero, none, that Sam could actually pull this off?"

"No, zero, none," Daniel said, jiggling fresh ice.

Moth frowned, a terrifying expression. He didn't like Daniel's answer.

"D, I don't want to psychologize you, but—"

"Please, don't."

"But your mom and dad abandoned you and turned you into the sad, pitiful mess of a person you are now. You can't protect the scared and lonely boy you were by suffocating Sam."

"Oh, god, I beg you, shut up."

"Why did you try to dump Sam on the Emmas? Why didn't you set out for Catalina *with* him?"

"Sam's not like us when we were his age."

The backrest of Moth's seat creaked as he leaned back. "Whose fault is that? Sam's got the Hierarch's magic, and you've just tried to keep it hidden away. All you did was seal it under higher pressure. You weren't ever willing to release him, so he finally released himself."

Daniel took another long sip. "You know that thing about true friends, how they're the ones who can tell you anything?"

"Yeah," said Moth, a little puffed up.

"I hate that thing."

"I'm not wrong, D."

Daniel massaged his temples. "I know. I wouldn't be so pissed at you if you were wrong."

"I'll live with it. So, what's next?"

"Sam might've gone down over the desert. Or over the Pacific. Land or water, I can't search thousands of square miles of wasteland. But if he's able . . . if he's still alive . . . he'll try to make it to Catalina. He'll stop in LA first to gear up, make connections, arrange some kind of transport to the island. That'll take him a while. Which gives me time. I won't find him in the middle of the desert or the Pacific, but I have a chance of finding him in Los Angeles."

Moth tried to make encouraging noises, but they both knew they were talking about grim prospects. Sam alive in Los Angeles was ridiculously optimistic. And even if he was, that only meant he was in the very place Daniel had spent the last decade keeping him away from.

Moth took a breath, filling himself with whatever vapors of cheer he could muster. "So, let's go get your boy, right?"

"What about your burger joint?"

Moth loved chili cheeseburgers. He was a connoisseur and cared about them passionately, the way fly fishermen cared about hacklers and muddlers. Owning his own shop was his dream.

"It can go a few days without me. Louis can run it while I'm gone."

"Louis?"

Moth grinned, bashful. "He's my guy."

"Shit, Moth, I'm sorry, I didn't know you had some-one." He got up. "I should go."

"This is how you congratulate me?"

"This is how I don't take you away from your life and drag you through my shit."

"I decide where I go and what I do."

Moth was giving him exactly what he came to him for: not just his physical strength and durability, or his counsel and his loyalty, all the qualities that made him invaluable on the jobs they used to run for Otis. But he was also offering to once again be Daniel's bedrock, to make sure whatever dark places Daniel walked into, he'd never be alone. That in a world where no rational person would ever trust anyone, there'd be one person he could trust.

Moth was always willing to be that person for Daniel. And Daniel would always accept it. He could rationalize good reasons. Saving Sam. Stopping Otis. Saving millions of lives. But he suspected the real reason he wouldn't turn Moth down was because Daniel was still a thief. Thieves took what they wanted.

NINE

Sam was empty. His veins and arteries were hollow tubes. His heart was a hollow box. He busied his hands and his mind on building a cairn. It was not the osteomancer's way to worry about a corpse—if it had magical value, you ate it, and if not, it was worthless. But Sofía Bautista was not an osteomancer, nor was her husband, and nor were her children. He would give her as much of an honorable burial as he could.

Em was looking over Sofía's rifle. She'd found it beneath more rocks. The barrel was crimped.

"We'll have to figure out a way back to the Bautista farm," Sam said. "We'll have to tell Fernando what happened."

Em set the useless rifle down in the sand. "No, Sam."

"How else is he going to find out? Somebody might come along and take the plane for salvage, but no one will care what happened to her. So we'll tell Fernando to his face. Then we'll drive back to the safe house. If your sisters have already ditched it, they'll have left a way for us to find them, right? We'll go back to the Emmas and Daniel."

Em came over and crouched beside him. She brushed her fingers over the cold stones of Sofía's cairn. Some of the rocks came from the fault creature's body. Sofía was dead because Sam blew it apart.

"Sam, I'm going to try to say this as kindly as I can. I didn't partner up with you because I have a crush on you. I didn't partner up with you because I was swayed by your charismatic leadership qualities. I'm not interested in being your sidekick while you seek redemption, or closure, or trot ahead on a quest to fulfill your destiny. Not everything is about you, Sam. The Emmas debated whether we should make the firedrake our problem. My sisters decided to leave it to someone else. And not because they didn't see the danger of a dragon in the hands of Otis and the LA osteomancers. They know it might lead to full-scale war with Northern California or an internal war that lays waste to half the Southern realm. None of my sisters saw a scenario in which the dragon gets built without a lot of people dying. But they won't do anything about it. Too risky, they say. But I think they're wrong. So I'm doing something. I'm going to Catalina, and I'm going to make sure the dragon never gets completed."

"With or without me?"

"No, *with* you, because I can't do it by myself. So get up, shake it off, and let's go."

"Shake it off. Is that what I should say to Sofía's kids?"

Em stood and picked up her bag.

"Tell me about Otis," Sam said.

"You know about Otis."

"Tell me what *you* know about him."

"Why?"

"Would you just? Please?"

Em took a breath. "Here's the first thing I was ever told about Otis Roth: he wanted golems. Because reproducible, disposable people are too useful to someone like him to pass up. So, he acquired some. But they didn't work out the way he'd hoped. They still had minds of their own. So Otis came up with a Plan B. He found the bones of some bird that could turn anyone into a programmable zombie, and he used them on street kids. Voilà, he had his wraiths, a collection of little operatives even better than golems. They're his cannon fodder, his suicide vests, whatever he needs. That's the kind of man Otis is. And that's why we don't want him to have a firedrake."

She hoisted her bag over her shoulder and stuck out her hand.

"Cikavac," Sam said.

"What?"

"That's the osteomantic bird he used to make the wraiths. The cikavac. And it was Daniel who processed the bone for him."

Em kept her hand out. Sam finally took it. She pulled him to his feet and they continued on, walking away from the wreck of the airplane and the scattered boulders of the giant and the corpse of Sofía Bautista.

An hour's hike from the crash site brought them to a place where the walls of the Abyss were lower, but still too treacherous to risk the climb.

"Feeling any better?" Em said. "At least physically?"

Sam wiped sweat off the back of his neck.

"I don't know. I've never used that much magic in such a short period of time. Or ever, actually. I'm weak as a baby lamb now. But for a while there I was pretty sexy, wasn't I?"

It seemed selfish to joke, but he was desperate for a sense of lightness, to lift himself above the awfulness of the last few hours. Daniel said he and his friends joked a lot during jobs. It helped them keep their nerves under control, and it reminded them of their best asset: each other.

"Baby lamb is redundant," Em said. "Hey, what kind of birds are those?"

Sam shaded his eyes from the midday sun. Small black birds circled in the searing sky. They were little more than dots, but something about the way they jittered in flight set off his alarms.

Not birds. Bats.

He grabbed Em by the wrist and raced for the canyon wall. They huddled among some rocks the size of cantaloupes and a scraggly chaparral bush that might have been sufficient to hide a small rabbit.

Bats didn't rely on sight. At least not normal bats. They relied on echolocation, and in this case, maybe smell. He went for his kit and shook out a few grams of yellowish powder into his palm and blew it into the air.

The meretseger serpent was associated with the silence of tombs, and its osteomancy could dampen noise. Sam didn't know if it would help conceal them from the bats, but without a better place to hide and no way to cloak his scent, he couldn't think of anything else to do.

Peering through twigs at the sky, he watched the bats flutter in circles.

"Think they saw us?" Em whispered.

A dribble of small rocks and sand rattled down the canyon wall, peppering Sam's hair. He twisted around and looked up. A man stood on the precipice, eyes hidden behind mirrored sunglasses.

He aimed a rifle down at Sam and Em.

"Got 'em!" he called out, and in seconds he was joined by half a dozen other men and women, all of them armed with black, chunky, complicated-looking guns. Down on the floor ahead, a quad bike closed in, raising a cloud of dust.

Sam screwed his eyes shut and ignored everything around him. He dug for smells of the sea bottom, for darkness and a rain of biomass falling to the ocean floor. Pins and needles pricked his fingertips, but that was all. No kraken storm.

The quad bike came to a stop mere feet from them. A bald fat man with a sun-pinked face dismounted, along with a tall, lean black woman with eyes tattooed on the sides of her bald head.

The hound sniffed the air.

"Juicy," she said.

They taped Sam's and Em's hands behind their backs, bound their ankles together, and hammered them with fists and boots until they were spitting blood in the dust. Sam was relieved to be dumped in a hot-box trailer connected to the quad bike by a tow hitch. At least no one was hitting him now.

They bounced along, cooking in the desert heat. Em kicked at the door for hours until she gave in to exhaustion and sat with her back to the steel wall of the trailer, legs curled up, silent.

"On the bright side," Sam said, "we're getting a free ride out of the Abyss."

Em made a sound that could have been a moan or a laugh. "I never even pulled my gun," she breathed, sniffling a trickle of blood from her nostril.

"Nothing you could have done. They got the drop on us, Slick." Each rut and rock they rolled over felt like a fresh blow to his punished body. Sam maneuvered close to her. Gently, painfully, he leaned his head into hers and wiped away her blood with his hair. "We'll be okay."

"Oh, Sam. You're a nice guy, but you're really stupid."

"Now I'm starting to wish I didn't have your blood in my hair."

"Seriously, I've been in some fuck-ups before, but this one gets the blue ribbon. Any ideas?"

They hit another jarring bump and Sam felt bootheels in his ribs and kidneys. His head throbbed with every pulse beat, and he rode up and down waves of nausea. But this had to be better than whatever they'd be facing when the quad bike stopped.

Yet, he was not afraid. He found that curious. Maybe because he was with Em, who, even beat up and miserable, somehow managed to pick him up. But he began to suspect it was something else. He still sensed things below: large, potent forces of deeply embedded osteomancy. And as the feeling persisted, he started to wonder if what he sensed was under the earth, or under his skin.

"It'll be okay," he said again. "We just have to wait."

The locking mechanism rattled and someone opened the trailer.

"Out," barked a pudgy white man with a cauliflower ear. Accompanying him was an ugly-looking crew, all bad skin and bad teeth and bad haircuts, and all with guns. The pudgy man had Em's confiscated gun in the waistband of his dirt-coated jeans. Sam wished he knew a way to make it fire remotely and shoot the guy's pecker off.

Instead, he obediently stepped down from the trailer. They were at the edge of the Abyss, on a plateau of sand and soil and low scrub. Nearby, a thirty-foot box truck idled beside a pickup truck with a long flatbed trailer and a pair of motorcycles. Quite a little convoy.

Sharp cliffs stood in purple shadow many miles away. The sun was almost gone over the horizon, and the air felt deliciously cool after the stifling trailer.

The band of uglies loaded them into the box truck, already crowded with twenty or thirty other captives in the airless dark. No room to sit, Sam stood shoulder to shoulder with the others. The truck bumped and swayed over desert terrain, sending Sam stumbling into others.

The air crawled with the stink of sweat and urine and vomit, the only airflow coming from a tiny vent in the ceiling. As Sam's eyes adjusted to the dim light, he looked more critically at his fellow captives. They ranged in age from a woman in her seventies who'd apparently been snatched from her home in her housecoat to a toddler scrunched up against his mother's thigh. Sam thought of the Bautista children and looked away.

A few stood out: a middle-aged man with slits in his neck, like gills; a chubby teenage girl with bad acne and a pair of what looked like condor wings growing through carefully seamed slots in her T-shirt. She kept the wings folded close to her back and winced whenever someone bumped into them.

Sam didn't understand. He'd assumed he and Em had been specifically targeted. But this was starting to look like something different.

"Where are they taking us?" Sam asked no one in particular.

"Heading to the cannery," said a man.

Sam squeezed between several people to reach him.

Round as a walnut, he stood chest high to Sam. He gazed up with giant, unblinking eyes, yellow as a fire hydrant and bordered by black rings. His pupils were half the size of pennies.

"What's the cannery?"

"Cannery? You know. A glue factory. A skinning house. Hooks, knives, hoses, tanks. They cut you open, let you drip out into a pan. Wring the magic out of you. Press your eyes like olives. Dry your skin out, crack it into flakes. Pulverize your bones. Harden your tendons like jerky. Smoke it. Add hickory flavor."

"Leeches," Em said. "We've been captured by leeches. Swell."

That explained the armed men and women, the hound, and the truck stuffed with what looked like a random assortment of people. But it wasn't random. Everybody in the truck had osteomancy in their system. Some were probably just occasional users, ingesting magic for medicine or adventure. Some might be practicing osteomancers. When they confiscated Sam's osteomancy kit, they probably assumed he was an osteomancer, but hopefully not which osteomancer. He was still drained from the seismic creature, and the hound with the tattooed eyes probably hadn't smelled his full potency. If they'd known what he really was and how much rare magic was packed in his system, they wouldn't have put him back here with the rest of the human cargo.

"Where's the cannery?" Em asked the owl-eyed man.

"Towers. Canals. Magicians at war. Whole nests of people, millions of them, all on top of each other, hungry, always hungry."

"You mean Los Angeles?"

The owl-man blinked. "City of Angels."

Em shook her head with irritation. "I'll be damned if I let myself get vivisected just so some limp-dicked accountant from Pasadena can eat my pelvis."

Sam nudged closer to her and stood with his back to

hers. They brushed fingertips. It was as close as they could come to holding hands.

Dripping with sweat in the fetid darkness, he shut his eyes and searched his bones for magic.

The leeches opened the box and forced the blinking captives out of the truck and into a stockade beneath blue sky. Gulls wheeled overhead and the algal stink of canals wafted on an oven-dry breeze.

The stockade's steel bars rose eight feet high. At one end, a ramp sloped down to a pier. Docked there was a 150-foot vessel with a black, shoebox-shaped deckhouse. Chimneys belched black smoke. A dinghy on a tow rope floated behind it.

Sam shuffled along with the rest of the captives and tried to get his bearings. Cargo cranes lifted steel containers onto barges. Acres of parking lots separated clusters of drab, rectangular buildings—warehouses and government buildings and freight inspection offices. Fast-food restaurants and gas stations and motels stretched off in the distance to the foot of brown hills fronting snow-dusted brown mountains. Sam had never been here before, but this must be the San Gabriel Grand Port, where the desert roads ended and the Los Angeles canal system began.

"Never see the capital now," the owl-man said.

"What do you mean?"

"Factory boat. They'll do us on the way."

Em came up beside Sam.

"Anything you can do yet?"

"Not yet," Sam said miserably. "I'm sorry."

"I really don't want to be canned, Sam."

He supposed they could try to make a break for it, but there didn't seem much hope with their arms bound and the high stockade rails and the leeches with guns. But maybe better to die now than in a glue factory.

A leech barked orders for everyone to get in line and move down the stockade. One of the captives, a man built like a lumberjack, decided instead to drive his knee into the leech's stomach. The leech squealed and doubled over, and the man lowered his shoulders and charged the stockade. Maybe he thought he could hit it hard enough to break through. Maybe he thought he could dive into the canal, and manage not to drown, and swim away before being riddled with bullets. Or maybe he just didn't want to die by knife cuts in the dark.

He never reached the stockade rails. A single gunshot cracked, and he fell. Sam didn't watch, but he heard the *chuk-chuk* of their cleaver-clubs biting into flesh and bone. He wondered who the man was, and where he was supposed to be today, and who would miss him when he didn't come home.

Anger pushed against his skin, like a bomb explosion contained by a barely adequate membrane.

The captives filed through a chute, onto the deck of the boat. They were met there by the woman with the tattooed eyes. Em was ahead of Sam in line and got to the hound first.

The hound's head flicked, but she said nothing as Em moved past her.

When it was Sam's turn, the hound turned her head. The black pupil inked on her temple shrank. Maybe it was a muscle contraction, or an optical illusion, but Sam felt as if he'd been truly seen.

"You have a very special smell." Her voice was a creamy alto. "I smelled it in Mecca, from miles away. I smelled it in the Abyss. You're frightened and angry, and your blood smells even more delicious."

She paused, waiting for Sam to confess something.

"Thanks," he said, as if she'd paid him a compliment.

She smiled without turning her head, keeping her tattooed eye fixed on him.

"I wasn't sure about you at first. I mean, nobody really is. There are descriptions, and there are stories, and there are legends."

Em, who was being led away with other captives toward the stern, gave nothing away. To dig in her heels, to turn around and face Sam, would signal that the hound was right, that Sam was something deserving this much scrutiny. There was only a stiffening in her shoulders that went unnoticed by everyone but Sam.

Sam was mesmerized by the hound's eye. It seemed to do more than merely see him. It seemed to be swallowing him.

"I'm known for the quality of my product," she said. "Most of my acquisitions are beneath the standards of my best customers, and I sell them off cheap. But sometimes I find special items. And I have some very, very exclusive customers in the market for a very special item. They gave me a sample of what I was to look for. Just a speck of essence. Little more than a mote. And it was the most wonderfully potent thing I've ever smelled. And do you know what?"

"I smell like a mote?"

The pupil closed to a small inky dot.

"Very much." She turned to one of her subordinates. "Don't leech this one. We need to deliver him fresh."

"What about the girl?" the leech said, indicating Em. "She was with him."

"She doesn't smell like much. Put her at the front of the line. We'll use her to calibrate our knives."

Sam lunged at the hound. The crack of the rifle butt on the back of his neck was like thunder. Hands caught him before he struck the deck. They were happy to hurt him, but they didn't want him damaged.

Sam's toes scraped the deck boards as the leeches dragged him by the armpits. He never lost consciousness, and so he took in the promised horrors of the enclosed deck. Buzzing fluorescents cast a pale blue light that would make healthy people look like they'd been dead for a week. Long steel tables with built-in drains ran the entire length of the deckhouse. Tools were stuck on magnetic strips— knives and cleavers and saws and scalpels and shears and picks. There were power grinders and drills and circular saws. Shelves were stacked with an exotic array of beakers and flasks and jars for storing osteomancy drawn from the bodies. Hooks and hoists on chains dangled overhead.

"Always a bad idea to tour the kitchen," Sam tried to say, but it came out as an unintelligible mumble.

With the exception of himself, no single one of the captives was likely very rich with osteomancy. These were users, mostly of watered-down magical preparations. But their combined magics formed a deep, crackling odor. To Sam's shame, he found it delicious.

A row of steel-barred cages lined the bulkhead. They were narrow, not much more than closets to tuck mops or an ironing board in, and each held a single captive. Armed leeches loaded the captives inside, and a single thug with a bayonet-fitted rifle stood guard, a job which seemed to largely involve keeping out of vomiting range.

Sam lifted his twelve-ton head to find Em but didn't see her. And now he began to resist. He tried planting his feet, but the leeches, a powerfully built man and a just as powerfully built woman, kept dragging him along. He twisted in their grip and managed only to earn a hard slap in the face. The woman adjusted her hold and took his thumb and pinky in one hand and did something that shot pain all the way to his jaw.

"Fuck you and your kung fu," Sam said, and she did something else that made him scream.

They pushed him into a cage. He lunged at the leeches as they slammed the cage door shut, and his face ran into the bars. The guard with the bayonet gave him a reptilian glare.

Magic should work differently, he thought. It should respond to anger. It should respond to need.

A whisper from the next cage. "Hey."

It was Em. A partition between them blocked his view.

"Hey," he whispered back.

The hum of the engines rose in pitch and the deck rocked as the boat pulled away from the pier. Technicians came down the gangway and took their positions at the table, arranging their tools and making small talk about sports and real estate.

"How are you feeling?" Em said.

He knew the full question behind her casual query.

"Not yet," he said.

"Your recovery time is kind of inconvenient."

"It doesn't take me this long to recover from everything, I assure you."

"Oh, please," she said. "You're totally a virgin."

"Not technically speaking, I'm not." He wished he could see her roll her eyes.

"Technically?"

"I think the amount of time I spend thinking about sex ought to count for something."

She laughed, just a little bit, and he realized he'd never heard her laugh before. It sounded glorious.

The guard came back to stand in front of Em's cage, and she hushed up. He gave a nod over to a technician at a row of switches on the wall. There was an electronic buzz and some mechanical noises, and Em's cage door sprang open.

"Out," snapped the guard.

And now Em's bravado shattered.

"No," she whimpered. "No, please, no." As wonderful

as the sound of her laughter had been, the sound of her fear and meek despair came from another reality.

There were noises of a brief scuffle, and they dragged her from the cage by her hair. Em shrieked now, sobbed, and Sam grabbed the bars of his cage, and he shook them and screamed, inarticulate with rage. He begged for the magic in his bones to erupt. He cursed the guard, he cursed the leech technicians, who didn't even lift their eyes from their work, and he cursed Daniel for being a poor teacher. He cursed himself for being useless.

Em's face was red, the muscles in her neck taut, and just then, Sam noticed that despite the pitiful sounds of her weeping, no tears fell. In fact, she was smiling. She twisted. Her foot went into the guard's knee. She had one of his hands, and then his arm, and she did something to his elbow that made his arm bend the wrong way, and then she had his bayonet. She drove the blade in and out of his eye. The technician who'd opened her cage reached for another switch, this one big and red, and Em shot him through the hand. The crack of the rifle sounded like a breaking bone. The leech at the gangway fired a shot in her general direction. It went far wide and he turned to race up the gangway. Em shot him in the head. She shot two more.

"Everybody sit down." She spoke just loud enough for her voice to be clearly heard through the deckhouse.

The technicians did as they were told.

A leech came down the gangway from the upper deck, firing. Em pulled the trigger and he fell.

She went to the switches.

Another leech came down the gangway. Em shot him twice, once in the knee, and then in the chest. She waited a few seconds to see if anyone else was coming down, then began throwing switches to open the cages. A few of the captives came out. Others stayed back.

"I've killed six guards," Em said. "You have their guns and a whole lot of knives. Stay below deck until you get an all-clear. Don't let the techs overwhelm you. Kill them if you have to. And keep your heads down. There's going to be gunfire above."

Some of the captives still wouldn't leave their cages. Some cowered. But a few stepped forward and gathered the guns of the fallen guards.

Blood streamed down Em's bayonet. She pushed away a lock of hair and smeared red across her forehead. Her eyes looked like stone.

So this was Em, being an Emma.

"How many above?" Sam asked her.

"I counted seven more, plus the hound."

"Any idea how we're getting off this boat?"

"Yeah," she said. She took a cleaver from one of the technician's racks. "You're not going to like it."

Em held the cleaver to Sam's throat. He felt a thin, cold line against his jugular. In her other hand she held the bayonet. Sam offered no resistance and let her walk him up the gangway to the deck.

The first obstacle they encountered was the pink-faced

man who'd first captured them in the San Andreas Abyss. He was waiting at the top of the gangway, his gun inches away from Sam's face.

"No bullshit," said Em. "I know you want him alive, and you want his lovely osteomantic tissues unspoiled by dirty metal. Throw your guns overboard or I shoot him."

Sam was wider and taller than Em, and there was no way for Pinky to shoot her without going through Sam. He flung his weapon over the side. It hit the canal with a satisfying splash.

"Good," Em said. "Now go jump after it."

Pinky snarled out the word "fuck" before Em thrust the bayonet forward between Sam's arm and side and punctured Pinky's belly. Pinky let out one long "Owwwww" and doubled over.

"What are they paying you guys?" Em called out.

Sam heard a noise behind him. He didn't get a chance to warn Em, because she pivoted around and tilted the gun up. There was another bone-crack from the rifle and someone fell, facedown, from the top of the deck. A pool of blood spread from his head. He didn't move.

"How much are they paying you?" she repeated.

"Two percent of the job," answered a voice. Sam didn't see its source. The rest of the leeches had hunkered down under cover.

"Your job's busted," Em said. "So, math problem: What's two percent of nothing?"

There were no answers. Sam supposed it was a rhetorical question.

"I make four of you left," Em said. "So I better see four people jumping overboard, or I'm going to kill my expensive hostage and then hunt you down and shoot your knees out just to hear your voices."

"Overboard, fellas," blared a voice from a speaker horn: the hound. She was probably in the wheelhouse.

One guy took a life jacket with him, but the rest just clambered over the rail and dropped into the canal.

The ability to impel someone to do what you told them, just with words, was a power as useful as magic. Sam liked how Em wielded it.

But she still had the cleaver to his throat.

"You can let me go now."

"Not yet. I don't want to lose my leverage," Em said, and Sam was seized by a queasy moment of doubt. Had he misjudged this situation? Had he misjudged Em?

"Shall we negotiate?" the hound said over the loudspeaker. "You must know what he's worth."

"I have your treasure, and you have no more thugs," Em shouted. "I don't need to share."

Drive head back into Em's face. Drive foot into her knee. Maybe she'd slice his jugular. Maybe bayonet him. Maybe shoot him. He'd need luck. He'd need chaos to work in sympathy with his intent.

That was Daniel thinking.

Sam let her hold him there, with her cleaver on his skin.

He chose this moment to trust Em more than he'd ever trusted anyone or anything. He was going to ridiculous lengths to prevent Otis and his Pacific firedrake from killing people beyond his ability to count, and he decided that if he couldn't trust Em, the world wasn't worth saving.

"You're still on my boat," the hound said. "And you're not going to take the wheelhouse while I'm in it."

"That's why I'm taking your dinghy," Em said.

"My boat's a lot faster than the dinghy. I'll just follow you."

"I think you're going to find yourself delayed.

"All clear," Em called down the gangway. The captives came up cautiously, led by a few who'd claimed the guards' guns and others who took up knives and cleavers. The owl-eyed man blinked in the harsh sunlight.

"It's a nice day to go boating," he said.

"The boat's not yours yet," she told him and the others. "The hound is in the wheelhouse, and she's more dangerous than the others. But there's only one of her, and there're a lot of you."

"Even odds?" said the girl with the stunted condor wings. She'd claimed a handgun.

"Maybe a little less than even," Em said. "But better than the steel tables."

The captives began moving toward the wheelhouse, and Em finally took the cleaver from Sam's throat. He felt something larger than relief.

"Thanks," he said, rubbing his Adam's apple.

They made for the stern and hurried down a ladder to the dinghy. Em took position at the outboard motor and Sam untied the tow rope. Gunshots rang out as they zipped away from the factory boat and raced through canal traffic at full throttle. Em stared straight ahead, her jaw set like granite. Tears glimmered in her eyes.

"Are you okay?"

"I hate shooting people," she said. "I just fucking hate it."

Sam watched out for police and for the factory boat and for more leeches as Em sped on, steering the dinghy and weeping.

Sam and Em arrived in Los Angeles on a vivid afternoon. The snowcapped San Gabriel Mountains loomed behind the jade and azure towers of downtown. Palatial clouds sailed overhead. Daniel always described LA as big and messy and sprawling. But never beautiful.

"Quit gawking," Em said, guiding the dinghy through midday traffic. "You look like a rube."

"I am a rube. I didn't think the buildings would be this tall." He craned his neck to watch an airship approach the mooring tower of an emerald-green skyscraper at least eighty stories high.

Em steered around a cement-mixing scow, its drum rotating on its way to a construction site.

"How many times have you been in LA?" he asked Em.

"Three times, on rescue missions. My first time, we broke golems out of the Playboy Mansion. That was weird."

She'd been acting like herself since the leeches, but there

was a strain in her manner, in her posture, in her voice. She'd killed people on the glue factory boat. It weighed heavy on her. But she was still with him.

After a brief stop at a hardware store to shoplift some tools, she drove them to a range of foothills off the La Cienega locks, where they left the dinghy in a dead-end canal. With shovel and crowbar over their shoulders, they hiked up a trail of green and yellow grasses. A sign said NO TRESPASSING. VIOLATORS SUBJECT TO MINISTRY OF JUSTICE DISPENSATION PENALTIES. Sam wanted nothing to do with having justice dispensed at him, but Em ignored the sign and cut a hole in a rusted chain-link fence.

They crept through oil fields. Pump jacks cranked up and down, pulling dwindling amounts of crude petroleum and magic from deep underground. Climbing among the mechanical squeaks and hisses, Sam and Em reached summit, where they paused to catch their breath. From here, the Hierarch used to launch dragon flames at enemy aircraft from beyond his borders, or at rebellious osteomancers inside his borders. Now, the place was occupied by a few radio transmission towers and the cracked remains of wartime catapult bunkers.

The view of LA was spectacular. The Pacific Ocean glimmered blue in the west, with a gray bank of clouds sitting on the horizon like a wall. Sam could make out the purple-gray silhouette of the Catalina Island ridgeline. It seemed enticingly close, as if they could just wade out to it. The rest of the LA basin was filled with houses and offices and strip malls and dark green tufts of treetops. The

Hollywood sign stood out against an arrogant blue sky, and just right of it, the green copper domes of Griffith Observatory. If Daniel had claimed the Hierarchy, that would have been one of his palaces.

He looked for the site of the Magic Castle, where he'd been born, and where Daniel rescued him. He saw no sign of it. Daniel had set it aflame, and rains and mudslides took care of the wreckage.

For all the times Daniel told him spooky-boo stories of Los Angeles, Sam felt oddly as though he'd come home. He spread his arms and encompassed the city, just as the Hierarch might have done when standing on this very spot with his war machines.

"What are you doing?"

Startled, Sam turned to Em. "Just looking," he said guiltily.

"Well, golden god, you can help me look for the cache."

The Emmas had laid in a cache of bone near here, and if he and Em hoped to survive Los Angeles and do damage on Catalina, they'd need to arm themselves. But the cache had been here for going on a dozen years, and the chances of it going undisturbed this long weren't great.

Em took them into a field of asphalt broken by tufts of weeds. She stepped gingerly, as if walking through a garden and trying not to step on the flowers.

"What are we looking for?" Sam asked. "Some marking stone or sigil or something?"

She didn't answer, just kept picking through weeds and busted slabs of concrete.

"A big X, like on a pirate treasure map?" Sam ventured. "An informative frog?"

"I'll know it when I see it. . . . Oh! Here we are."

At Em's feet, a spray-painted face on the concrete looked up at him. It was just an outline done in red, but he recognized the nose.

"You drew your own face to mark where you left your stuff? That's ingenious."

"It's not my face. It's the Emma who buried the cache. To anyone else it just looks like graffiti, but to an Emma, it couldn't be more obvious."

"Okay," Sam said. "I'm sorry I made fun of you."

"When did you make fun of me?"

"When I said 'ingenious' I really meant 'incomprehensibly stupid,' but now that you explained it, I guess it's not a bad system."

They pried the slab away and started digging through dry, loose dirt and plant roots. Two feet down, Sam's shovel struck metal. Another minute of digging revealed a bread-loaf-sized ammo box.

Em brushed dirt away and unclipped the lid, and Sam joined her in staring into an empty box. He smelled only dirt and a tinge of rust.

"This is either the best sint holo invisibility essence I've ever not seen, or else it's an empty box," he said.

Em slammed the box shut and kicked it into the hole. Sam backed away from her, because she looked like she was searching for other things to kick. He grasped for an encouraging word, or at least something mollifying.

"Maybe we can find the person who stole your magic and make them suffer," he offered.

The *crack-pop* of gunfire rang out, and bits of concrete peppered their knees and shins. They dove into the dirt for cover, but instead of more gunshots, there was a shout.

"You leave my chickens alone!"

Sam lifted his head above the weeds. In the doorway of one of the bunkers, an ancient scarecrow of a man carried a rifle.

"We mean your chickens no harm," Sam called out.

"What chickens?" Em whispered.

"Whatever chickens he's upset about," Sam whispered back.

"Stand up so I can see you," the man said in a timorous voice.

Em clamped her hand around Sam's arm. She had an extraordinarily strong grip. "I think he means stand up so he can shoot us."

Another shot blast, and the sound of a bullet's ricochet.

"I can shoot you standing or I can shoot you snake-crawling. Your choice."

Sam wrenched free from Em's clutch. "I choose standing."

He cautiously lifted himself to his feet, hands in the air. Cursing, Em did the same.

The man's eyes were red rimmed and wild, and his hands shook so much it was hard to tell if he was aiming at Em and Sam or aiming at a cloud. Dangerous in any case.

From somewhere in the bunkers, a rooster crowed, and the man's legs began to tremble. He shifted from one foot to the other in a little dance of agitation.

"Seriously," Sam said. "We're not after your chickens."

The man squinted and leaned forward, and then his eyes popped wide and he fell to his knees. "Forgive me," he wailed. "I am a plunderer and a glutton." The more he shook, the more the bore of his rifle bobbed and jittered.

"Hey," Sam said, "could you maybe put the gun away?"

The man gawked at his rifle as if he'd suddenly discovered a python in his hands. He tossed it before him. Sam and Em both flinched. Luckily, there was no accidental discharge.

Sobbing, the man buried his face in his hands. "I dreamed of this day. I prayed for it."

Helplessly confused, Sam turned to Em. "Is this like an LA thing, or . . . ?"

"I don't know. Every other time I've been here it's just been a lot of running around and shooting and explosions."

The man wiped an arm across his sloppy nose. "The chickens are yours," he blubbered. "It's all yours." He spread his arms in an all-encompassing gesture, uncomfortably like the one Em caught Sam giving the vista of Los Angeles.

His eyes shot skyward, and then he hastily rose to his feet. "Come on," he said with a manic grin. "I'll hide you." He disappeared into the shadows of his bunker.

"Hide us from what?"

"That," Em said.

He followed her gaze. A helicopter, small in the distance, approached from the office towers of Century City. Maybe just a news chopper, or a rich person's transport. Or maybe it belonged to an osteomancer on the hunt.

The bunker started to look like a good idea. They followed the man inside.

Inside, a gas camping lantern cast a yellow glow over a shopping cart stuffed with what looked like random garbage, but were probably the man's life's possessions. Among newspaper pages and crumpled plastic bags were books and a trombone missing its slide and plastic water jugs. A radio was plugged into an extension cord that snaked off into the dark unknown. Chickens clucked in the shadows, and the stench of chicken shit hung everywhere.

The man held a finger to his lips as the hum of the helicopter resolved into the rhythmic chop of rotor blades. They huddled in the cramped space until the sounds passed overhead and faded.

"You're safe now," the man said, smiling shyly at Sam.

"Who was that in the chopper?"

"Looters and lessers, sire, the whole lot of them. They buzz the sky like vultures, picking on the remains of your kingdom."

Em gave Sam an *uh-oh* look, which matched the feeling in his belly.

"What do you mean, *my* kingdom?" he asked, though he knew damn well what the man meant.

The man giggled, like they were all in on a delightful secret.

"You don't have to hide from me, majesty. I'm your most loyal subject, always have been, and my daddy before me, and his daddy before him."

Sam didn't quite know what to say, and Em was no help.

"Come on, I'll show you my chickens."

He cantered into a deeper part of the bunker. Em began following, but Sam blocked her way.

"What are you doing? He thinks I'm the Hierarch."

"Apparently. So?"

"So," Sam sputtered, "I've spent my life trying to avoid situations just like this."

"No, you've spent your life trying to avoid people who want to vivisect you. This guy is your number one fan. And we need the magic my sisters cached. If nothing else, I want to see these chickens."

Exasperated, Sam went along with her. In a larger chamber, rails in the floor led to a pair of steel doors, probably for the deployment of a war engine. The device was nowhere in sight, and a carpet of weeds and dry plant bits indicated the doors hadn't been opened in a long time. The smell of chicken shit was stronger here, and clucks and shuffling sounds came from cages set up on sawhorses, partially covered by a plastic tarp. But when Sam's eyes adjusted to the dark, what drew his attention was a wall plastered with newspaper and magazine pages, and drawings and photos and postage stamps, and a small fortune in currency, all depicting the Hierarch's face: strong, grim, with eyes like two pinpoints of light in a coal shaft, ageless, but a chin and nose that unmistakably also belonged to Sam.

The man could barely contain his glee. "The pretenders said you were dead. They said Blackland ate your heart, and the rest of the osteomancers divided up your kingdom and squatted in your sacred places and ate your magic. But

I never believed them. I don't know how anyone who ever saw you could believe them. But me, I *did* see you. You wouldn't remember me, I was just a boy, at your Blessing of the Animals ceremony. I gave you a chicken and you ate it live on the spot, right in front of me. You honored me, sire. *You* honored *me*." He got blubbery again. "Oh, sire. The Hierarchy without you . . . We are excrement and gas. Where have you been, my liege?"

"Oh," Sam said. "Wandering the desert? Yes. I have been wandering the desert."

This answer seemed to please the man. He rubbed his hands together. "Gathering your malice and power. It is what I hoped."

"Yes, exactly," Sam said. "I have been wandering the desert, gathering my malice and power."

"So, your chickens," Em prompted.

The man drew himself up to all the haughty dignity he could muster. "Not my chickens. The Hierarch's chickens."

He pulled the tarp away, scaring up a cloud of dust and disease vectors. The animals in the cages weren't chickens, but they used to be. Now, they were the size of beach balls. Their heads were featherless, more feline than avian. Vestigial rear legs grew from their hindquarters. They were covered in sand-colored fur.

"You fed them magic from the box," Em said.

The man nodded, proudly at first, but then shrank once he realized he may have displeased Sam.

"They were always scratching there," he said, defensive. "You know how chickens are."

"Griffin magic in the cache?" Sam asked Em.

She nodded.

Sam did not relish eating the chickens in hopes of extracting traces of griffin.

Em gave the man a cross look. "Poaching the Hierarch's magic is a death sentence."

Even Sam winced at her punishing tone.

"I am sorry, majesty." Tears clung to the man's eyelashes.

And now Sam had to decide what to do. There was protocol in case someone ID'd him. The man didn't know he was the Hierarch's golem, but him thinking he was the actual Hierarch was maybe even worse. Daniel would have fogged the man's brain, but Sam didn't know how to summon lamassu magic. Would Daniel have killed him?

Yes, to protect Sam, certainly.

But there was another option. Sam could actually assume the Hierarchy.

He imagined the old Hierarch standing on this hilltop, commanding everything from the sea to the mountains and beyond.

"You have failed me by stealing my magic," Sam said. The man peered up at him, as if to glimpse the ax coming for his neck. "But the Hierarch is merciful. And he rewards those loyal to him. So, I shall forgive you."

"Oh, your most beneficent majesty—"

"And I do more than forgive. As I honored you before when I ate your chicken, so I shall again. I have a task for you."

Shivering in unseemly ecstasy, the man bowed his head.

"You will be my herald. When my people hear word of my return, they will hear it from you. But not until the time is right."

The man was sobbing uncontrollably now. "I am unworthy, your majesty. But I shall do your bidding. Only . . . how will I know? How will I know when it's time?"

Em gave Sam a "yeah, good question" look.

"You will know only when you hear it from my lips."

On his way out, Sam stopped in the doorway of the bunker and looked at the wall and all the money pinned to it, with all the versions of his face. It was a sizable collection.

"One more thing."

"Yes, your majesty?"

"Do you suppose you might spare your lord and liege some of this cash?"

Em rented a two-seater pedal boat and bought a couple of ice cream sandwiches. The ice cream would help them look like tourists, she explained. Sam was skeptical, but he wasn't going to turn down ice cream.

This was a peaceful place, with walking paths winding through green lawns and palm fronds gently swaying in the breeze. Vendors sold snow cones and papaya spears. Children chased soap bubbles and dogs chased butterflies, and couples and families in row boats meandered around

Echo Park Lake, a blue pond reflecting white clouds. Sam saw nothing frightening here. None of the horrors Daniel talked about when he spun his tales of LA. At least not at first.

Sam and Em pedaled across the pond, past lazy flotillas of ducks and geese, out to a tiny, grassy island in the center of the pond. A half dozen stakes were planted in the grass, and upon each stake was mounted a severed head.

The island's only living inhabitant was a prematurely wrinkled man tanned like a horse saddle. He wore a straw boater, a blue pinstriped seersucker jacket, and white trousers. A shiny metal change dispenser was clipped to his belt.

Flashing bleached teeth, he called out his spiel: "Fifty shells a piece gets you a ten-minute visit and an oral history of the island and its denizens. Oh, excuse me a sec. Yaw!" He thrust a pole at a pigeon that had landed on one of the heads. The pigeon cooed and flapped away, but not before depositing a white blob.

"Do you have to clean that?" Sam asked.

The Keeper of Heads glanced at the head. "His relatives are behind on maintenance fees, so, no. You kids want the tour or not? It's free to look at the heads from the pond, but once you're landed . . ." He squinted at Em. "You look familiar. Do I know your family?"

"You might have met some of my sisters," Em allowed.

He didn't look excited to see her. "You're very young. Why'd they send you?"

"Can't say. Operational security. Speaking of which . . ."

A couple who looked as wholesome as a white picket fence approached in a rowboat. They even had a picnic basket.

The Keeper stopped talking about anything to do with the Emmas and went back to his tourist spiel: "Starting from the far left, we have Adrienne Chu, who worked in the kitchen of Sister Tooth. As I'm sure you've read, she attempted to sneak basilisk venom into our dear matron's soup. Sister Tooth was wise to the diabolical Miss Chu from the very moment she was hired, of course, and the soup never had a chance of reaching her lips."

Chu's head was just a skull with a few shiny patches of snail-colored skin and strands of hair. The crime and trial and execution must have all happened some time ago. Probably all on the same day.

The Keeper continued to tell the tales of the executed criminals. Each violator had committed a heinous crime, and each came off as hideous and evil but inadequate to the task of achieving their goals. The message was clear: mess with power and you'll end up as the most gruesome kind of lollipop.

"What do you need?" the Keeper said to Em, once the couple in the rowboat was out of earshot.

"We need a source for bone. Someone we can trust. Preferably someone who's worked with my sisters. Sint holo, meretseger, seps, salamander. Processed is okay, raw is better."

The Keeper whistled. "Is that all? You got that kind of money to spend?"

She showed him the edge of the wad of bills they'd collected from the chicken man's wall.

"For that, I can give you an address. No guarantees my contact will have what you need, but it's the best I can do right now."

Sam was satisfied, but Em wasn't. "I know the stuff we're asking for is rare, but there's got to be more than one person in LA dealing it."

"There used to be two," the Keeper said. He pointed his pole at one of the heads. It had no eyes and no lips and only the left half of its nose. "Now there's one."

They took the address.

The neighborhood off Melrose Canal was an unlikely place to find an arms dealer. Jacaranda trees sprinkled vibrant lavender petals over narrow waterways. Neat little Moroccan- and Spanish- and Tudor-style houses lined the canals.

Em docked the boat in front of a pink cottage. They went up to a door painted with flowers and bees and hummingbirds, and Em knocked.

The woman who answered was younger than Sam had expected, near Daniel's age, in her early thirties. She was short, in a tight gray T-shirt that exposed strong shoulders and biceps.

Sam realized he knew her. They'd met ten years ago, right before Daniel took him away from LA.

"Oh, for fuck's sake," she said. She recognized Sam, too.

She ushered Sam and Em inside as if she were taking delivery of some embarrassing package she didn't want the neighbors to see and shut and locked and dead-bolted and chained the door.

"You're Daniel's kid," she said accusingly.

"I go by Sam now."

Em looked back and forth between them.

"Em," Sam said, "this is Cassandra Morales. Old friend of Daniel's. Cassandra Morales, this is—"

"An Emma. I know the look."

"Her name is Em," Sam said pointedly.

"Is Daniel with you?"

Sam knew a lot about Cassandra Morales. She and Daniel had grown up together, pulled a lot of jobs together. Her areas of expertise included mechanical locks, electronic locks, sphinx riddles, alarms, osteomantic wards, and shooting.

"Daniel couldn't make it," Sam said.

"What does that mean?"

He saw the fear cross her face and remembered that she was more to Daniel than an ex-associate. They'd been a couple. Daniel didn't talk about that part much at all, but he'd let it slip a few times, and when he did it was one of the rare times he painted LA as something other than just a corrupt shithole to avoid. It was a place where he'd left behind people he loved. Staying away cost him.

He told Cassandra about the tsuchigumo attack.

"He's strong," she said, too quickly. "He'll be all right." Sam couldn't tell if she was reassuring herself or him.

"That doesn't explain why you're not with him. Or what you're doing in the last place he'd ever want you to be. It's risky for you to be walking that face of yours around Los Angeles."

"I was hoping you wouldn't recognize me," Sam said. "Not everyone does."

"There's an artist's impression of the Hierarch as a boy hanging in the Norton Simon Museum, and it might as well be you."

"We weren't planning on being in LA," Em said. "Plans changed."

Cassandra picked up a big black cat nuzzling her shins, which somehow made standing in her living room slightly less awkward. Her little pink house was as charming on the inside as it was on the outside, the spaces filled with knickknack crockery themed on hens and roosters and sheep and cute red mushrooms with white dots. Light spilled in through the back windows with a view of a back-yard vegetable garden. Something must've been cooking in the kitchen, because the smell of onion and garlic made Sam's mouth water. He hadn't spent much time in houses. He decided he liked houses.

Cassandra put down the cat.

"Come to the kitchen. I was about to have lunch."

They sat around Cassandra's little round table, with its red-and-white-checkered tablecloth and rooster and hen salt and pepper shakers and mismatched, hand-painted wooden chairs. She served up bowls of *albóndigas* soup. Daniel, who was an excellent cook when he had a kitchen and ingredients, couldn't make soup this good. Sam wanted to sit in this quaint little house and eat this soup for the rest of his life.

Cassandra ate and listened without comment while Em and Sam told her everything, from Gabriel Argent showing up at the Salton Sea to getting her address from the Keeper of Heads.

Cassandra chewed a panko-breaded meatball. "Why did you come to see me?"

"We need munitions," Em said. "Explosives. And stealth magic. Something that can destroy a Pacific firedrake."

"Let me see these plans Argent gave Daniel."

"We lost them in the plane crash," Sam said.

"That's a problem."

"We'll see." Em asked for something to write with, and Cassandra fetched a pen and legal pad and set them in front of Em with an air of challenge.

Over the next ten minutes, Em reproduced Argent's map of the island and diagrams of the facility. She included doors, cable tunnels, ventilation shafts, known guard locations—everything, as far as Sam could tell. Sam had looked at the plans. He thought he'd studied them. He realized he and Em had different standards for what constituted study.

If Cassandra was as impressed with Em's memory as Sam, she didn't show it.

"How recent is your intel?" she asked, once Em lifted her pen.

Em looked embarrassed. "We're not sure."

Cassandra placed a Día de los Muertos saltshaker on

the part of Em's drawing labeled "hangar." The ceramic skull grinned.

"When this was the Hierarch's fortress, they used to launch airships from here. It's the only area big enough for assembling a dragon. There'll be some kind of tank for all the osteomantic goop to grow tissues in and whatever else it takes to turn bones into a living creature. This here," Cassandra said, indicating the center of the facility, "is the power plant."

"The power plant is the key to our plan," Em said. "We cut the lights and the alarms, and then we make our way to the hangar and blow it up."

"How?"

"Salamander resin would do it," Sam said.

Cassandra shook her head. "I'm always in favor of being equipped for boom and mayhem, but you can't blow up a Pacific firedrake. A dragon like that is basically a living explosion inside an impenetrable shell."

"Poison, then," Em said.

Cassandra thought it over. "Maybe."

"You'll help us," Sam said with confidence. "Because you know what could happen if that dragon gets built."

"Actually, now that you've told me your plan, I know what will happen if I let you go to Catalina Island. And that's why I'm not letting you go."

Em put down her fork. "Let us go? You can't stop us."

"Oh, honey. You wanna bet?"

"I'm a combat-trained Emma. He's the Hierarch's golem, trained by Daniel. You like your odds?"

"Easy, Em. She's a friend."

"I'm *Daniel's* friend," Cassandra corrected. "So I know what keeping you safe means to him. You're the embodiment of the man who ate his father. Yet Daniel left his home, and his friends, and any chance he ever had for comfort and relief, all to make sure nobody rips the bones from your flesh."

"I know what he's given up," Sam said. "I've been with him every waking moment of the last ten years."

"Then you know he wouldn't want you going anywhere near Catalina."

"He'd be going himself if he could. And he'd be asking you to come with him."

Cassandra looked off at nothing in particular. "In that case, Daniel would be disappointed." She picked up the cat and scratched behind its ears. The cat gave Sam a reproachful glare.

"This is a really cute place," Em said. "You carry firedrake insurance?"

Cassandra smiled at her. "That was subtle. I have other places. Not as cute, but remote enough that I won't be worrying too much about firedrakes if Otis decides to raze Los Angeles."

"And the firedrake can be someone else's problem," Em said with contempt. "You can sit in your remote hideaway and watch Los Angeles burn on TV."

"That's right. You should come with me. It's what Daniel would want."

Sam found he couldn't be angry with Cassandra. She'd just enumerated what protecting Sam had cost Daniel, and now, with Daniel possibly dead, she was proposing to uproot her life with its knickknacks and kitchen and garden and take up Daniel's burden. This, after having known Sam less than half an hour.

"We'll go somewhere else if you won't equip us," he said.

"There is no one else."

"That's not true. There's Mother Cauldron."

Of all the Los Angeles osteomancers, Daniel feared Mother Cauldron most. She was potent and knowledgeable and unpredictable. She might sell Sam what he needed. Or she might make him an ingredient in one of her soups.

Cassandra surely knew this. She pressed her lips together, and for a while, the only noise was the kitchen clock ticking.

She scraped her chair away from the table. "Come with me."

Her backyard was bordered by a high brick wall crawling with bougainvillea and bean vines. There was a birdbath and hummingbird feeders and a red chicken coop where plump white hens clucked away. She took Sam and Em into a shed done up like a little red barn. Inside were some gardening tools, a lawnmower, a bicycle with a wicker basket.

"Give me a hand here."

Sam and Em helped her roll back a rug, revealing a plywood door in the floor. She pulled it up by a rope loop and they followed her down a ladder into a storage space twice the size of the shed. Lights flickered on, illuminating steel shelves neatly lined with army-green ammo boxes, mason jars, caskets. A refrigerator hummed in the corner. Small rockets and sabertooth bayonets lined racks.

Sam examined a heap of rukh eggs the size of hand grenades.

"Where did you get all this stuff?"

"I was a thief for a long time," Cassandra said. "Now I'm a smuggler. This is what I do when I'm not working in my garden."

She walked the length of the storage area, depositing packets of magic in a fruit basket as if she were shopping at a farmers' market. "You'll need sphinx skeleton oil for locks and alarms. Some seps venom corrosive enough to melt through stone and steel." She tossed a few packs of bandages in the basket. "These are soaked in eocorn and hydra regen. You're going to get hurt at some point. It's diluted, so don't expect miracles."

She opened a footlocker and lifted out two sets of black thermal underwear. "These are impregnated with sint holo and meretseger bone dust. They won't make you invisible or silent, but they'll help make you less noticeable when you're sneaking around, right before you step into a trap or a detail of armed thugs or fall into a hole filled with acid or blow yourself up. Some people like conspicuous deaths, but I say there's nothing dignified about being a spectacle. Let's see, you'll also want night vision, rope, field rations. . . . Do you have guns?"

"No." Em had ditched the leeches' captured bayonet before coming into the city. If they got pulled over for inspection, it would have been too hard to explain away.

"Can't help you there, sorry."

"Don't like guns?" Em asked.

"I'm an expert marksman, actually, but I only deal what I steal." From a locked cabinet, she produced a vial of polished bone, no bigger than a perfume bottle. "I got this from Mother Cauldron's kitchen. No guarantees, but it might be toxic enough to foul a firedrake."

She tucked the bottle in the basket with the rest of the groceries.

"I think that should do it. Any more and you won't be able to haul it to Catalina. I'll give you a couple of bags." She turned to them with finality. "That's it. Except for a little advice. Take all this stuff and dump it in the canal. Forget the dragon. Get out of LA. Get as far away as you can. Enroll in school. Pick up a musical instrument. Try out for the drama club. Go out on some dates. Reach adulthood."

Em wasn't charmed. "Does the advice help you sleep better?"

Cassandra smiled in a way that made her look older. "Who sleeps anymore?"

When they returned to the dinghy, someone was sitting at the tiller. Gray haired, neatly trimmed, with sharp dark eyes under a high brow and a nose that Sam could only think of as precise, he was handsome enough to model suits on a billboard. Sam smelled predation on him.

"My name is Max. I work with Gabriel Argent. If I meant to harm you, I would have done so before you ever left the Salton Sea."

"You're Argent's hound," Sam said.

"I believe that's more or less what I just said." He didn't wait to be asked what he wanted. "We have an operative on the island. Her objective is to provide Daniel Blackland with intel about the island's most current conditions. We are not in continued contact with her, so she doesn't know that Daniel's injured and not coming. Our operative's instructions are to leave any intel she gathers at a dead-drop." Max gave them the name of a café in Avalon, Catalina's former tourist settlement.

"If you have people there, then why do we have to do this?" Sam said. "We're not professionals."

Em took exception to this. "Speak for yourself."

"Mr. Argent is risking enough by placing someone on the island," Max said. "As it is, this woman doesn't even know who she's working for. She just knows she's being paid an outsized amount of money to observe. The fact that I'm in your boat, talking to you, constitutes an even more ridiculous risk. But Mr. Argent wants the firedrake destroyed. And on that note." Max sprang from the boat, onto the sidewalk.

"Wait," Em said. "If this is all so important, give us some real help. We don't even have transport to the island."

Max gave the dinghy an appraising look. "No, you don't. This thing will capsize at the first wave. I suggest you steal something better."

With that, he set off down the sidewalk through a gentle rain of jacaranda petals.

"You ever get the sense we're being used?" Em said.

Sam pulled the start cord. "I never feel any other way."

ELEVEN

Daniel and Moth entered the lobby of the Ministry of Water and Power, Los Angeles headquarters. Gabriel Argent had done a nice job on the place. Waterfalls cascaded down the four-story atrium into a reflecting pool. The air echoed with the sounds of water trickling over rocks and pleasant rain. This was still the kind of place where you took a number and sat in a chair until summoned to a customer service window, but you could fool yourself into thinking you'd come here to enjoy the scenery instead of waiting to ask a question about your bill.

Daniel walked up to one of the service reps.

"I don't have a number," he said, preempting the obvious question. "I want to see Gabriel Argent. My name is Daniel Blackland. Tell your supervisor and pass it up the chain. I'll be right over there."

Without waiting for a response, he took a seat on a nice leather couch and skimmed a pamphlet about water conservation.

"We should go see Cassie after we're done here," he said.

Moth glowered. "No."

"What do you mean no?"

"By no, I mean the customary thing usually meant by no."

Daniel tried again. "We need to talk to her—"

"You *want* to talk to her. That's not the same thing."

"—to see if she knows anything about the kids. If the boy made it here, he might have gone to her."

"Then I'll go and ask. But you're not seeing her. Not now."

"Look, she and I are totally cool. You know how well we still worked together after we broke up. I've even talked to her on the phone a few times the last couple of years, just to check in and catch up."

"And after this job is over, you can go check in and catch up and even hold hands at the malt shop. But not until after."

Daniel needed to stop talking. He didn't want to start raising his voice in Gabriel Argent's stronghold.

"Moth, what's your—" He cut himself off and tried again with less volume. "What's your problem?"

"My problem is that if you go see her now, when there's stakes, when she sees you're in trouble, then she's going to want to help you. And you'll try to talk her out of it, you'll say it's out of the question, you don't want her involved, yadda and so forth. But you won't mean it. You'll *think* you'll mean it, but not enough to turn down her help."

"I can turn down her help."

"You didn't turn down mine."

"I . . . I just want to check with her about the kids."

Moth sighed. "Okay, I'll try something else." He held up his left hand, fingers splayed out. "See this?"

"It's kind of in my face and super huge, so, yes."

"Chopped off by a helicopter rotor last year."

"I don't even want to know." Daniel turned the page of the water-conservation pamphlet. Apparently you could save entire riparian habitats by putting a brick in your toilet tank. "Fine. Tell me. What was your hand doing in a helicopter rotor?"

Moth made a fist. "That's beside the point. The point is, it grew back, because I can't be hurt."

"Sure you can. It's just more trouble than it's worth."

"My *point* is, you can be hurt. And Cassie can be hurt. And if you go see her, she'll sign on with us, and I'm not having it."

"And you're deciding that? She doesn't get a say?"

"D, when we're on a job, you're the boss. But when it comes to protecting my friends, I am."

"Our friends," Daniel said. "I think you meant protecting *our* friends."

"Come with me."

Gabriel Argent's hound stood before them, hands clasped behind his back, dazzling with his good haircut and light-gray suit.

Daniel snatched a number from the ticket dispenser, just for fun, and they followed Max from the lobby. A private elevator took them deep into the wells of the building, and deeper into the wells of the earth.

"You know, last time I was here I was being extorted," Daniel said conversationally.

"Last time I was here, I was held prisoner inside a coffin filled with water," Moth said.

"Man, why you always gotta one-up me?"

Max closed his eyes with great weariness. "I don't like buddy movies. In any case, that was Gabriel's predecessor. He's dead."

"Right," Moth said. "William Mulholland. You shot him through the back of the head. You'd think Argent would wear a helmet."

"I do, too. Alas, he doesn't listen."

The elevator doors opened on Argent's throne room. He sat on an elevated chair, some thirty feet above a pool of flawless black water. Hundreds of copper pipes descended from a glass-domed ceiling, like the tendrils of mechanical jellyfish. Almost hidden in the nest of pipes, Argent turned valves and wheels, his movements quick, controlled, and sure. Daniel knew what skilled sorcery looked like.

"You're being awfully indiscreet, coming here," Argent said without looking away from his work. "I thought I made it clear I don't want my association with you publicized."

"Your desires aren't my lookout, Argent."

"It's dangerous for you, too. Puts an even bigger target on your back. And compromises the Catalina mission."

"I don't care about the Catalina mission. Sam is missing."

"So you said." Argent looked up to the ceiling. Behind the glass dome, more pipes spread out in a complicated web. He turned some more valves. "Why call on me? If you think he might be in Los Angeles, why not confront the people you think want to do Sam harm?"

"Because, you fucking drip, your water goes into every last capillary in this city. If you don't already know where Sam is, you can search for him. You can find him."

Daniel suppressed the buzz of kraken storm building under his skin. He didn't want to have a violent confrontation with the chief water mage in his own stronghold. Or at all, really. He and Argent weren't friends, but neither were they enemies.

He kept his electricity below the surface, but it crackled in his bones.

Max took a warning step forward. Moth took a countering step.

Argent looked down at Daniel briefly before turning his attention back to pipes and valves. "Sam is of the Hierarch's bones, and the Hierarch had defenses that prevented my predecessor from keeping tabs on him. But even if I could find Sam, I wouldn't look for him. The reason why should be obvious."

"Because if I find Sam, and he's still alive, I'll stop him from going to Catalina. And you want the dragon slain, so you'd much rather he go to Catalina even if he dies in the process."

Daniel watched Argent's face. He wanted to see some clue that he'd misrepresented Argent. He wanted Argent to deny what Daniel was saying, for him to clarify or correct.

No such indication came. Daniel was surprised how sad it made him.

"You once said you didn't want to be enemies," Daniel said. "I always considered you at least an ally. Not a comfortable one, but still." He turned his back on the water mage and headed for the elevator. "That's over, Argent."

"Can you wait a second, Daniel? I just want to show you something." Argent spun some more valves. Concentric ripples spread out across the black pool, and the glossy dark surface of the water gave way to images of devastation. Mountains of debris, and sideways houses ripped from their foundations, and a tangled mass of cars and boats spread across a field of mud. Torrents of brown water pushed along a cargo of torn-away roofs. The bloated carcasses of cows and horses bobbed like rafts. People were pressed against a flumeway overpass, the water risen at least forty feet, debris building up behind them, crushing them.

Argent climbed down from his throne. He was close enough to touch. Close enough to burn.

"Mother Cauldron once poisoned the Ivanhoe Reservoir. I responded by cutting off the taps to her possessions for eight hours. No water, no power, canal traffic frozen. What you're looking at is her response. She dissolved the Ivanhoe Dam. One hundred and sixty-seven people dead, easily four times as many homeless. Not to mention the economic loss. This is what happens when the powers squabble, Daniel. If it's known I sabotaged the Catalina dragon, it won't be a squabble. It'll be war, and I'm not strong enough to take on the combined forces of Otis Roth, Mother Cauldron, and Sister Tooth. We can't have war, Daniel."

The image shifted to the inside of a house. The waterline was a foot below the ceiling. Amid the floating papers and sofa cushions was a family of four, two adults and two children, clinging to one another as a disaster they had no hand in making took their lives.

Daniel had some sympathy for Argent. He knew what it was like to have nothing but bad options.

"If harm comes to Sam, you'll have a war with me, Gabriel."

Argent looked into the water. "Yeah. Life's funny."

Daniel knew exactly what he meant.

The Enamel Tabernacle loomed above an Orange County labyrinth of strip malls and cul-de-sac canals lined with sand-colored stucco houses. Two towers fashioned to look like basilisk tusks spiked the blue sky, sunlight glinting off their pearly surfaces. On weekends, thousands of worshippers passed between the towers through a great arch of mammoth, mastodon, and monocerus tusks. On a late Wednesday morning, Daniel and Moth entered the church alone.

The place's official name was the Church of Dantis, but Daniel had always called it the Enamel Tabernacle, Bicuspid Basilica, or the Molar Mosque. Once inside, his smart-ass names no longer comforted him. Sunlight came through panes of translucently thin dragon enamel, casting the space in a warm, milky glow. The floors and walls and even the pews gleamed with polished ivory. Above, tusks the size of telephone poles formed a dome.

"The only known world-elephant tusks in existence," said a man, walking down the nave toward Daniel and Moth. He was yellow haired and white, smiling in a blue blazer and tan slacks. "It's something to behold, isn't it?"

"That's a lot of magic," Moth said. Daniel heard cash-register bells in his voice.

The man maintained his pleasant smile and clasped his hands. "It certainly is, but it's just a reflection of the grace the Lord invested in all of us. Is this your first visit to the church?"

"I'd like to see Sister Tooth," Daniel said.

The man was only momentarily taken aback by the absurdity of Daniel's request. "Of course. She'll be leading our Sunday-morning service. It begins at nine, but we advise worshippers to arrive no later than eight if they want a seat, though there is standing room in the balcony. In the meantime, you're welcome to explore the visitors' center and library, which are just past the drinking fountain to your left."

"I'm Daniel Blackland and she'll see me now."

The man's smile faltered. "I see. I'll have to check if—"

"Thank you, brother." From the distant altar, Sister Tooth approached, her heels echoing off the bone-mosaic floor. She wasn't wearing her full helmet and armor, just a long, wine-red dress under a breastplate fashioned from a spade-shaped tooth of some gigantic creature. This was the first time Daniel had ever seen her face unobstructed. Her skin was white as marble, the contours of her cheeks and jaw forming sensual curves. If she was a monster, she was a beautiful sort.

The grip of an ivory sword peeked from the scabbard belted to her hip. Legend held that the sword was a single dragon fang.

"Lord Blackland," she said with a gracious little head bow.

"I'm not a lord. You can call me Daniel, or mister, if you're feeling formal."

"If you'd chosen a different path, I might be calling you Lord Hierarch."

"Turns out I like truck stops more than palaces."

"The point is, my lord, that castle or campground, it was your choice to make."

"Did you try to kill me?" he said.

She seemed neither surprised by the question nor affronted.

"Did someone try to kill you, my lord?"

"It didn't work, obviously, but I can't let that go unanswered."

She seemed to take this as a given. "There are any number of people made nervous by the fact that you're still alive. I acknowledge that I'm on that list, but I shouldn't think I'm at the very top."

"The venom was custom designed for me. Whoever crafted it must have had access to my essence."

"Ah," she said, as if she'd just solved the last clue in a

crossword puzzle. "Your teeth. Yes, I do know your teeth. Your father brought them to me when he wanted to know how to extract the most magic from them. He wanted to use them to make a golem from you. I did try to warn him."

The light changed, growing cooler, darker. Clouds outside must have drifted in front of the sun.

"Warn him?"

"That it was an ill-advised notion, making a golem from teeth. Teeth are potent sources of osteomancy, but they are fire, and rending, and consuming passion. For a golem, you need large bones, through which great quantities of blood have flowed, soaking their osteomancy into the hollows. Or else the golem is a sad thing. Broken. Incomplete."

Daniel had met his golem, very briefly, when they were both children. He was just as Sister Tooth had described: damaged.

"The attempt on me was to snatch the Hierarch's golem," Daniel said. "And now he's missing. Do you know anything about that?"

Sister Tooth's unblinking pale eyes were almost white. "I have tried to procure your boy many times. I don't want you as an enemy, but the Hierarch's golem is simply too rich a treasure to leave alone. Nonetheless, I would never send assassins for you."

"Why not?"

"Because when I take your teeth, my lord, I'll have them from your living head." She smiled. Her teeth didn't match. They were many colors. Many shapes. They came from many different creatures. "I have answered your questions.

Now I have one for you: Will you fight me, here, in my own house? Or will we wait another day?"

"Moth, by the way," Moth said, waving. "My name is Moth. I'm standing right here, part of the world."

Daniel remembered the satisfaction of plunging his hands into the Hierarch's chest. Cracking through his breastbone. Grasping his heart and pulling it free. He remembered biting into it and tasting the flavor of his magic. Sister Tooth wasn't as richly osteomantic as the Hierarch, but she'd make someone a very fine meal.

"Later," Daniel said.

The La Brea Tar Pits were the historical heart of osteomantic power in Los Angeles. The first magic excavated by the Hierarch came from there, and it was the land upon which was built the byzantine castle of the Ministry of Osteomancy's headquarters. The Ministry now made do with drabber quarters on less hallowed ground, and the castle belonged to Mother Cauldron.

The building had been closed to the public for nearly a decade and showed its neglect. The flags that once snapped defiantly, regardless of the breeze, were now limp tatters. The plaster sculpture of a mammoth that spent decades trapped in the tar, bellowing to her mate and calf on the grass shore, had finally succumbed and rotted into black muck. Only the rusty steel skeleton of her superstructure remained.

Daniel and Moth went around to the side of the building, where a bored-looking guy sat on a stool in front of a door, reading the racing forms. He looked like a shlub, but he gave off smells of smilodon and short-faced cave bear and dire wolf and griffin. He was no shlub.

Daniel approached him, with Moth striking a menacing loom behind.

"I'm Daniel Blackland, son of Sebastian Blackland, and I want to see Mother Cauldron."

The guy folded his newspaper, got up off his stool, and went through the door and locked it behind him.

Moth shook his head, exasperated. "I think your subterfuge might be a bit rusty. You keep using your real name."

"And my dad's name. I'm the guy who killed the Hierarch, Moth. I can't move through the capital without people finding out who I am. It'd be like John Wilkes Booth catching a matinee at Ford's Theatre the morning after."

"Which he was not stupid enough to do, I can't help but point out."

The door opened. The guard had brought two bigger friends with him. They loomed at Moth, but Moth was simply the best loomer Daniel had ever met, and he made them look ridiculous.

"This way," the guard said.

He brought them down a long metal staircase barnacled in red rust, many levels down, into heat and steam and bubbling and hissing. The smells of sulfur and charred dirt blanketed the inside of Daniel's head.

The guard stopped on a rather rickety and crowded landing. "You go one more level down. She's expecting you." He smiled. "Good luck."

He and his two big friends climbed back up the stairs, leaving Daniel and Moth alone.

Daniel peered down the rest of the stairway. He couldn't see the bottom. Just steamy darkness.

"Wait up here," he said to Moth. "I won't need you for this."

"Right-o," said Moth, and when Daniel continued down, Moth remained glued to his back.

They pushed their way through the steam, Daniel leading the way by smell, moving toward the sounds of running water and clanking metal. Overhead turned a great contraption of wheels and blades, like a giant egg beater, clearing enough air to reveal a vast kitchen. Ovens burdened with copper kettles stretched into the mist. Hundreds of spoons and spatulas and knives and cleavers hung from racks. Bowls of powders and bones and bales of dried herbs covered marble-topped islands. All of it was built atop a concrete platform hovering over sluggish tar.

The air was nearly solid with the aromas of griffin and sphinx and gorgon and dozens of other osteomantic creatures. And in the center of it all was Mother Cauldron.

Daniel had always heard Mother Cauldron was an enormous woman with flesh the color of cooked mushrooms, with as many as six arms to stir her pots. Indeed, she was all this. But when she favored Daniel with a warm smile, he could see nothing monstrous about her. She seemed kind, welcoming, comforting. And that's how he knew how dreadfully powerful she was.

"Come in," she said setting down several spoons. "Are you hungry? I'm making soup."

In fact, she was making at least a dozen pots of soup, and it all smelled amazing, and he was tempted.

He moved around the kitchen, leaning over the various pots and kettles and reaching into his cells for regenerative hydra essences, just to be careful, just in case he touched something poisonous. Mother Cauldron was the best osteomantic mixer in the realm, and most of her preparations were deadly, weaponized magic.

"I'd just like to talk to you," he said.

"Whatever about, dear?"

"The Hierarch's golem."

"Is he for sale? If I recall, I once sent representatives to negotiate for me, but you weren't persuaded."

"You sent nine guys with cleaver-clubs to raid the motel where we were staying."

"And that was the last I ever heard from them. I inferred that you weren't interested in my offer. Have you changed your mind?"

"No," Daniel said.

"Then it seems doubtful we have anything to talk about."

"I was visited by more negotiators this week. They attacked me with tsuchigumo venom. It was potent stuff. It even managed to make me queasy."

"I would imagine so. I can still smell its traces on you."

She sprinkled herbs into one of her kettles. "You think that was me?"

"Sophisticated osteomantic poisons are kind of your signature move, Mother."

She lifted a spoon to her lips and tasted her soup. Trilling a little song, she shaved some slivers of bone into the pot.

"Poisons are only part of my repertoire. Some of my mixtures are crafted for delight. Some for love. Some for the most wondrous things."

Daniel moved to a small green kettle, simmering on a stove. A spoon immersed in a pea-green paste rested against its side. "This one actually smells good. What is it?"

"Just a tummy-warmer. It's very nutritious. Try some?"

Daniel dipped the spoon in and lifted it to his nose. He did not inhale.

"Jesus," he croaked, jumping back and flinging the spoon away. "You just tried to kill me, didn't you?"

She sighed. "Why are picky eaters always the most dramatic?"

He backed away from the kettle as if it were a hooded cobra. "The tsuchigumo was yours, Mother Cauldron. No one else can cook something that nasty."

"Well, dear, I'm flattered. You're absolutely correct. Tsuchigumo is my recipe, and it can't be reverse engineered. If you were attacked with it, it was mine."

"Mercy me," Daniel said. "You just admitted to the man who ripped the Hierarch's heart from his chest that you tried to kill me."

She smiled sweetly. "I admitted to providing the mechanism to have you killed."

"The subtle difference eludes my angered perception. Who'd you sell the poison to?"

She frowned and wagged a finger. "I don't reveal my customers." And then she laughed and flounced with all her hands. "But of course, it was Otis Roth. Who else could afford it? He's always wanted your boy, and I like his money very much." She flicked her tongue at Daniel, as if tasting him. He shuddered. "But you already knew this. What do you really want, Daniel?"

"My boy is missing. I think he might be in LA, and I want him back."

She adjusted the heat on a few of her burners.

"I don't have him."

"Who does?"

"Perhaps you might consider asking Otis," she said, with withering sweetness. "Though it's really not any of my business. My kitchens provide half the magic in the realm. I certainly can't be held responsible for its deployment."

"I could make you responsible," Daniel said.

"Yes, you could fight me. You're a very powerful young man. Perhaps you would even rip out all my hearts. But it would cost you, and I think you might want to save some strength for whatever confrontations lie in your future. Don't spend yourself on tantrums, my dear." She dipped a spoon into her cauldron and lifted it to her nose. Strands of black, viscous fluid oozed down. "Are you sure you won't have some soup before you leave?"

Daniel turned to the stairs, but Moth held his place.

"I'm just going to point out one thing," Moth said.

"Daniel's still alive. So, you might want to keep working on that tsuchigumo recipe of yours."

Mother Cauldron slurped from the spoon. "Why, dear heart, what is it you think I've been doing?"

On their way back to the boat, Daniel whistled a happy little tune. Moth eyed him.

"Okay, why are you being so smug?"

"You'd be smug, too, if you were the best thief in the kingdom."

"Daniel . . ."

"You know when I almost ate from the green kettle and freaked out and threw the spoon?"

"I was there," Moth said. "I would have laughed at your lack of dignity except I was scared to make a peep."

Daniel fished out a jar of bone from his pocket.

"Misdirection, my friend. Sleight of hand."

Moth rumbled a laugh. "That's my boy. What is it?"

"I don't know, exactly. But if there's a toxin capable of melting a patchwork firedrake, this is it."

Moth leaned away from the jar. "So that's what this drop-in was about?"

"No. But when opportunity knocks . . ."

"You make sure it knocks you right in the teeth."

TWELVE

Gabriel Argent shepherded a flock of headaches, from his throne.

A tugboat had gone over the embankment of the 405 flumeway and landed in the 10 flumeway, bringing traffic to a standstill between West LA and downtown. That was in addition to the jammed 110 and 5, caused by a baseball game at Chavez Ravine.

He turned some valves and diverted water to spillways to bleed off at least some of the afternoon commuters to surface canals. The red alarm light on his map turned yellow.

A new red light appeared on a different part of the map, at the Hyperion water treatment plant. A cracked pipe had sent eight hundred gallons of untreated solid waste into the sea off Playa del Rey. Gabriel turned some more valves and leaned over the edge of his seat to peer into the black pool below his throne. Colors swirled in the water like drizzled paint. Images came into focus, and he watched

plant operations with his remote eyes until he was satisfied the leak was being dealt with. Still, some heads would
have to roll. Not literally, of course. But the longer he
stayed in this job, the more he feared that "literally" would
become inevitable.

Incompetence was one thing. Not a good thing, but not
a thing he was willing to kill people over. Sabotage, however . . .

He paged through a leaflet the Northern California
Kingdom had airdropped over the border. It instructed
saboteurs on simple, safe techniques they could use to in-
hibit the Southern realm's ability to make war.

Transportation: *Make train travel as inconvenient as possible for enemy personnel. Issue two
tickets for the same seat on a train in order to
set up an "interesting" argument.*

Telephone: *At office, hotel, and local telephone
switchboards, delay putting calls through, give
out wrong numbers, cut people off "acciden-
tally," or forget to disconnect them so that the
line cannot be used again.*

Organizations and Conferences: *When possible,
refer all matters to committees, for "further
study and consideration." Attempt to make the
committees as large and bureaucratic as possible.
Hold conferences when there is more critical
work to be done.*

Employees: *Work slowly. Think of ways to increase the number of movements needed to do your job: use a light hammer instead of a heavy one; try to make a small wrench do instead of a big one.*

Managers and Supervisors: *To lower morale and production, be pleasant to inefficient workers; give them undeserved promotions. Discriminate against efficient workers; complain unjustly about their work.*

Deliberate incompetence as sabotage: fiendishly simple to execute yet difficult to detect, and more likely to get under Gabriel's skin than an open air raid.

"Gabriel." Max stood at the edge of the pool.

"You have news?"

"Yes, but I'll give it to you later. Otis Roth is here to see you."

"Did you make noise at him about not having an appointment?"

"Yes. Shockingly, it had little impact."

Gabriel kneaded his eyes. He sighed. "Show him in."

He fiddled with his valves as Otis entered the chamber. Disappointingly, Otis looked well.

"Are you here to complain about something, threaten me, or both?"

"I don't like to have my options limited. But let's say a little of each. Come on down from your high chair." Otis stepped to the edge of the pool.

"Sorry, but I'm too busy. I'm a terrible delegator." He opened another valve that sent water flowing through a newly completed part of the city's mandala. "This is about power, I assume?"

"When isn't it? You agreed to provide Catalina with twelve gigawatts a day."

"And I'm betraying you horribly by only providing 11.86. That's a lot, by the way. So there's your complaint. Let's move on to your threat."

"Aw, there's no threat, Gabriel." Otis sounded a little wounded. "If we're going to run things as a triumvirate, we have to get beyond the old habits of an eye for an eye."

"Or a dam for a warehouse," Gabriel said.

Otis chuckled. Because collateral death was funny, Gabriel supposed.

"I'm just asking that you care about the firedrake as much as me and Sister Tooth," Otis said.

"My first responsibility is to the people of this city and this kingdom, and it's going to stay that way, even when we've established our power trio. I'll try to get some more electricity to the island. Can we please get to the subject of Daniel Blackland, which is the real reason you're here?"

"How did you know?"

Gabriel spun more valves, increasing water flow and traffic speed through the Sepulveda Pass.

"Every time you flush a toilet, I know a little more about you and your activities. You might lay off the fried food, by the way. Daniel visited Sister Tooth. He also visited Mother Cauldron."

"And he visited you as well," Otis said.

"He did. He lost track of the Hierarch's golem. He's convinced he's in the city and thought I might know his whereabouts."

"Do you?"

"Regrettably, I wasn't able to help him."

"Interesting," Otis said. In that one word, Gabriel heard a trap snap shut. "The golem must be good at holding his bladder, then, because he's in the city, yet you can't find him."

"Maybe he doesn't flush. But this is good news, isn't it? You need him . . . *we* need him . . . for the big Frankenstein moment when we throw the switch and bring the firedrake to life."

"Indeed. Which is why, as an equal partner, I wanted you to know that we're all going to be working together to find him."

"I'll keep an eye on the urinals," Gabriel said.

Otis began climbing the stairs to Gabriel's throne.

Max stepped out from the shadows, but with a look from Gabriel, he withdrew.

Standing before Gabriel, Otis moved in close. His normally twinkling eyes glinted like polished knives. "I hope you know I'm serious, Gabriel. I want the golem. If you're not telling me something, I worry for our continued friendship."

"And I'm serious, too, Otis. You're a smart and careful man. If you can't secure Sam Blackland, I'm sure you have a backup plan. Is it Daniel?"

Otis gave him a tight smile. "Who else could it be?"

"I'm not sure that bringing Daniel Blackland down on you is the best idea you've ever had."

"Angering an enemy seldom is, Gabriel. But sometimes, there's little other choice." Otis turned and headed back down the stairs.

True enough, thought Gabriel. It was true with Otis. And if Daniel found out that Gabriel knew where Sam was but kept it to himself, it would be even more so.

THIRTEEN

Pelican squadrons skimmed over the harbor amid the squawking laughter of gulls. Cranes lifted containers off ships, while tugs brought in barges piled with mineral ore to be loaded onto train cars. Hundreds of scows backed up to the warehouses lining San Pedro harbor, waiting to deliver cargo all across the realm. The smoggy air roiled with diesel exhaust and metallic aromas.

For this last errand, Daniel came alone. He walked down the train tracks to a warehouse where three guys in tracksuits and gold chains glowered. They crossed forearms the size of hogs.

Daniel sincerely hoped he wouldn't have to break bones. These were just Otis's foot soldiers. He'd practically been raised by guys like this. Some of them had the morals of plywood, but they weren't all bad. They taught him to shave and helped him with his homework.

"I'm Daniel Blackland and I hate it when I have to hurt the help, so may I just come inside, please?"

At the mention of his name, the men went pale around the lips.

Daniel climbed up to the dock and approached the thugs. The top of his head barely came up to the clavicle of the shortest man. They stepped aside for him and he entered the warehouse.

Crates stacked on pallets rose to the ceiling. Forklifts beeped, and people with clipboards called out orders, and the air reeked of magic. In the old days, Otis was a master of hiding in plain sight, and he ran his various criminal enterprises behind a screen of boring, legitimate businesses. These days, as the realm's unchallenged main supplier of osteomancy, he was bigger in Los Angeles than ever, and any question of his legitimacy was rendered moot.

"Otis at home?"

The forklifts halted. The people with clipboards fell silent. Nobody answered.

"That's okay. I'll look for him myself. But you guys have thirty seconds to get out of here."

He heard the bolt of a rifle.

"Twenty-nine, twenty-eight . . ." And when nobody moved, he roared in a voice that was everything but human. Clipboards clattered to the floor. Forklifts were abandoned with the engines still running. The retreating footsteps sounded like rain.

Alone, Daniel paced the floor, surprised by a pang of nostalgia. He'd spent so many hours in places like this. Otis hired fugitive osteomancers to teach him what his father hadn't been able to before he died. If they hadn't known his father personally, they'd certainly known of Sebastian

Blackland and respected him. Like Daniel, they'd lost homes and loved ones during the Hierarch's purge of rivals. They expected the Hierarch to catch up with them one day, and they expected to die in a glue factory. They predicted the same eventual fate for Daniel and so were kind to him.

He'd hung out with Moth and Punch and all his friends in a warehouse like this. He'd fallen in love with Cassandra in a warehouse like this.

He found a disheveled office with signs of recent occupation. Cold coffee at the bottom of a carafe, an uncapped pen. On the wall hung a framed photograph. It was Daniel's father, neat and trim in a starched white shirt and gray slacks, sitting behind a piano, his marvelous fingers stretched in a keyboard-spanning chord. Daniel's mother leaned on the piano, her eyes closed and mouth open, singing. There was an arrangement of Victory Day candles and palm fronds. Daniel had no memory of his parents like this, singing songs in a house decorated for the holidays. But he must have experienced it, because there he was, sitting next to his father on the piano bench. From his size, he must have been around two years old.

He lifted the photo from the wall, gently, as if it were an ancient artifact that might crumble in his hands, and he stared at it for minutes, examining every detail. Blurred in the background was an achingly familiar dining room table, laden with more Victory Day candles. People sat around it, friends of his parents, he assumed. And there, to the side, almost out of frame, was a large red-headed man, smiling and looking right into the camera. Even blurry, Daniel knew it was Otis.

Otis wasn't a sentimental man. His offices were always decorated by promotional giveaways. Calendars. Notepads. Practical things. He didn't keep souvenirs. He didn't display mementos. The photo was for Daniel's sake.

Daniel placed it back on the wall. With a flick of his Zippo, he set about the business of burning the entire place to the ground.

With black smoke boiling into the sky and burning wood crackling behind him, Daniel returned to his boat. A black van was parked close behind it, bobbing in the oily canal water. Face hidden under the hood of a sweatshirt, a figure leaned against the side of the van. Daniel's heart quickened and his tongue went dry.

"Did you expect to find him at home?" she said.

"I thought there was an off chance."

Cassandra pulled her hood back, and Daniel experienced a telescoping sensation, as if she were close enough that he could brush his fingers across her cheek, yet so impossibly distant. She was here, a foot away from him, and she was ten years in his past. Even when she stepped forward and gave him a brief, strong hug, her physical presence did little to steady him. He'd spent a decade imagining some version of this moment.

"How'd you know to find me here?"

"Barometric pressure changes when you're around. The birds fly differently. Dogs and cats become unsettled. I just had to read the signs."

"Moth told you, didn't he?"

She came just short of laughing. "Yeah."

"And did he tell you I'm trying to track down Sam?"

"He did. But you can stop looking for him. Sam came to see me. He's fine. Both him and the Emma."

"Oh." Iron bands around Daniel's chest loosened, and he took his first unrestricted breath since waking up in the Funeral Mountains and learning Sam was gone. "Oh, thank god. Really, he's not hurt or . . . he's okay?"

She touched his arm for brief comfort, and when she drew her hand away, he felt the faint tingling ghost she left behind. Cassandra wasn't an osteomancer, but she always made him feel as though she were.

"I got the feeling he's been through a lot," she said, "but he was okay. And that Emma girl he's with is about as Emma as Emmas come. They've got a good partnership. He's a smart kid. A good kid, I think." From Cassandra, who hadn't met a lot of people she considered good, this was a tremendous compliment. "He seems strong," she added. "Really strong. Like, almost as strong as you."

"Yeah?" Daniel said with a twitch of dread.

Cassandra knew him well enough to notice. "Shouldn't he be strong?"

"I think I've been harmful to him, Cass. I'm here in Los Angeles, soaking in the magic, and I feel really good. And mostly, in the desert, I've felt the same, osteomantically. But when I wasn't near Sam . . ."

"You were poisoned. You were sick. Of course you didn't feel the same."

"Yeah," Daniel said. "That sounds good. Okay, I'll believe that."

"You think you've been using him."

"Yes."

"He wouldn't even be alive if it weren't for you."

"Where's he now, Cass?"

Cassandra answered with a guarded expression. "I don't know where he took off to after he left my place."

Daniel was sure he was misunderstanding her. He *had* to be misunderstanding her.

"He came to you and then left? Why?"

"Because he got what he came for. Magic and gear."

"You armed him for Catalina and then let him go? Why didn't you hold him?"

"Hold him. You mean keep him prisoner." Cassandra's eyes narrowed dangerously. "He's an osteomancer, and his friend is an Emma. How was I going to stop him? I didn't want to get into a firefight in my own house. And if I didn't outfit him, he'd have gone to Mother Cauldron, and I didn't want to be responsible for that. And, in case you need this pointed out to you, I'm not his jailer."

"I'm not his jailer, either. But I am his protector. And sending him to the island . . . Jesus, Cassie."

He stopped himself before saying more. He was being unfair. No, Cassie wasn't Sam's jailer. And she was right. Sam would have gone straight to Mother Cauldron, or even tried to rip off Otis. And then this wouldn't be a rescue mission. Instead, Daniel would be trying to recover his corpse.

"I'm sorry," he said.

"Forget it."

"No, I really am. And I'm sorry for always having reasons to say, 'I'm sorry.'"

Most unexpectedly, the corners of her mouth quirked in a mischievous smile. "Will you quit being morose if I give you a present?"

"I dunno. Depends if I like it."

She slid open the side door of her van. "Have a look."

Daniel poked his head in.

Otis sat on the floor. His ankles were bound with leg chains, his hands cuffed behind his back. He was blindfolded. Several strips of duct tape covered his mouth. And even bound up and humiliated, Daniel saw him as dangerous, this man who raised him as surely as did his own mother and father.

Cassandra slammed the door shut. The steel of her van didn't seem thick enough to contain Otis.

"If I couldn't keep Sam safe for you, I figured the least I could do was hobble one of his threats."

She made it sound so simple. But you didn't just bag Otis Roth and go on with your day. There would be repercussions. She would be hunted. In her own way, she'd done the equivalent of slaying the Hierarch. And life hadn't gotten simpler for Daniel after eating the Hierarch's heart.

"Cass . . . I don't know what to say."

"Just say thanks."

He couldn't. The word was too small.

"How'd you find him unguarded?"

"Got a tip."

"Argent?"

She scoffed. "I'd never deal with Argent. I know Otis's locksmith. I could have taken him years ago. Just didn't have a good enough reason."

"Let me take him off your hands."

She didn't consider the offer for a second. "I can take care of your dear old uncle. You've got your own stuff to deal with."

"You just made my stuff a little easier."

She frowned at him, the distinct frown she used whenever she thought he was being stupid. In the old days, it used to put him on defense, but now it just made him miss her. "Just because I've got him trussed up in my van doesn't mean he's out of the picture," she said. "He's already set things in motion. He's still dangerous."

"I know, but at least now he can't improvise. This is big, what you've done for me. And for Sam."

"You really like that kid, don't you?"

"He's my kid. I love him."

"Weird world."

Fireboat sirens wailed in the distance, coming closer, and Cassandra took that as her cue to depart. She climbed into the van and shuffled over to the driver's seat.

"Am I going to see you again?" Daniel asked, hand on the door.

"Probably. Good luck on Catalina, D."

"You should really kill that son of a bitch."

"We'll see," she said.

"Oh, and Cass . . . Thanks."

He was right. It was just a tiny word.

He moved his hand away. The sirens came closer and closer, and he watched her motor down the canal until she turned a corner and left Daniel behind.

FOURTEEN

Sam chose the Ships Coffee Shop on La Cienega because he and Em needed to steal a boat and the diner had a great window view of the docks across the canal. But as soon as he saw the mint-green tabletops and the battered toasters bracketed to each table, he realized he'd been here before. This was the first place Daniel took him after killing the Hierarch. He'd set Sam up at the counter with a bowl of tomato soup and a glass of milk, and that small act of kindness meant nearly as much to Sam as saving him from the Hierarch.

The waitress brought Sam soup and milk and coffee. Em got pancakes and hash browns.

"So what about the black one?" Em said, looking out the window.

"The forty-footer?"

"Yeah, it's a bateau. Should be seaworthy."

Sam shook his head. "Nah, something smaller. Sneakier. Faster."

"The red Stiletto?"

"Well, it's fast."

The docks were part of an all-day marina stretching half the length of the block. The day price was low but the hourly rate was high, which meant people who left their boats there weren't planning on coming back for a while. There was a single dock attendant who hadn't strayed from his little booth for as long as Sam and Em had been watching her.

Sam blew on his coffee. "Oh, check out the purple Baja Jumper."

"The pimp ship with the sparkles?"

"Why not? Those can hit fifty knots."

"Unless we hit rough seas, in which case we'll be at the bottom of fifty fathoms."

A woman slipped into the booth next to Sam. She had eyes tattooed on the sides of her shaved head. A man as thin as a flagpole took the seat next to Em.

"Twelve-foot seas, wind gusts up to forty miles an hour," the hound said. "That's the forecast for tonight."

Sam slurped his tomato soup. "How'd you find us?"

"Is that a trick question? I'm a hound. I smelled you."

"Out of all the millions of people in Southern California, you tracked me to this city, to this neighborhood, to this diner."

"What can I say? You stink good."

Em brought a forkful of hash browns to her mouth. "Can we at least finish breakfast before you start bothering us?"

The hound leaned back in the booth, relaxed. "Take your time. You're not going anywhere. I didn't bring cannon fodder this time. I brought Bennie."

The thin man carried a certain nonspecific lethal aspect about him.

"Who's Bennie?" Sam asked.

"Bennie's my gun. Say hello, Bennie."

Bennie made a pistol with his thumb and forefinger. The nail of his index finger was a black, gleaming, corkscrew-shaped thorn. It looked like the tip of a manticore spine.

"Remember, I'm a hound. If I smell you start to use magic, the girl's life is over."

Bennie pointed his finger-gun at Em's head. "Boom."

Em made a shadow-puppet rabbit back at him.

The waitress came to the table. "Can I get you anything, hon?" she asked the hound.

The hound's smile was thinner than a paper cut. "No, thank you. I'm perfectly fine."

Sam took a huge swig of coffee. "I could use a refill when you get the chance."

"Sure thing, hon." The waitress pocketed her pad and pencil and went off.

"Now, I've gotten to know you two a bit over the last couple of days," said the hound, "and I know what a tremendous mess you're capable of making. I don't like messes. So I'm going to offer you a deal."

"What do you say, Em? Are we interested in a deal?"

"Absolutely, considering Screw Finger's scary manicure is pointed at my head."

Sam set his mug down. "What's the deal?"

"You come with me, and I conduct you safely to my employer. Your girlfriend goes free. Simple as that."

"Otherwise?"

"Bennie spills her brains all over your breakfast."

"Simple as that," Em said. "Who are you working for?"

"My employer wishes to remain anonymous."

"It's Otis Roth, isn't it?" Em said. "Come on, just tell us."

The hound sighed.

Em nodded. "Ha, yeah, I saw your head-eyes flick. It's Otis."

"Wasting time."

The waitress came with her coffee carafe, and a few things happened.

She leaned over the table to fill Sam's cup.

Sam grabbed her wrist, snatched the carafe from her hand, and splashed scalding black coffee in the hound's face.

Simultaneously, Em threw her arm out like a crane flapping its wings. Her wrist made contact with Bennie's, and then she drove her elbow into the inside of Bennie's elbow. She used her other hand to control Bennie's finger-gun, turning it toward his own face. With a soft pop, the manticore nail shot away from his finger, embedding itself in his forehead.

Meanwhile, Sam drove his fork into the side of the hound's head, right in the pupil of a tattooed eye.

She shrieked.

The waitress screamed.

And Bennie's face turned to liquid, melting away like hot candle wax.

"Call the cops! Call the cops, Lloyd!" the waitress hollered, running into the kitchen.

Sam scrambled over the back of the booth seat and Em shouldered their bag of gear and scooted under the table. With every customer in the diner gaping at them, they bolted out the door.

They'd left the dinghy in the small slip yard behind the restaurant. Just the tip of the prow emerged from the water. The hound had taken the precaution of sinking their boat.

A police siren wailed.

"How fast can you hotwire a boat?" Sam asked.

The siren sounded very close.

"Not fast enough. Hoof it."

They walked down La Cienega at what Sam hoped was a brisk city pace and not a guilty-looking sprint. With luck, the cops would stop at the diner, and he and Em would have time to steal a boat or wave down a taxi. But the sirens kept coming. Someone must have told the cops which way they'd gone.

A yellow speedster with chrome pipes and pontoon stabilizers pulled up alongside them. The boat was so glossy Sam could see his own face reflected in the finish. A blacked-out window whirred open, revealing a guy with blond curls at the wheel. He looked about Sam's age, but they might as well have been from different planets. He was magazine-cover handsome, the sort of looks one is born with and then improves upon with money and expertise. He was cool.

He smiled, showing teeth so finely sculpted that Michelangelo would have been proud of them. "You guys need a ride?"

The police sirens were getting closer.

"Yes," Sam said. "Yes, we do need a ride."

"*Mi barco es su barco.*"

"We're being chased by cops," Sam said, hating himself for the weakness of honesty, but it wasn't long ago that he'd built Sofía Bautista's cairn, and he didn't need the guilt of more collateral damage.

"I get it," the guy said. "Hop in."

"We're being chased by other people, too," Sam added, hating himself even more. "Really dangerous people."

"I eat danger for breakfast." He seemed really excited.

A pair of gull-wing doors lifted and Sam wasted no more time diving into the front seat. Em tumbled into the back. The doors shut, and with an alarming but satisfying engine roar, the boat reentered traffic.

"Hold on," the guy said. He throttled up, swerving around slower boats and sending a wake splashing against the canal wall. The traffic buoy ahead changed, and he gunned through it.

"I think you ran a red there," Sam said admiringly.

"Oh, whoops." His laughter was the sound of childhood delight.

He maintained the boat's speed, sometimes straying into the opposite lane. There was a moment of terror when Sam was sure they were going to be sideswiped by a gondola bus, but the guy acted like he drove this way all the time. Strangely, Sam felt himself relax as they tore along the canals. The sirens faded in the distance, and there were nothing but civilian boats behind.

"I think you lost them," Sam said.

"Well, this one goes to me. They do catch me sometimes, which is why I don't have a license. Technically, I'm a criminal." He grinned those magnificent teeth and laughed again.

"So you do this a lot."

"It's not always running from cops. Usually it's paparazzi."

"You're a . . . celebrity?"

The guy blinked, surprised. "Well . . . yeah." Then, the laugh. "You really don't know who I am? You got in a boat with a complete stranger? I *like* you guys."

"His name is Carson," Em said. "He used to be in Boysquad, but now he's solo."

Carson looked back at her in the rearview mirror.

"Are you a fan?"

"No," she said, but Sam could tell by how vehemently she denied it that she was.

"Okay, I really do like you guys. So, what's your story? Runaways? You steal something?"

Em just looked at him.

Carson slowed to a more reasonable pace, though it was still above the speed limit. "That's cool, you don't have to say. Sorry to be nosy."

"Why did you pick us up?" Sam asked.

Carson made a *pff* sound. "Cops," he said, as if that was all the explanation anyone could need. "So, where to?"

They'd come to the split of Wilshire and Santa Monica canals in Beverly Hills. Across the canal, a cop dismounted his canal skimmer, but he didn't look up at Carson's boat, only got out his ticket book and walked toward a bank of docking meters. Still, Sam didn't feel comfortable here.

"Look, why don't you hang with me for a while. We can grab a bite, maybe smoke a little griff; no one will bother us."

"Why are you being so nice to us?" Em said.

"I don't really have much else to do today." For just a moment, Carson's confident élan fell away, and Sam caught a shade of loneliness. He was probably a skilled enough performer that he could draw on that aspect for breakup songs, but it seemed authentic enough.

Carson's winning smile returned. "But it's not like you're my hostages. I can let you out wherever you want."

Sam and Em exchanged a look. Carson had money, access, and shelter.

Best of all, he had a boat.

"I guess we can hang for a while," Sam said.

Carson kept rooms at the Beverly Hills Hotel, a complex of pink Mediterranean bungalows and birds of paradise and attractive invasive plant species and a swimming pool filled with water the color of blue mouthwash.

"I'm renovating my house," he explained, leading the way down a red carpet flanked by potted palms to the main building. "I can't create with hammers banging in my skull, so I come here to relax when I'm in town. I just finished up my Asian tour, and before that was Oceania, and before *that* was South America, so I need a lot of relaxing. God, São Paolo."

Sam shook his head in commiseration. "São Paolo."

The only thing Sam knew about São Paolo was that a lot of Andean wolf bone got trafficked through there.

Carson hadn't gotten more than three steps into the lobby before a managerial type in a good suit rushed out to greet him. He nodded graciously at Sam and Em without registering visible distaste or disapproval, but he was clearly dazzled by Carson's glamorous photons.

Sam had stayed in plenty of motels. He had cataloged sixteen distinct shades of mysterious brown stains peculiar to such places. He doubted he'd find any brown stains here. When the manager opened the door to Carson's room, the very first thing Sam noticed was the baby grand piano. Sam had never before seen a baby grand piano, much less one in a living room. Some distance from the piano was a marble fireplace. There were couches that looked like Greek monuments outfitted with pillows. There were tables that existed only to support a single statue or bouquet of flowers. There were chairs placed throughout the room, presumably in case you wanted to sit next to the wall, far away from other people.

Carson asked for a tray of "snacks and drinks and stuff" and passed the manager some paper money in a secret handshake.

"Where do you sleep?" Daniel asked after the manager left. "Do the couches fold out?"

Carson gave him a curious look. "I've got three bed-rooms here. Plus a kitchen, two bathrooms, and a powder room. It's a suite, you know? The Hierarch's Suite."

Sam pretended to be very interested in an abstract painting next to the fireplace. "The Hierarch's Suite? Does that mean the Hierarch stayed here?"

"Nah. Lord Verridan owns the hotel. I think this is just his way of saying he's going to be the next Hierarch. Verridan also owns the Dragon Pearl Hotel downtown, and they've got a Hierarch's Suite, too. Not as nice as this one."

Carson went to the piano. Standing, he played a few nimble one-handed runs. "I wrote 'She Stopped Dancing' on this thing. Kind of my good luck charm."

A bellhop brought up a tray of chocolate, caviar, oys-ters, and sandwiches filled with exotic lettuces, along with fresh-squeezed orange juice and champagne. Em and Sam nibbled pricey delicacies while Carson played a medley of his greatest hits in an effort to impress Em. Her head swayed gently with Carson's sappy ballads of love gone wrong, and her knee bounced along with the up-tempo parts. Carson addressed the more suggestive lyrics to the piano keyboard and looked Em in the eye for the goopy, heartfelt parts.

She did a good job of pretending to be impressed.

At least Sam hoped she was pretending.

For his own part, as he tried to figure out what advan-tage he could draw from Carson's acquaintance, Sam felt as though he were pretending, too. Here he was, in all his grubby glory, squatting in this chamber of riches with a member of Los Angeles aristocracy. How old was Carson, anyway? Nineteen? Twenty? Not much older than Sam. And he didn't fear cops.

In another version of the world, Carson wasn't Sam's patron, or even his peer. Especially not in a suite named for the Hierarch. In another version of the world, people like Carson groveled before Sam.

Carson finished a song with the inspiring chorus of "Yeah, girl, yeah, girl, girl, girl" and bashfully accepted Em's applause. Sam clapped with as much enthusiasm as he could muster.

"So," Carson said, "you wanna smoke a little griff? No pressure if it's not your thing, but I hope you don't mind if I partake. I'm always wiped by the end of a tour. Griff helps me feel human again. But I can go in the powder room if it bothers you."

Eat when you can. Sleep when you can. Take magic when you can.

"I don't mind."

They moved to one of the couches. Carson filled a pipe with a pinch of powdered griffin bone, lit it with a platinum lighter, and took a deep, slow puff. He blinked a few times and shuddered. Griffin transferred properties of strength and energy. People of Carson's socioeconomic class used it as an eye-poppingly expensive pick-me-up.

"Em?" Carson offered the pipe to her.

"No, thanks," was all she said, and Carson didn't push. "Sam?"

Sam accepted the pipe. He took a deep puff and closed his eyes. His body already contained essences of sixteen distinct griffin species, including the one he was now smoking. This was Colombian griffin, specimen 623.B, extracted from a single femur taken from the La Brea Tar Pits in 1948.

There was no way he should know that. This sort of finely tuned feel for osteomancy was in Daniel's bag of tricks, but had never been in Sam's.

Maybe Em was right about Daniel siphoning off his osteomancy, and the longer he was away from him, the closer to the surface Sam's magic rose. But he also suspected something else was at work. This was Los Angeles, the Hierarch's home. The Hierarch had worked magic here for almost a century. He'd fed magic to his people. They'd breathed magic, sweated magic, pissed magic into the water, and when they died, their bodies were burned and their magic entered the air, or they were buried, and the earth drank their magic. Los Angeles was the Hierarch's great cauldron. Maybe Sam was finally getting his due.

He held his breath and let the osteomancy stew in his lungs and soak into his cells. His bones grew restless.

He passed back the pipe. "Nice stuff."

"So, Carson, tell us," Em said. "What were you going to do tonight if you hadn't rescued us from the cops?"

Carson settled back on the couch. "I was just going to go to the pleasure barge, but I don't know. It's getting a little boring. Unless . . . Yeah, hey, you guys wanna come with me? I can totally get you in. I mean, I know I just said it's boring, but that depends on who you're with."

"What's the barge?" she asked.

"It's a floating club, three miles off the coast. It's pretty cool." He said cool as if "cool" wasn't necessarily something to be desired. "Hollywood stuff, all the glitter and plastic. But if you know the right people, you can get good magic. I mean, really good magic. Even unicorn. And tonight's Tuesday."

"What's special about Tuesday?"

"That's when El Tiburón shows up in his submarine."

Em leaned forward, enraptured. "Submarine?"

And Carson talked.

The barge was a floating party for the frothy cream of LA. It was owned by the Duchess of San Pedro, who partnered with the Baja cartel and let them use it as a delivery stop for their magic trafficking. Sam gathered that getting invited should make him feel like Cinderella. What excited him, though, was the cartel's mode of transport—a garage-built submarine, designed to get through Mexican and Californian security and rival cartels' obstructions. As one of the cartel's best customers, Carson claimed to have actually been given a tour of the sub. He said it was primitive, using a lot of off-the-shelf gear, but that the superstructure was the fossilized rib cage of a sea serpent. Likely a gunakadeit, from his description.

In the hotel suite's powder room a few hours later, Sam wrestled his arms into a suit jacket and regarded himself in the mirror. He felt constricted, but the shoulder padding and taper of the jacket made him look better than the sweatshirts and T-shirts that comprised his usual wardrobe.

He put the tie up to his chest and understood that there was no magic in the world that would help him figure out how to put it on, so he stuffed it in his pocket and unbuttoned his shirt collar.

"I'm the Hierarch's kid," he whispered to himself. "I

am a rightful prince of California." And then he laughed at himself, because the notion was absurd. And then he stopped laughing, because, truthfully, it wasn't.

The clothes were courtesy of Carson. He wanted to make sure his guests looked good, and with a single phone call, he'd summoned a team of clothiers with trunks and racks. Another phone call brought hair and makeup stylists. Sam didn't like the suggestion that their appearance lowered property values, but Em told him to think of it as costuming, and that helped him swallow it.

Besides, he *did* look good. And he felt even better.

He found Em in one of the bedrooms, testing her ability to maneuver in her shoes by vaulting over a dressing table. They were shiny black things with straps, but the heels were low and they actually had some tread.

"They'll do on the barge," she said.

She looked spectacular in her little black dress. Sam found himself staring at the curves of her bare shoulders and the slender muscles of her arms until she caught him looking and he had to pretend he was assessing her outfit for practicality.

An hour later, Carson's stretch catamaran was motoring into black water beneath a star-sprayed sky. His crew included a skipper, a first mate, a bartender, and two bodyguards, all to serve Carson and his two guests. Sam stood at the prow, salt wind in his face. He saw no barge, no lights, nothing but the dim gleam of the catamaran's running lamps over the waves.

"The barge is painted black," Carson said, picking up on Sam's unease. "It doesn't have windows or exterior lights. And the duchess hires a tug to move it from time to time. If you don't know where it is, you'll never find it at night. But don't worry, we're really close now."

"So, the barge is basically illegal," Em noted.

"Hell, yeah it is." Carson laughed. "But the duchess is the sheriff's sister-in-law, and her brother is head of Accountability in the Ministry of Osteomancy. You can have fun tonight and not go to jail, I promise."

After another half hour, the catamaran drew up alongside a pier jutting from a building so dark it looked like a hole in the world. Carson took them down a gangway to a bald, brawny doorman who stank of cave bear. Refined cave bear tooth was a popular magic fed to soldiers, bodyguards, gladiators, anyone who needed ferocity and speed and strength and had an employer rich enough to provide it.

"I'd tell you everyone you're going to meet is cool, but that'd make me a liar," Carson said. He was serious now, not the glib charmer. "If anyone bothers you, you just let one of my security guys know, and it'll be taken care of. You're my guests. That means something."

The bear guy opened a door, like tearing a seam in the darkness, and out spilled hazy light and pummeling music and the smells of cigarette smoke and osteomancy. They entered the noisy miasma.

Sam watched the crowd of perfectly dressed and adorned and coiffed gorgeous people make a path for a smiling Carson, who effortlessly exerted the force of his fame and charisma. Em nudged Sam, and they followed in Carson's wake.

The club confirmed Sam's worst fears. It was painfully loud, stuffed with people, and lit with bursts of color. Tanks bubbled with swirling water, like giant cocktails. The chairs and tables looked like extruded, hardened goo. Bare arms glittered with fish scales, rustled with feathers. Faces smiled with predators' canines and feline eyes. A lot of money and resources were being spent here on cosmetic osteomancy. By tomorrow, the scales would fall off, the feathers would molt, and the teeth would shrink to small, aching, human nubs. But tonight, everyone was magic.

A silver man appeared before Carson: silver hair, light-gray eyes, white suit, preternaturally perfect nails. A host of some kind. Carson exchanged a few words with him, but they were blotted out by the music, and Sam couldn't hear.

The silver man guided the party up some steps in the middle of the floor to a raised platform outfitted with bloodred sofas and a table already set with hors d'oeuvres, along with champagne in silver ice buckets and a dozen different kinds of bottled drinks.

Em sat and looked like she belonged here, and Sam sat and felt like a donkey in a tutu. They were joined by two raven-haired girls and one raven-haired guy. Sam assumed they were siblings, maybe even triplets. They all had gleaming black talons for fingernails.

"I've got some business to do," Carson said over the din. "My friends are going to keep you company until I get back. Okay?"

Sam gave him a thumbs-up and Em did nothing yet still managed to convey consent, and Carson left them with the talon siblings.

Sam wasn't happy with this arrangement. Now he and Em would have to find a way to ditch their babysitters. And Sam felt on display. The clubbers below weren't shy about staring with curiosity at Carson's new friends. Their attention was probably supposed to be considered some kind of honor.

The talon brother said something in Em's ear, and Em laughed at what must have been a supergood joke.

One of the sisters cuddled up to Sam. She said something to him, close enough that he felt her warm breath on his cheek. But if there was an osteomantic essence that enabled people to actually have conversations in this fashionable torture chamber, Sam lacked it.

"What?"

"You're the Hierarch," she screamed.

Well, this was a nightmare.

Maybe he should pretend he didn't hear her.

Maybe he should kill her.

He rejoined with, "What?"

Meanwhile, Em and the other two talons were laughing and carrying on like they'd formed a lifelong bond.

The girl took a twenty-crown bill from her handbag and held it up. "See? You look just like the Hierarch."

"Thanks," Sam said.

"I mean, not just like him, but you could be his great-grandson."

She beamed as if she'd just told him something wonderful.

"Thanks," he said again.

"You must get that a lot. Do you get that a lot?"

"I do," Sam said. "I get that a lot."

Em was shouting something at Sam.

"What?"

She shouted again.

Mushroom? Was she shouting "mushroom"? Why was she shouting "mushroom"?

"Bathroom!" she hollered. "You have to go the bathroom!"

"Oh! Right!" He turned to the talon sister. "I have to go to the bathroom!"

"What?" she screamed back at him.

Em pranced down the steps, into the crowd, and Sam fled after her.

They found a little space behind some potted plants that muffled just enough of the music to let them talk as long as they shouted directly in each other's ears.

"I thought guys like Carson had private rooms at clubs," Sam said.

"He sings up on stages in front of tens of thousands of shrieking fans. It's possible he's an exhibitionist."

"You seem pretty comfortable here yourself."

"Are you kidding me? Forget our mission, I want to blow *this* place up. Let's find the back access."

Sam scanned the club floor the way Daniel would do it, looking for opportunity. He spotted a waiter shouldering through a swinging door.

"That way," he said.

They followed him into the kitchens and ran into another waiter carrying a silver tray upon which sat a single toothpick. Sam braced himself to get yelled at for trespassing. Instead, the waiter acted like he'd been caught in some heinous act.

"I'm so sorry, sir," he said. "May I be of assistance?"

Man, it was good to be fake rich and glamorous.

"Our table is out of those swirly cheese things," Sam said. He only assumed that there must have been some manner of swirly cheese things. "And our waiter just totally disappeared."

"I'm so sorry, sir. Which table?"

"The elevated one."

The waiter's sense of urgency increased, suggesting Sam's VIP status had climbed even higher in his esteem.

"I'll get right on it." He turned to retreat into the depths of the kitchen, but Em held him up.

"You know, it's pretty stuffy out there. Anywhere we could get some . . . you know, privacy and fresh air?"

Some sort of understanding passed between Em and the waiter that completely eluded Sam.

"Well, there's a smoking deck, but it's kind of employees only." He looked off in the direction of nothing in particular as Em slipped some cash in his palm. "But if you go through those doors, down the corridor and to the left, you can get out to the loading dock. There's an old sightseeing crow's nest on the roof. The ladder's gone, but if you move some barrels around . . ."

"He was awfully helpful," Sam said, suspicious, after the waiter went back to the land of toothpicks and swirly cheese things.

"You owe him big time."

"What for?" He hurried to keep up with Em as she navigated the barge's back gangways.

"He thinks he's helping you have sex with me."

Sam's cheeks burned. "I don't need help."

"Oh, sweetie," Em said.

Cramped in the basket of the crow's nest, they hunkered down and observed activity on the barge's seaward side deck. A small crowd gathered there: the silver host, a uniformed LAPD officer, some assorted muscle, Carson's bodyguards, and Carson himself.

A white V appeared in the water, with a stovepipe at its point. As it neared the barge, the stovepipe rose higher atop a nub of a conning tower, a low wedge of black metal with a pair of grimy, pancake-sized portholes. Sam could hear a chugging engine now, and the dirty smell of diesel fumes coated his nostrils. The group on the barge grew more tense as the sub approached, except for Carson. He seemed as happy as a puppy.

The craft fully surfaced. It was an unlikely conveyance, with external fixtures and pipes that might have been salvaged from a toilet, and sloppy welds and hammer marks where its steel skin had been pounded to curve around the structure. Corrugations suggested the ribs of the sea creature beneath.

The sub bumped up against truck tires lining the dock.

"I am not getting in that thing," Em whispered.

Which was the only sensible reaction to the sight of the junkyard submarine. It didn't look sturdy enough to endure a swimming pool, much less the Pacific Ocean. But Sam couldn't help but grin. It was a *submarine*. They were going to steal a *submarine*.

With the squeal of unoiled metal, a hatch lifted and a man emerged. He was not the fearsome, scarred, tattooed visage Sam expected of a magic trafficker. His round face was fringed with a white beard. He gave the group gathering on the dock a jolly smile and spread his arms in greeting.

"Hola! Hola!"

Hampered by a large duffel bag strapped across his chest, he climbed out of the hatch. A pearl-handled, gold-plated revolver weighed down each hip. He gripped external pipe fixtures to steady himself and clambered out on top of the sub. One of the muscle guys on the dock tossed him a rope, and between the two of them, they tied the sub off.

With help, he hopped to the barge, all smiles and embraces. Carson got the biggest hug. To the cop, he passed a small parcel wrapped in brown paper—a bribe, Sam assumed. He did it with as much cheer as General Griffin-tooth tossing presents to children on the Hierarch's birthday.

So this was the deadly El Tiburón, the Shark, head of the Baja cartel. He exuded more happy walrus than shark, but Sam remembered something Daniel had told him about heists: whenever something looks too easy, it's a signal that things are about to go to shit.

Three more men climbed from the hatch, and they did not look jolly. Their backs and arms and shoulders were covered with pebbly growths, like glyptodon armor. Thick, bludgeonlike tails with eight-inch spikes on the ends grew from their lower backs. The armor and spikes were cracked and grayed, not fresh growth. That meant these guys were fed enough magic that they never lost their osteomantic attributes.

The head count on the barge was now up to a dozen, including lots of osteomantically enhanced muscle. *How many guys does it take to equal a job gone to shit?* Sam wondered.

Maybe it wasn't too late to change plans and steal a boat. But the submarine was just too perfect to abandon. Sam *wanted* it.

Gifts and bribes and hugs and pleasantries finished, most of the party proceeded into the club.

"There's your diesel," one of the club muscle said, pointing at a fuel barrel shoved up against the wall. "You don't need our help, right?"

"We got this," said a glyptoid, his voice incongruously high and squeaky.

The muscle followed the rest into the club, but the glyptoids remained behind.

"We're going to have to strong arm this," Em whispered. "And I'm using 'strong arm' as a euphemism for suicide."

Sam rummaged in his kit and picked out a vial of hypnalis. "Meet Plan B."

"That's just a mild sedative," Em said.

True. But Sam felt ready to try something.

He dialed the flame of his torch and held it beneath the hypnalis. It needed to be heated to just above 920 degrees. Daniel kept cooking temperatures and times in his head, but it didn't really matter. That was all recipe. Deep osteomancy relied on smell.

Sam didn't pay attention to anything but the contents of the vial. Not the salt air, or the persistent bobbing of the barge, or the distant geysers of whale spouts. Just the little bottle of magic. The sense of falling into cool clouds threaded its way to his nose. He spat in the vial and killed the flame.

"I need something to soak this up. Little bits of cloth or something."

Em got out her pocketknife. "Untuck your shirt."

From his shirttails, she cut a few postage stamp–sized squares of cloth. Sam wadded them up and soaked them in the vial.

"How's your throwing arm?"

"I throw like a girl," Em said. "By which I mean with strength and accuracy. But those little spit wads aren't going far no matter what. They're too light."

"Easily fixed."

He sprinkled a few grains of prepped Colombian mammoth on the wads to give them more heft.

Two of the glyptoids carried the fuel barrel over to a hatch near the sub's stern. With a wrench, one of them unscrewed the gas cap and affixed a nozzle to the barrel.

Em slid on a pair of gloves from Cassandra and weighed the wads in her palm. "You know, you might actually be a real osteomancer after all."

There were three glyptoids, and Sam had supplied her with only four magic-saturated bits of his shirt. She'd have to hit them in the face, the only unarmored targets they presented.

When the glyptoid pulled the barrel away from the fuel hatch, Em stood and started hurling the wads. She nailed the nearest glyptoid above his left eye. The second one caught a wad in the cheek. The third one ducked, and the wad intended for him went over his head and hit the deck. The glyptoid stared up at the crow's nest. His pebbly little eyes narrowed. He saw them.

This was the moment things went to shit.

Em fired off the last wad. To Sam's utter disbelief, it landed inside the glyptoid's mouth. The glyptoid paddled his arms backward and made a sound like dry heaves as he fell. He lay still on the deck, as did the other two.

Scrambling down from the crow's nest, Em went to shut the fuel hatch, while Sam untied the mooring line. He leaped onto the back of the sub and crawled to the main hatch. As he climbed down the steel-runged ladder into the dark, he finally understood what Daniel meant when he talked about being simultaneously terrified and elated.

He squeezed into the cockpit, ducking his head under exposed wood and sloppily trimmed fiberglass. The air stank of diesel fumes, machine oil, human sweat, and glyptoid urine. The pilot's seat was an office desk chair with the back removed, situated behind a steering wheel salvaged off a car and a two-lever control system off a ski boat. Various electronics were arrayed around the dashboard with a nest of cables so unruly it made Sam itch. A pair of valve wheels crowded his knees.

Em came down after him, sealing the hatch. "Move over," she said. "I'm driving."

"No way. You're in charge of air and . . . other submarine stuff."

Em didn't like it, and Sam couldn't blame her. Who wouldn't want to pilot a sub? But with a standard steering wheel and boat throttle, driving would be the easiest part. She squeezed into the stuffy tube behind him, crammed with suitcase batteries and thin mattress pads for the crew. A compartment the size of a laundry closet contained the diesel engine.

With the turn of an ignition key, the engine chugged to life. Sam eased the throttle lever forward and whooped when the sub moved through the water. Once clear of the barge, he turned portside and pushed the throttle up. Within seconds of taking the sub, they were out to sea.

"Em, we just stole a submarine, and I'm not even kidding."

He spun around in his seat to face her and found her grinning.

"Okay, how do we submerge?" he asked.

Em stared blankly at him. "How should I know?"

"I thought you said you knew how to work a sub."

"When did I say that?"

"You implied it."

"With my silence on the subject?" She leaned over his shoulder. "The controls look pretty straightforward. I think we can do this."

"Good," Sam said. "So. Submerging?"

"Well, that part, I'm still not sure about."

"Submerging is kind of the most important part, Em. That's why they call it a *sub*marine."

"It's one of those two wheels by your knees. One fills the ballast tanks to dive, the other empties them to surface."

Neither of the wheels was labeled.

In a TV monitor mounted over the dash with bungee cables, a trio of chase boats glowed in night-vision green. Sam could make out people standing, aiming rifles over sloped windshields. Meanwhile, the sub pushed along, full throttle, at seven knots.

"How do I put down the periscope?"

Em glanced back at the pipe above her head. "I don't think it goes down."

"I am starting to hate this sub."

"So steal the Nautilus next time. Oh, there, it's that toggle." Em clicked a light switch, and the periscope descended. "Now move your knee so I can fill the ballast."

Bursts of lime-green light flared in the TV monitor. Bullets struck the conning tower.

"If those breach the hull—" Sam said.

"I know how holes work." She squatted down and reached between Sam's legs for the wheel on the left. Only the fact that they were being shot at helped distract Sam from the location of her hand.

Em gripped the wheel and, with a grunt, began turning it. There was a gurgle, and then the sound of rushing water— hopefully the sound of the ballast tanks filling and not the submarine flooding. Water rose up the portholes with a cascade of bubbles, and the sub sank below the surface.

"Think we should turn around?" Sam said. "Back toward them?"

"Like a Crazy Ivan? Operative word being 'crazy'?"

"Just to throw them off our trail."

Em shook her head. "Right now they probably think we're headed to the mainland. Or maybe south, back to Mexico. Not out to open sea. And even if I'm wrong, it's a big, dark ocean."

Creaks and groans sounded all around, like a haunted house. Sam expected the skin and the rib cage to cave in and let in an avalanche of cold Pacific seawater. But the sub was holding together under ten feet of pressure. At least for now.

As far as Sam knew, Daniel had never stolen a submarine off a Mexican osteomancy cartel. He hoped he'd get the chance to tell him about it someday.

FIFTEEN

Avalon was a dead town. Bathing suits hung in mildewed tatters from racks inside the shops. Rental bicycles rusted in place. Signs in the filthy windows still said OPEN. Sam could just make out the cake-shaped old casino in the fog, looming over the ruins like the fading spirit of an extinct beast. Tourism in Catalina's main settlement hadn't been hopping since the Hierarch turned the island into a fortress.

Sam and Em crept down the sidewalk in their sint holo–impregnated suits, hoping to be no more conspicuous than the stray cats prowling the beachfront street. Sam imagined they were stirring the ghosts of sailors on leave from Los Angeles.

They found the wreck of a Spanish-style building with peeling stucco skin. Warped, chipped boards covered the windows, and over the door, Sam could still make out the scar of an old sign: PELÍCANO. Just like Max said.

One of the boards over the windows rested on the sill and wasn't nailed in place. Em slid the board aside, and they both slipped into the restaurant. Filmy glasses were racked over the bar. Salt and pepper shakers and ketchup bottles gathered dust on the tables. The floor was a mess of splintered wood and plaster, seagull guano, and rat droppings. Over by some booths, a mural provided a simple map of the island, two diamond-shaped landforms connected by a thin isthmus. The insertion point to the facility was supposed to be a small, hidden cove at the isthmus near the fishing settlement of Two Harbors, where a sea cave opened to the tunnel complex.

Behind the front counter was a stack of menus. The plastic laminate was yellowed and brittle, but the menus were mostly intact. Em withdrew the seventh menu from the top and opened it to the appetizers. Inside were three blank slips of paper. They'd found the operative's dead-drop.

Sam unscrewed the cap on a pot of sphinx oil from his kit. Odors of hot sand and abrasive wind wafted up at him, whispering secrets and riddles in his sinuses. He rubbed an oil-dampened sponge over the papers, and the oil reacted with the ink on the paper. Though the writing remained invisible, the whispers grew louder and more distinct.

Sam repeated the whispers to Em.

"Insertion point viable. Conditions may change if delay persists."

The operative had expected Daniel a day ago.

The next message read, "Insertion point compromised. Await instructions."

Things got even more discouraging with the last mes-

sage: "My presence on island possibly discovered. Will
make final attempt to determine new insertion point and
relay to you."

Sam tucked the papers back in the menu and returned
the menus as he found them.

"What do we do now? Wait here?"

"For how long?" Em said. "We don't even know if the
guy's still alive."

"He is."

The hoarse whisper came from the kitchen. A woman
aimed a gun at them made of some clear substance, like
water suspended in stasis, not quite exactly like ice. She
was decked out in camouflage, her face smeared with partially sweated-off black paint. Scratches on her cheeks
and forehead made her look a little wild.

"What day is it?" she demanded.

Em responded with the code phrase supplied by Max:
"It's the day to get things done."

The woman didn't lower her weapon. "You're not who
I was expecting."

"He was injured and couldn't make it," Em said. "We're
his replacements."

"Who injured him?"

"Otis Roth's people," Sam said.

"You're lying. You caught Blackland and tortured him
for the pass phrase."

"How do we know you didn't?" Em countered.

The woman changed her grip, and the gun seemed to
solidify. It'd be hilarious to be killed by a water pistol,
Sam thought. But she lowered her weapon.

"You're Sam and Em. The home office told me you might make it."

"What do we call you?" Sam asked. "Agent H_2O?"

"You can call me the unlucky bastard who had to wait for you to lollygag your way here."

Sam shook his head. "She's not a real spy."

Em tensed. "What makes you say that?"

"She said 'lollygag.' Real spies don't say 'lollygag.' "

"Actually," Em said, lecturing, "I met a spy in Lompoc, and she said 'lollygag' all the time. And she was a really good spy."

"Are you two done?" The spy looked ready to shoot them right now.

"Sorry," Sam said. "About the lollygagging."

"I found you a new insertion point. Not as easy to get to as the original, but that's what you get for being late."

"For lollygagging, you mean."

Sam wasn't sure why he wanted to give her such a hard time. Maybe messing with people who were poised to harm you was a trait he inherited from Daniel.

She described a route to the island's interior, up to the thirteen-hundred-foot summit of Mount Torquemada. Adjacent to an old antiaircraft gun emplacement, they'd find a ventilation shaft leading into the facility.

"Nice of them to leave that there for us," Sam said.

"Nothing nice about it," the woman shot back, her eyes bulging a little. Sam was getting the sense that her time on the island hadn't been easy. "Sister Tooth is still using it as a gun emplacement, manned by a team of three. They check in downstairs by radio once an hour. You'll have to figure out how to handle that. Where'd your plane land, anyway?"

"No plane," Em said. "Crypto-sub. Anchored it in a cove. We're hoping it'll still be there when we're done."

"Submarine. That's nice." Her estimation of them seemed to rise a little. "Much cushier than swimming from LA."

"You swam here?"

She spread her fingers and showed them the webbing in between. "And I've got eight hours until the magic wears off. Which means I should have been gone a long time ago."

"Will you be able to make it back?" Sam suddenly felt responsible for her, as he did for Sofía Bautista, and Em, and the leech captives, and even, in a way that felt new and burdensome, for Daniel. He shouldn't have made fun of her.

The woman responded with a smile that made Sam think his question didn't have a happy answer.

"Good luck," she said, departing through the kitchen.

"You, too," he said, though she was no longer there to hear him.

By now, the sun was rising, so they decided it was better to wait for dark, even though it meant holing up and spending an entire day in the decrepit restaurant. They dined on their ration of cereal bars and water and listened for sounds of approach. Rodents rustled in the ruins and pigeons cooed in the rafters. With little else to keep him occupied, Sam brooded.

He wanted to ask Em about growing up with her sisters, about what it was like to have a family, to share a common purpose. He wanted to ask what it was like to be away from them. He wanted to tell her how, in this damp and foul place, he felt as if he were where he was supposed to be. Part of it was because he had sort of fallen in love with her. Just as he had fallen in love with Valerie at the Salton Sea. As he had fallen for any number of girls with whom he'd had momentary contact, because his heart was the vacuum which nature abhorred. And, possibly disconnected from these ridiculous feelings, he loved her because she was the first real friend he'd ever had.

Once or twice, he caught her looking at him, and he wondered if there were things she wanted to say but couldn't, because she didn't want to risk being heard by a patrol party, or because she feared how stupid she'd sound if she spoke her words aloud. And so they sat in silence, and Sam hoped that when this was all done they'd both be alive and maybe they could sit at a table with good food in a house with furniture and have a conversation without worrying about leeches and guns.

They left the restaurant after sundown and made their way to the trail Argent's operative told them about. Fog thickened around the island like a slow flood as they hiked into the interior toward Mount Torquemada. Limbs of mahogany twisted like arthritic fingers from cracks in the schist, reminding Sam of the San Andreas creature's grasping claws.

The trail dipped into a hollow where thicker fog gathered. Sam couldn't hear Em's footsteps, yet the breaking surf at the bottom of the hills seemed mere yards away. The brush rustled with creatures. The air did weird things to sound. It was too easy to imagine every fox or shrew darting across the scrub was actually something worse.

As they headed up the next rise, Sam heard something worse.

A breath. A snort. Something large. Wads of mist swirled ahead.

Another snort, and a whisper-soft bulk emerged from the gloom. At first Sam thought it was a bison—there were still bison on Catalina, descended from a herd brought over in the 1920s for a silent Western—but as the creature came closer, Sam made out curving tusks, crossing at their tips, and a trunk swinging low to the ground.

Sam's breath caught in his throat. The animal wasn't huge. The top of its head didn't even come up to Sam's chin. But it was nonetheless magnificent.

Em clutched his shoulder, and he felt she was the only thing holding him to the ground.

"That's not an elephant," Em said in a gruff whisper.

"No. It's a mammoth."

Its breath smoked, and as it approached, scents of grass and dung and magic rolled over Sam in waves.

Judging from the length of its tusks, it was an adult, but its modest size meant it must be a pygmy Colombian mammoth. Their remains were known on some of the other Channel Islands, but they'd gone extinct eleven thousand years ago.

Sam's cells contained inherited mammoth osteomancy, which the Hierarch had gained by eating mammoth bones, but his sense of this creature's magic was so much stronger. It was potent, and beautiful, and wrong. And it was proof of concept that osteomancers could take bones and vat-grown organs and cultured flesh and combine them into a patchwork animal. Imagining a living Pacific firedrake, Sam was struck with dread and delight.

The mammoth came to a rest on the trail before them. It raised its trunk and snorted, drawing in air.

It's smelling me, thought Sam.

He pulled away from Em's grasp and extended his hand out into the few feet of space between him and the mammoth. The mammoth reached out, curling the fingerlike extensions on the end of its trunk around Sam's hand. Sam was touching living magic.

Over the last few days, he'd wondered how he was different from the Hierarch. Now he knew. The Hierarch would see the mammoth as a resource. He would consume it. But Sam never would. Sam considered the mammoth his kin.

Releasing his hand, the mammoth lowered its trunk. Sam and Em stepped aside to let it pass and watched as it retreated into the fog, becoming a ghost in the gray world.

At the peak of Mount Torquemada, a woman and two men huddled around a long piece of plumbing mounted on four knobby tires. Sam and Em watched them from the cover of an ironwood tree.

"Antiaircraft gun, twenty millimeter," Em whispered. "Looks like war surplus."

They would have met the gun had they arrived by air as originally planned. But Sam couldn't feel good about avoiding that fate. Not with Sofía Bautista's body lying under a pile of rocks in the desert.

In addition to the big gun, the crew was equipped with thermos bottles, black rifles, and a radio set. The radio was the biggest problem.

On Em's go signal, they set off across the distance to the gunners.

Darkness and fog assisted their suits' osteomantic stealth properties, but as they approached the three from behind, Sam felt as though he were tap-dancing in broad daylight while playing bagpipes. One of the men yawned. Another arched his back to stretch. Em leaped ahead. She struck one gunner behind his ear and hit the woman at the base of her skull. Both went down.

Before the third could raise his gun, Em dropped low, thrust a leg out and swept it in a circle, taking him down at the ankles. By the time he hit the ground, Em was back on her feet with his gun aimed at his face.

The two gunners she'd sapped were still conscious, and they were Sam's responsibility. He took a lump of gray caked powder from his kit—processed gorgon bone—and crunched it between his molars. His tongue grew cold and numb. He forced it down, past his dry, brittle throat. Within seconds, an icy sludge crawled through his veins. He blinked, and his eyelids felt like they might flake away. He blinked again, and they felt normal.

He blew a cloud of particulates into the air. They crystallized in the cold and precipitated onto the two gunners. The gunners stopped writhing. Their moans fell silent. Their faces grew gray as concrete, and they froze in rictus horror.

With the sound of cracking walnuts, Sam stretched his neck and flexed his fingers.

"It's time for you to check in," Em said to the third gunner. "If you don't, your friends downstairs will know something's wrong, and they'll send someone up to check. Right?"

"That's how it works," he said. He had pimples and was working on a mustache.

Em cupped the radio mic in one hand and put it in front of the gunner's mouth. She keyed the mic and whispered, "Talk."

The gunner cleared his throat. "Base, Mount Torquemada Station, all clear. Over."

"Thanks," Em said. "Except for the part where you used your distress code. You were supposed to call this 'High Vent Station.' Fortunately, I changed the frequency, so that went out to Guam."

"Well, that's the best you're going to get out of me," the gunner said, with a gleam of defiance. "You can go ahead and shoot me now."

"We're not going to shoot you." From his kit, Sam removed a tiny vial, filled with a golden, pearly fluid.

"Cat piss?" the gunner asked.

"Lamassu," Sam said, leaning over him. "Ever heard of it?"

The gunner swallowed. Clearly he had.

"With enough of this stuff, I could convince you to shoot your own mother dead and eat her for dinner." Sam felt like a heel, making threats. The guy probably wasn't ideologically invested in Otis's operation, and he might not even know anything about the firedrake. But fear was a better weapon than fisticuffs. "I'll try not to use that much. Just enough so you'll make the radio call and then take a nap. But if you're going to struggle, I might get sloppy. Hold still, okay?"

Em put him in a headlock and turned his head so Sam could reach his ear. He let three drops of the lamassu fall in. The gunner did not fight him. He even bit his own arm to muffle his scream.

Sam and Em opened the hatch to a freight elevator shaft that plunged into the mountain's interior. "Hopefully, the car won't come up and smear us into paste," Em said, starting the way down iron ladder rungs stapled into the bare stone.

The ladder reached bottom in the back of a high-ceilinged vaulted chamber lined with chain-link pens. Sam and Em hunkered behind a stone pillar and surveyed the room. Housed inside the pens were a few dozen men, women, and children. The occasional cough or moan broke through the din of air handlers.

With only some banks of fluorescent fixtures dropping weak light, Sam couldn't get a good look at the occupants, but from his time on the leeches' glue-factory boat, he could guess what kind of prison this was.

A lone watchman paced up and down the cages, none too watchful. His attention was buried in a paperback book, held in one hand. The other lazily swung a cleaver-club by its strap. Sam could make out the walnut grip of the holstered gun and the dried blood on the blunt edge of his cleaver. Whoever the prisoners were, they must not be considered much of a security threat.

Sam wanted the guard to keep coming toward him. He wanted to see a brief look of surprise register on his face. He wanted to see his hand fumble at his snapped-shut holster, and maybe even an instant of pain as Em broke his neck. To Sam's mind, the difference between the gunners upstairs and this guard with blood on his cleaver-club was vast.

Without lifting his eyes from his book, the guard turned and headed back down the floor.

"Leech victims?" Sam whispered.

"Maybe," Em said. "But what for?"

"A project like this needs a lot of osteomancy. They're probably wringing it out of any low-level osteomancer or user they can find."

"Suppose so. Anyway, when he comes back this way I'm going to shoot him, unless you have a better idea."

"Too noisy," he said. "This'll have to be Em-quality fisticuffs."

"I knew it," she said with a sigh.

At the end of the chamber, the guard turned and started his next circuit.

Em untied one of her boots and removed the lace. She made eye contact with Sam and pulled the lace taut between her hands. Sam understood.

The meretseger-impregnated soles of her boots made no noise as she rushed the guard in several long strides. With her bootlace, she reached over his head, put a knee in his back, and pulled down on the lace, garroting him.

Sam was right behind her. Kneeling, he grabbed the guard's face with both hands and exhaled gorgon essence. Like the sentries above, the guard stiffened and turned gray. When Em loosened the garrote, he fell, and the sound of his cheek striking the floor was stone grating against stone.

"We can stash him in one of the pens if there's an empty one," Em said.

"Why does it have to be empty?"

"If it's not, we have to deal with prisoners trying to get out."

"So?"

"Effecting a prison break's not part of our mission objective."

"Then let's change our mission objective. I say we bust them out."

Em arched an eyebrow. "And do what with them?"

"They can climb out the way we came in. The gunners we left up top aren't in any condition to do anything about it, so maybe they'll make it to a beach."

"And then what?"

"And then maybe they'll steal a boat. Whatever, at least they're spared the glue factory."

"Not part of the mission," Em whispered.

"We were being held with people like this just yester-day. And a breakout could be a useful distraction." Daniel used to tell him about the use of deliberately introducing chaos: fire alarms, actual fires, massive explosions.

Sam could tell he was winning the argument. Missions of liberation were kind of Em's thing, after all.

"Fine," she hissed.

Sam went to one of the pens. He didn't recognize any-one from the leech boat in the desert, but these people would have fit in with them: Some had fading scales or molting feathers. One woman had scimitar incisors curv-ing over her bottom lip. He tried to ignore the faces star-ing at him through the diamond-shaped gaps in the fence and concentrated on the gate. It was held shut with a heavy chain and padlock.

"The guard's got the keys somewhere on him," said a boy in the pen Sam was examining. He couldn't have been older than ten.

Em fished a key ring from the guard's pocket, but didn't toss it over when Sam held out his hand.

"If we let you out, it's going to cost you," she said to the boy. "You tell us everywhere you've been in this com-plex, everything you've seen, everything a guard's ever said to you. Everything."

"It's a trick," said a man from an adjacent pen. Flaking horns grew from his temples. "Don't tell them anything."

"This room's the only one we've seen," the boy said, ignoring him. "We were all picked up by leeches and they sold us to some people in San Pedro and they put us on a boat, but we were under the deck so we couldn't tell where we were going, and then we were inside and they locked us up here. They took my mom and my sister yesterday."

The woman with the scimitar teeth nodded. "They move a few of us out every day. At different times, not on a schedule."

"Where do they go?"

The woman didn't answer, but she didn't need to. They were being processed for their magic. Whatever was left didn't matter.

The horned man turned to the others in his pen. "We don't know what happens to the ones they take away. Maybe they're still alive. If we try to escape they'll just capture us again. They'll kill us. Maybe they'll do worse."

"There is no worse," the boy said flatly.

Em unlocked the gate and swung it open, then moved to the next. She let out the woman with the scimitar teeth.

"There're three gunners up top," Sam said. "I magicked them pretty good. But the rest of the island could be crawling with sentries, and there'll be even more once they find out you've escaped. But if you can make it to Avalon, maybe you can steal a boat—"

"And in the meantime, we're a diversion so you and your partner can do whatever you came to do?" the woman said.

"Yes."

"And what is that, exactly?"

"I'd rather not say. But we're going to hit the people running this place as hard as we can."

The woman took up the guard's pistol and cleaver-club. "If we run into anyone, we'll hit them even harder."

Sam turned to gather up Em and go but froze when he saw the man with the horns at the room's entrance. His hand was on the pull-switch of an alarm box.

"Don't—" Sam said. But it was too late. The man stared him straight in the eyes and pulled the alarm.

"You know that thing Daniel told you about jobs going to shit?" Emma said.

"Let's have a nice conversation about that after we've hauled ass out of here."

They ran from the chamber, into unknown parts of the facility, while the alarm bells clanged. They did not lollygag.

SIXTEEN

Moth wiped sea spray from the binoculars and handed them back to Daniel. From their inflatable commando boat a hundred yards offshore, Daniel watched the opening to the sea cave. They were supposed to make their entry here, but it didn't look promising.

In addition to a sandbagged machine-gun nest, an operator sat behind an array of eight war tubas—giant horns with a complex of tubes that fed into the operator's ears.

"Can he hear us?" Moth mouthed.

Daniel shook his head. "They're aimed at the sky, for airplanes."

"We can take these guys," Moth said, pleading. He was more of a smasher than a sneaker, and too much hunkering made him cranky. "We rush them with overwhelming force, fight our way in, make it to the dragon, you drop in your little jar of poison, we bash our way out, and then it's nothing but the finest meats and cheeses for the conquering vandals."

"You're an adorable ape. But I want to find Sam and the Emma. That means we sneak."

"They must have found a way in," Moth offered, as if this were a sound argument for storming the castle.

"Okay. So we find another way."

"Can you sint holo both of us?"

"If I extend confusion miasma to you, you'll just get confused. I could maybe walk you across a room, but over rocks and a minefield . . . ?"

Moth massaged his temples, as if he had a headache. "All the things I could have done with my life. I could have been a bank robber. I could have been a jewel thief."

"Come on, it'll be just like old times."

"Terrific. I so miss the hellish disasters of old times. Okay, how about this: I storm the beach and let them shoot me. And they're like, 'Oh, holy shit, we just shot that guy!' and they come down to look. Then, when my guts grow back, I'm all, 'Ha-ha, suckers!' and I bash their heads together, and we're in!"

"Will you please take this seriously?" Daniel said.

"I'm willing to get my guts shot out and you don't think I'm taking this seriously?"

"How long does it take your guts to grow back?"

"Okay, about a day. You're a jerk. So, what's your bright idea?"

Daniel landed the boat on a narrow apron of gravel, about 250 yards north of the machine-gun nest. From there, they picked their way over sea-carved sandstone, trying not to slip on green slime coating the rocks. Where passage was impossible, they waded into the water.

The current alternately tried to suck them out to sea and smash them against the rocks. Moth had an easier time with his strength and bulk, and his firm grip saved Daniel from becoming driftwood a few times. But when they neared the sea cave, it was up to Daniel to get them both inside, alive.

The machine-gun nest was tucked in front of the cave opening, on a ledge six feet above a rocky shelf. It was a problem, but not insurmountable. Daniel was more concerned about the mines he smelled.

"We could go in bold," he suggested, "like those Norwegians who took the Nazi hydroplant in the Global War."

"I don't know that one," Moth said. "Where the fuck's Norwegia?"

"God, Moth, read a book some time."

"Crumville ain't got a good library." He sighed. "I guess we go beetle, then."

Daniel unhappily agreed. He unsheathed his knife, covering the blade with his hand to prevent its gleaming black iridescence from drawing attention. The blade was impregnated with shinjin-mushi beetle shell, an abrasive essence good for tunneling. To conceal the noise of digging, he timed his attacks to coincide with the incoming surf. His blade dug into the cliff face, chipping away at soil and scrub root and sandstone as if it were rock candy. But even with his digger's best friend, this was going to take a long time.

He and Moth took turns chipping away until Daniel's shoulder started screaming from fatigue and Moth took over completely, hacking away like a miner with gold fever.

He muttered "Fuck you, cliff," between blows, and by the time he broke through he was almost frothing at the mouth.

"You scare me sometimes," Daniel said.

"That's just because you don't know what hard work looks like."

"It looks awful."

"Don't be an aristocrat, Daniel. It's ugly."

They climbed through the chasm Moth had made with Daniel's weak help and emerged inside a latrine. The tile walls echoed with the sharp ringing of alarm bells. Hiding behind a doorway, they watched a patrol of guards jog past.

Some carried firearms, others cleaver-clubs or lances tipped with serrated teeth. All wore black shirts and trousers, tucked into boots. Otis's guys usually wore suits, so Daniel assumed Sister Tooth was providing security.

Daniel disliked the prospect of knocking out guards just to steal their uniforms. For one thing, it left you with the burden of finding an out-of-the-way place to stash their unconscious deadweight, and unconscious deadweight was *heavy*. Even more burdensome, you didn't really want to permanently injure or kill anyone.

Unless you did.

In which case, everything became much simpler.

A pair of guards met each other in the hallway. The smaller of the two was about Daniel's size. The larger one was bigger than Daniel, but still four inches shorter and fifty pounds lighter than Moth.

"What's going on. Break-in?" asked the bigger guy.

"More like a break-out. The livestock we were holding upstairs got out of their cells."

"I didn't even know we were holding livestock. For leeching, I guess?"

The smaller guy shrugged. "Not my department. They had Beaumont watching them."

"Beau-moron? No wonder they got out. So what's the big deal? There's no way they're getting off the island."

"Bells ring, we scramble; that's all I know. Get your team and head upstairs."

"Aye aye," the bigger guy said, long-suffering.

Daniel exhaled with relief. They weren't looking for him and Moth. And, better yet, they weren't looking for Sam. The "livestock" were just a convenient distraction. Or, if Sam had actually paid attention when Daniel lectured him on heistcraft, maybe a deliberate distraction.

Moth pinched the cloth of his shirt and gave Daniel a questioning look.

Daniel nodded.

They stepped out into the hallway. There was less than a second of surprised hesitation from the guards, which was enough for Moth to drop both of them in one-armed chokeholds.

Minutes later, Daniel was comfortable in a slightly-too-roomy uniform, and Moth was grinding his teeth, trying to button his trousers.

Several pairs of footsteps sounded down the corridor, coming closer.

"Kill them?" Moth mouthed.

"Hold off," Daniel mouthed back.

He knelt and covered the stripped and unconscious guards' faces with his hands and thought back to the first time he'd tasted sint holo bone. It had been prepared by his father, scalding hot from the kettle, refined well enough to render Daniel invisible and enable him to walk right past the men who were busy cutting his father to pieces on the living room floor.

He used remnants of his father's gift that still remained in his cells, pushing it through the palms of his hands.

"Hurry," Moth whispered.

Five guards arrived, halting before Daniel and Moth. A tall woman with gray hair stepped forward.

"What's this?" she said, looking from the guards sprawled on the floor to Daniel and Moth.

"Two of the livestock," reported Daniel crisply. "Looks like they were trying to exit through the cave."

She looked them over, her eyes slightly glazed. "Are they still alive?"

"Yeah. We managed to take them down with nonlethal force. I don't think they're feeding them much upstairs. Should we take them back?"

The woman sluggishly brought her attention back to Daniel and Moth. She peered into their faces, regaining her focus.

"Good work," the woman said. "Take them to Storage B, and then join up with your team. We've got to get the rest of these cows rounded up. Sister Tooth doesn't want any delays."

"Yes, ma'am."

She led her team off, but stopped and turned around several yards down the corridor.

"You," she said, aiming a sharp finger at Moth.

Daniel tensed.

"Your pants are undone."

"Sorry," Moth said. But she was no longer listening. She turned and jogged away while Moth heroically tried to meet button to buttonhole.

"Moth, quit futzing with your pants and help me figure out how to get to the power plant from here."

"Did you see the look on her face? Like I was the worst, slobbiest guard she'd ever seen. Like I'm not super-overqualified to work here."

The power plant was the first target. Cutting the facility's power would mean no alarms, no surveillance cameras, and no lights—an even better distraction than escaped prisoners. Since the power was still on, that meant Sam and Em hadn't gotten here yet. Or else they had but something prevented them from getting the job done. Which suggested any number of bad possibilities.

"Moth . . ."

"I tell you one thing, there wouldn't be any escaped prisoners running around if I was in charge of this place."

"Moth!"

"Find where the power cables come out and follow them back to their source."

The alarm bells finally stopped clanging. Either all the prisoners had been accounted for, or else everyone who needed to know they'd escaped knew. Some of the guards and sentries would be returning to their normal stations.

"Grab 'em and let's go," Daniel told Moth.

Moth hoisted an incapacitated guard on each of his shoulders and followed Daniel down corridors carved from the rock. They came to a door, behind which hummed air handlers or some other equipment. A young man came out with a tool belt and gray overalls. He looked surprised to see Daniel, and when his eyes fell on Moth and his now-moaning cargo, he made a startled hiccup.

"Can we stash these guys in here?" Daniel asked quickly. "Or are you still working?

"No, no, I'm done. Uh . . . you want to leave them in *here*?"

"Just temporary until the holding pens are secure. But if you need to be going in and out, we can find somewhere else."

"No, it's fine. I gotta go reset some alarm boxes. Man, the infrastructure here . . . I'm telling you, if I was in charge—"

"That's exactly what I was just saying," Moth said. "Hey, you got a safety pin, by any chance? I got a problem with my pants."

"Sorry."

"No sweat," Moth said, despondent.

The technician left them alone, and Moth dumped the guards on the ground and proceeded to duct tape their wrists, ankles, and lips.

Daniel found a fuse box, with conduit branching to the bare stone ceiling. There was no open vent, but the blade of his shinjin-mushi knife would dissolve the rock like a seltzer tablet.

"Hey," Moth said as Daniel climbed up on a junction box to reach the ceiling.

"Yeah?"

"I know this is serious shit, but I'm having fun. You know?"

Daniel wasn't having fun. He was too worried about Sam to have fun. But having Moth with him helped make the worry something he could push back so he could keep moving forward. He grinned at his friend.

"I know."

It was slow going in the shaft. Like the rest of the complex, it was carved from the bare stone, most likely by the Hierarch himself, and it gave Moth only enough room to pass without scraping his head too often.

They followed the thickest of the power cables, and though they took some false turns, Daniel got the sense they were moving deeper into the complex. After a while, he stopped following cables and instead followed scents. His nose detected odd things—the aromas of magma, of pressures ascending from tremendous, subterranean depths. He smelled kraken storm, much brighter than any he'd ever smelled before. And also, dim traces of osteomancy that smelled like Sam. Most strangely, he caught a whiff of something that reminded him of himself. It was like looking at a mirror in a darkened room.

They turned a corner, and Daniel found himself facing a woman with a bayonet.

In the dark, Daniel had a difficult time focusing on her. Her aroma was confusing. Some kind of sint holo essence in her clothes, he suspected. But he recognized her face—the thin blade of a nose, the gray eyes, the cheeks, narrowing down to a mouth that seemed set in a mocking half smile.

"You're an Emma," he said. "You're Em."

Her eyes widened a little. "And you're Daniel Blackland." She didn't lower her weapon.

From behind her in the shaft, like a light emerging from a cave, came Sam.

Over the past few days, Daniel had thought about what he'd do when he found him. In some scenarios, he was too late, and he was mourning over Sam's body. He was building a fire with the hottest flame he could summon to make sure nobody would ever consume his boy's magic. In others he was screaming himself red in the face over Sam's reckless disregard for self-preservation. Daniel had given up ten years of his life trying to keep him safe, only to have Sam traipse into his enemies' stronghold.

"You're alive," whispered Sam, and he rushed at Daniel and wrapped his arms around him, and Daniel returned his embrace, and his tears of relief fell into Sam's hair.

And he could already feel his cells awakening, nourishing themselves on Sam's magic.

Sam pushed him away.

He felt it, too.

———

The reunion was brief and consisted mostly of exchanging pertinent information. Like Daniel and Moth, Sam and Em were trying to make their way to the power plant. From there, they would get to the firedrake hangar and poison the dragon in utero.

"Looks like you're just in time to join us," Sam said.

"I didn't come here to destroy the dragon, Sam. I came here to get you."

"That's not quite true," Moth said.

Everyone turned toward him.

"Moth—"

"I'm sorry, Daniel, but that's not true. Each one of us is here by our own choice. If Sam and Em want to get off the island, that's fine, I'm all for it, I will lead the way home. But none of us gets to withhold from the others. Team, right?"

Sam fixed Daniel with an unyielding stare. Maybe it was the light, or the tension between them, or the ordeals he'd suffered coming here, but his face looked older, leaner, harsher. He looked more like what he actually was: a younger version of the Hierarch.

"What are you not telling me, Daniel?"

There was a lot he wasn't telling him. But now wasn't the time for confessions. Focus on the job, Daniel told himself.

He reached into his bag for the small jar of bone.

"It's a coagulant," he said. "I stole it from Mother Cauldron. It'll kill anything. Or almost anything. Maybe a firedrake."

Sam held his hand out. "If you're not willing to use it, then let me have it."

Daniel slipped it back into his bag. "What if we make a deal?"

Sam's eyes narrowed. "What kind of deal?"

"I don't want Otis or Sister Tooth to have a Pacific fire-drake any more than you do. But the only thing I want even less is for them to have you."

"Okay? So?"

"You get off the island, and I'll slay the dragon."

Sam's expression softened, just a little. "No," he said gently.

"Just think for a minute, Sam. This way, we both get what we want. No more weapon of mass destruction, and I don't have to lose sleep wondering what else I could have done to keep you alive."

"No."

"Sam—"

"I'm sorry, Daniel. Please listen to me. Ten years ago, you charged into the Hierarch's castle and found me. One minute you had no idea I existed. And the next minute you devoted yourself to protecting me. You didn't raise me on stupid notions of heroism. You just showed me that when people do stupid things for the right reasons, sometimes they can live with themselves. Well, millions of people need me to do a stupid thing, and I need to do it, too."

All it would take was one strong kraken jolt to the center of Sam's chest. Enough to stop his heart. And then hydra regenerative and eocorn to keep him alive. Moth could haul him out, the Emma could go with them, and Daniel could finish the dragon business alone.

"There's something else you're not telling me," Sam said.

And here it was. Daniel forced himself to look at the boy.

"Did you know?" Sam asked him.

"No," Daniel said, his whisper in the stone tunnel like a weak exhalation. "Not until you were already gone. I really didn't. I would never knowingly consume your magic, Sam. Please believe me."

Sam nodded sadly.

Daniel reached to ruffle his hair, just like he did when Sam was small. And just like Daniel's father did when Daniel was small.

Sam stepped away. "Don't," he said.

Em and Moth watched all this. Discomfort and love was evident on both their faces.

"The power plant's this way," Em said. "And we're all going together."

Moth offered her his hand.

"I'm Moth, by the way."

"Em."

"I don't suppose you have a safety pin?"

She rummaged in her bag and found one.

"Em," Moth said, fixing his pants, "I'm fed up with everyone on this team but you."

Daniel peered through the vent, thirty feet down to the power-plant floor. There were two entrances, one at either end of the room, each manned by a pair of guards. Curiously, he spotted none of the surveillance cameras he expected. He supposed since this wasn't a shop or casino there was no reason to keep cameras hidden. Or maybe something about the environment made cameras inoperable.

Next, he took in the cables and steel latticework and apparatus, like the guts of a giant radio. He located the transformers, the circuit breakers, and control equipment. There was a ring of six glass tubes the size of phone booths set on a raised concrete platform. Cables snaked from the bottoms of the tubes through a gap in the floor, presumably a cable tunnel. The glass was darkened, and Daniel didn't know what the tubes' function was, but he wasn't sure he needed to. The equipment was pretty densely packed, and it wouldn't take much finesse to bring the whole place down. A few clusters of salamander-resin charges ought to do the trick.

So, drop a few rukh eggs to stun the guards, rope-ladder down to the floor, place the charges, grab the ladder, and have Moth pull him up before things went boom. Simple, violent, and nice.

A sharp scream cut through the noise. The tubes flared, illuminating human forms inside: six people, naked, suspended in standing positions by brackets under their arms. Their flesh was punctured by wires that fed into coiled devices at their feet. Arcs of lightning played over their skin, and they jittered and screamed. Daniel's cells responded, sending spikes of pain from the depths of his bones to the surface. His head flooded with scents of brine, with the delicious rot of the ocean floor and the fearful moans of fleeing sperm whales. The facility was being powered by kraken storms induced from the osteomancers inside the tubes.

Whenever Daniel thought he'd encountered all the ways in which Otis used people, Otis never failed to come up with a new twist. This had his fingerprints all over it, using osteomancers as human resources.

Should have killed him, Daniel thought. *Should have killed him before he teamed up with Sister Tooth and his other collaborators, before he got his hands on a Pacific firedrake skull. Should have killed Otis a long time ago.* Because Otis might be wrapped up in the back of Cassandra's van where he couldn't pull strings, but there wasn't much comfort in that. Otis had already pulled all the strings he needed.

Daniel turned to his companions. "We have a problem. They're powering this place with human kraken batteries. We blow the plant up, we kill six people."

Sam nudged Daniel aside to get a better look. "I thought Argent was supplying electricity. Why's he using an osteomantic power source?"

"This isn't Argent. This is Otis."

"Of course it is," Moth said. "What's the procedure, then?"

"No salamander charges," Sam said. "Not until we disconnect the batteries."

Daniel found himself feeling proud of him. "Agreed."

They quickly sketched out a revised plan. Regrettably, it would entail more risk than simply blowing the shit out of the place.

Daniel cut through the vent grate with his shinjin knife.

"Shut your eyes and hide your faces."

In rapid succession, he lit and dropped three rukh eggs to the floor. Searing-hot daggers of light struck his eyes through closed eyelids. Cracks of close-distance thunder punished his ears.

"Everyone still alive?" he said, blinking away spots.

They all were, though Moth professed to not be sure.

Below, the guards were rolling around on the floor and looking generally miserable and nonlethal. That wouldn't last, and the commotion of rukh thunder would probably bring more reenforcements. So things from here would have to move quickly.

The team descended the rope ladder, except for Moth, who remained in the shaft, ready to haul them back up. Spreading out, Em and Sam went to disarm the stunned guards and bind them up with duct tape. Daniel made for the glass tubes.

His skin prickled as he approached, even though the tubes had gone dark and quiet. He spent a few seconds examining the various connections and mechanisms and decided he didn't have time to understand them. He chose a tube at random and drew monocerus essence from his cells. The skin of his right hand burned and cracked and turned gray, and he hissed in pain as armored plating formed over his knuckles. He pulled back his fist and drove it through the glass. Shards fell with a musical scream.

Daniel at first mistook the man inside for a child. He barely reached five feet, and his eyes looked too big for his head.

"Can you hear me?" Daniel barked at him.

The man mumbled something and turned his head.

"Tell me how you're hooked into this thing. Can I just yank the cables?"

"My name is Tom." His voice was weak, but Daniel saw awareness and intelligence in his eyes.

"Hi, Tom. I need your help. I want to get you out but I don't want to hurt you."

"Too late for that." He showed the weariest smile Daniel had ever seen. "Do whatever you have to."

At least a dozen wire bundles emerged from Tom's flesh. How deep they penetrated was impossible to tell. Severing them might kill Tom or electrocute Daniel, but at least thirty seconds had passed since he'd dropped the rukh eggs and there wasn't time to perform a thorough study.

The blade of his knife sliced easily through the first bundle of wires.

"Still with me?"

Tom moaned. "Keep cutting."

He cut through a second bundle and watched for Tom's reaction.

"Still good?"

"Keep cutting," Tom said.

Daniel cut through the third bundle, and waited before cutting the fourth. "One more left, Tom. How are you doing?"

Tom closed his eyes and smiled. "Cut me free," he said.

Daniel sawed through the last bundle, and Tom sagged. His arms slipped out of the brackets supporting him, and Daniel caught him as he collapsed. He lowered him to the floor.

"You gotta walk, my friend. Get to the ladder and my big, strong buddy will haul you up."

By the time he finished the sentence, he realized Tom was dead. His mouth was twisted in a grimace of pain, but not as much pain as when he'd been alive. His open eyes stared at nothing.

Otis was so clever at getting Daniel's hands to commit his crimes.

And now what? Continue cutting the rest of the batteries free and hope they survived disconnection longer than Tom did? Go with the original plan and blast the power plant to rubble?

"Daniel," Sam called from his position at one of the entrances. "Something's coming."

Daniel smelled it, a redolent, billowing confusion of flame and kraken mixed with his father's aftershave and, incongruously, the raw-egg odor he associated with golems.

Sam identified it before Daniel did: "It smells like you."

Sam was right, and Daniel was afraid.

"Evacuate," he said. "Up the ladder, now."

Em and Sam hurried over from their respective positions. Em got there first.

"You and Sam go back into the cable tunnel. Make sure you replace the vent grate. Then get to the firedrake and finish things."

She looked at him, questioning. "What about you?"

"Just climb," he said. He meant for it to sound like an incontrovertible order, but the tone of pleading in it was unmistakable. Understanding, Em started climbing, and Daniel decided he liked her very much.

"What's going on?" Sam said when he reached Daniel.

"Too complicated to explain. Follow Em. I'll be right behind you."

"That smell . . . is that who I think it is?"

"I think so."

"Well, come on, then."

The odors fell on them like a collapsing wall. The last time Daniel had encountered osteomantic force this strong was when he'd faced the Hierarch. He'd barely survived that encounter. He staggered, but Sam held steady.

"Do you trust me, Sam?"

"I have to," he said at last.

The hesitation in Sam's answer broke Daniel's heart.

"Then for this last time, do what I tell you. Go with Moth and Em. Destroy the dragon. Let me deal with this."

Sam lingered.

"Whoever finishes their job first comes for the other," Sam said.

"Sure."

"Promise me, Daniel."

"I promise."

Sam turned and followed Em up the ladder.

From the vent, Moth looked down on Daniel, waiting for him to come up.

"I'm staying," Daniel said. "Strawberry field."

Moth's eyes widened. He looked down on Daniel as if he were already dead.

———

Daniel plunged his hand into his bag and found the jar of poison he'd stolen from Mother Cauldron. He reached into his cells for sense memories of confusion, of alluding perception, essences from the sint holo serpent, and concentrated them around the cold, polished surface of the jar.

He was standing in the middle of the room when the source of potent osteomancy arrived, alone.

He had more muscle than Daniel. His skin was a light, pasty beige, probably from spending time indoors. His face was hard, his cheekbones more prominent than Daniel's. Above his left eye was a rough, carnation-pink patch of skin, which Daniel knew was the legacy of a horrific wound. He didn't quite look like a twin, even though he was even more closely related to Daniel than that.

He stepped up to Daniel, examining him with keen fascination.

Daniel raised his hands in the air and surrendered to his own golem.

SEVENTEEN

Daniel followed his golem. There were no hand-cuffs or chains or weapons or guards. Nobody took his osteomancer's kit away.

He hoped they'd fight. It would be a good distraction. But this was better. He'd been caught in the act of sabotage alone, and maybe Sam's team could make it to the dragon hangar undetected.

Daniel and the golem went down tunnels and back corridors without speaking, except for an occasional "Watch your step" or "Don't bump your head" from the golem. Of all the things Daniel dreamed of feeling when meeting the closest thing he had to a brother, the very last thing was shyness.

"What do I call you?" Daniel asked him when the silences became too awkward to bear.

"My name is Paul."

"Paul Blackland?"

"Paul Sigilo."

"Mom's name."

Paul gave him a sideways glance. "Huh. Strange hearing someone else call her 'Mom.' I grew up an only child."

"Me, too."

They arrived at Paul's private quarters, a room carved out of the sandstone. Tapestries and a Persian rug and warm lampshades made it seem less like a hole and more like a grand sultan's tent. To gather his thoughts and courage, Daniel made a point of calmly examining the furnishings. The silks were embroidered with scenes from the Far East, of Chinese dragons laid out in osteomancers' workshops, being stripped of scale and skin, of cauldrons full of boiling osteomantic preparations.

"You're a better decorator than I am."

Paul shrugged. "You're always on the move. I've been here for five months."

There was a bed and a writing desk, but the room was dominated by a hefty oak table, arrayed with glasswork and burners and jars of tissue samples. Bones, both prepared in jars and raw, were scattered across the table amid books and loose-leaf papers. It had been a long time since Daniel had seen an osteomancer's materials of this quality. It reminded him of his father and induced a pang of something: nostalgia, sorrow, envy.

"I have to search your bag," Paul said apologetically.

Daniel unslung his satchel and handed it over. Like any good osteomancer, Paul used his nose first, opening the bag and sticking his face in. Only then did he reach inside and begin pulling out items: rukh eggs, salamander-resin charges, packets of meretseger, a bottle of seps venom, matches and spare knife and med kit. He searched inside all the pockets, ran his hands into every little fold, smelled the air in the bag, around the bag, around Daniel.

He handed it back.

"And now you. Sorry."

Daniel put his hands in the air and let the golem pat him up and down and go through all his pockets.

"You're only carrying basic gear. How were you planning to sabotage the firedrake?"

"I got attacked with tsuchigumo venom a few days ago. It's still in my system. I figured I could just bleed it into your dragon."

"That wasn't a very good plan. It'd take a lot more than that to harm a Pacific firedrake."

"It was very cleverly prepared tsuchigumo. It almost did me in."

Paul shook his head and looked uncomfortable, as if Daniel had said something socially awkward. "Was Otis Roth behind the attack?"

"Afraid so."

"I'm sorry."

The sint holo miasma he'd placed around the bottle of toxin from Mother Cauldron's kitchen had escaped Paul's notice, but Daniel was eager to change the subject. He turned to the work table. "Looks like you're a real osteomancer."

"I was trained by some of the best. Go ahead, look closer. I can tell you're dying to."

"It's funny that you said 'dying,' because usually when

someone invites me to examine their nefarious plans, it's a precursor to trying to kill me."

Paul laughed. It sounded familiar. "You associate with a vile crowd, brother."

Daniel took a slow circuit around the table. He examined skeleton diagrams, detailed studies of muscular and circulatory systems, pages written in osteomantic notation, much of it beyond Daniel's training and knowledge. But not all of it.

"The first time I met you," Daniel said, measuring his words, "it didn't seem like you'd ever be capable of this kind of work." He gestured at the table. "This is amazing."

"I actually don't have memories of that day," Paul said, moving over to a wood-and-brass cabinet. "I came out of the jar brain damaged. But once Mother brought me to San Francisco, she found some osteomancers who got things working right." He tapped the side of his head. "But you remember me?"

"Kind of hard to forget. Dad . . . my dad . . . was freshly murdered. I went to Mom at a safe house, and she was there for less than three minutes before she introduced me to you and then put you in a car and drove off. I never saw or heard from her again. So, yes, I remember you. That was kind of a big day for me."

Paul looked at Daniel with sympathy but no pity. It seemed like he wanted to say something but was holding back, and Daniel felt embarrassed.

"Want a beer?" Paul said finally, pulling two bottles from the cabinet. "My own brew." He popped the tops and handed one to Daniel.

So here I am, thought Daniel, *having a beer with my no-longer-brain-damaged, genius golem-brother. Oh, life.*

"You must have more questions," Paul said.

"Only very sensitive, personal ones."

Paul clinked his bottle against Daniel's and took a swallow.

Daniel took his own sip. The beer was cold and richly dark. "You were shot, on your knees, in a strawberry field. Shot in the *head.*"

"How'd you know about that?"

"I consumed some lamassu before a job. Lamassu is a—"

"We call it Sumerian sphinx up north. Very tricky stuff to work with. So you ate some, experienced psionic backlash, and connected with the part of your essence invested in me. Interesting." He cocked his head and smiled, as if waiting for praise. "Well, yes, that happened. Mother came back for me and they were able to repair me in San Francisco. Again, that's just what I've been told. I don't remember it. Fortunately."

"All right. So, your brain got better, your head got fixed, you grew up in San Francisco, got some outstanding osteomantic education, and no doubt there are thousands of other things that happened to you and turned you into the person you are. But I think for now, I'd like to skip ahead. This is great beer, by the way."

"I'm happy you like it."

"What are you doing in Southern California, Paul?"

Paul picked up an articulated model of a skeleton. It was sleek, with a long, spiked neck and wings.

"I'm here for the same reason you are. The dragon. Though I suspect our intents with regards to it are in opposition."

"You talk kind of funny," Daniel said. "But, yeah, I came here to destroy it. That's my role. I'm here to foul things up. What's your role?"

"I'm building a dragon. It's my dragon." He made the model's wings flap.

"Your dragon? Otis Roth might see that differently."

Paul made a dismissive gesture. "I needed Otis for the resources. Firedrake remains, osteomantic materials, this facility, which is conveniently distant from my rivals up north. I mean, you're correct, Otis thinks the dragon is his. But he's going to be disappointed. I don't suppose you've seen him recently?"

Daniel mulled it over. "Oh, why not tell you? I've got him packed away. You probably won't be seeing him again."

"Well, I have to thank you for that. He was useful, but he's an untidy thread."

Daniel laughed. "It's funny, because that sounds just like something Otis would say. He calculates the value of human lives on an abacus. He's like you. He's cold."

"Yet you're the one who has him 'packed away.'"

"That's not cold. That's red-hot rage."

Paul shrugged. "In osteomancy, extremes of cold achieve the same ends as extremes of heat. Sebastian Blackland's Law of Absolutes."

Daniel had learned that law when he was eight years old, from the man who the law was named after.

"You didn't know my father." Daniel said it as a declaration of fact, but it was really a question, and he hoped the answer was no.

"I know his writings. It's standard material in the Northern realm. Though they've scrubbed his name off all his theorems."

"Then how—?"

"Mother, of course. She told me about our father, and about her life in the South. And about you, of course."

It bothered Daniel to hear Paul refer to Daniel's parents as his own. It was like having to share toys with his surgically removed appendix.

"Was it satisfying?" Paul asked. "When you killed the Hierarch? They say you ate him alive, over the course of days."

"That might be a bit of an exaggeration."

"I thought so. You strike me as a practical fellow. You'd want to get the job done and move on as quickly as possible."

"Well, he was the man who killed my father. I was motivated by being really angry."

"But you aren't driven by need for vengeance. You do awful things, but only those you feel you must."

It was simultaneously unsettling and pleasing to be so succinctly understood. It was something Daniel sometimes experienced with Moth and Cassandra, a release of personal gravity he felt when someone knew him well enough to articulate things about him he wasn't even fully aware of. But at the same time, it was like having his skin peeled back.

He changed the subject again. "Have you met the Northern Hierarch?"

"Met her? I'm one of her court osteomancers. Like Father was to the Southern Hierarch."

"You better hope you're not like my father was. You know how that ended for him. What's she like? Is she nice?"

Paul smiled. "I would love to introduce you to her."

Daniel set down his beer.

He still hoped Sam was out there with Moth and Em, getting closer to the dragon. He wanted Otis to be disappointed, and Sister Tooth, and now Paul, and the whole bloody lot of them.

"A Pacific firedrake, capable of destroying entire cities," Daniel said. "That's quite a toy you're building. And who's the osteomancer you're sacrificing to give it life?"

Paul looked pleased. Daniel had impressed him. "How did you know I'm sacrificing an osteomancer?"

"Paul, you let me read your notes."

"Ah, yes, I did."

"Are you surprised I understood them?" Daniel said, lifting the sheet of calculations. It confirmed that the firedrake required the vivifying force of a living osteomancer to activate it.

"Not at all. I'm just surprised you could decipher my lousy penmanship."

"It's the same as mine."

Paul inclined his head, conceding.

"I'm not sacrificing anyone," Paul said. "Not the Hierarch's golem. Nor you. Like I said, it's my dragon."

Daniel let that sink in. He broke into laughter. "Oh, my god, you're really not . . . You're going to invest your *own* essence into the dragon? You are going to jump into a seething vat of magic and pump your molten, osteomantic goo into a quiltwork firedrake?" Paul just looked at him, straight-faced. Daniel banged his fists on the table. "Oh, my brother. Oh, my poor, lost brother. They didn't fix your brain damage. They just used it."

Daniel's laughter abruptly died away. He could find no more bitter humor in any of this. "Who sold you on this idea? It was Otis, wasn't it? He's conned me so many times."

"It wasn't Otis. Like I said, he serves me. This is my project. I've been working on it for a very long time. While you were growing up, robbing warehouses, I was studying. While you were road-tripping, I was preparing. I know what I'm doing."

"Melting yourself into a dragon. You can't possibly know what you're doing."

"I think, Daniel, that we view the world and our function in it differently."

"You can say that again." He picked up the beer bottle and tilted it back, draining the rest in a single swallow. He wiped his sleeve across his mouth and belched. "So, when do you go swimming? Can I watch?"

"I'd be honored to have you there. But of course I can't let you anywhere close to my dragon. You came here to slay it."

Daniel folded his empty bag with angry, jerky movements, using the motions as a diversion while he slipped his hand inside. "So how are you spending your last hours as something resembling a human being?" While he spoke, he retrieved the sint holo–fogged bone jar and transferred it into his pocket.

Paul brightened. "I thought we'd have dinner with Mother. I know it's been a long time for you."

Daniel remembered times when he observed himself from the outside. His earliest such memory was from a morning on a cold beach, the first time his father fed him magic, when Daniel glowed like a sun with kraken storm. Another time was when he came upon the scene of his father's magic being harvested by the Hierarch's agents. He remembered silently cataloging his father's bones and muscles as they were revealed to him with knives and saws. And he remembered watching himself cowering, insubstantial as tissue.

But not all these times were horrific. There was the day he lost his virginity to Cassandra, and he saw himself as the thin, awkward kid he was, looking ridiculous as Cassandra helped him along.

Daniel theorized that when his brain couldn't quite process what was happening to him, it tried to bail out of his body like a pilot from a crashing plane.

Now, he watched himself be led by Paul to his mother's quarters. Paul looked self-possessed and confident. Daniel looked lost.

She sat at a desk with her back turned to him, her hair

the color of iron, her spine rigidly straight. Aside from the desk, there was a canvas cot with a thin pillow and blanket, and a table upon which sat a tray with a half-empty carafe of coffee and an uneaten sandwich.

She was on the telephone, her end of the conversation consisting of grunts, some sharp "no"s, and silences that sounded like condemnation.

"Mother, I brought someone," Paul said.

She waved a hand. "Just a moment. We've had a bit of a prison breakout."

"Sister Tooth can handle that," Paul said. "This is more important."

Exasperated, she snapped a final order: "Just keep them away from the hangar. I'm not changing the schedule for this." She hung up and spun around on her chair, and Daniel saw his mother's face for the first time in twenty-two years. He felt as if he'd been grabbed by a tide, yanking him free of the mooring to which he'd been desperately clinging.

It was his mother. Daniel loved her, and he was going to murder her son.

She rushed to him, her face registering shock, pain, joy, or some blend of all three. Ultimately, it was unreadable. Daniel held himself stiffly as she embraced him, and if she noticed, it didn't lessen the strength of her hold. Despite his intentions, he loosened and returned her hug. He was surprised by how slight she seemed, how small. Of course, the last time he'd seen her, he was only twelve.

When she finally pulled away, she studied his face in a way that made Daniel wonder if she was going to count his fingers and toes. She'd find his pinky missing, and he thought he might enjoy telling her the whole story of Otis's betrayal.

She sniffed and wiped tears from her cheeks, very much like a person weeping with authentic emotion, and stared at Daniel with frank wonder, as if he were a newly discovered kind of creature.

"Hi, Mom."

She stepped back and kept her hands on his arms and looked him up and down.

"Daniel . . ." she began, then paused to gather herself. "Daniel, my Daniel. What are you *doing* here?"

"That's not important," Paul cut in before Daniel could respond. "This is a busy time. But I wanted to be here to see this. To see my mother reunited with her son. And to have a last dinner with you. It's perfect. The family together, finally, during an amazing time."

He beamed. He really did seem so happy.

"I'm here to sabotage your Pacific firedrake, Mom. But Paul caught me. Please don't be too mad."

She opened her mouth but was at a loss for words. Again, she composed herself. "This is all so much. Paul, couldn't we delay?"

Paul took his time answering. "No," he said softly, as if it pained him. "I'm sorry. The timing's critical. We lost one of the storm generators—"

"My fault," Daniel said with good cheer.

"—which put us back at least half an hour. Any longer,

and the vitalizing mixture could go beyond the conversion point, or the dragon's tissues could necrotize. I don't want to risk it. I'm sorry."

Daniel liked the way Paul described immensely complicated osteomantic processes without pomp. Then he realized why he liked it: it reminded him of his father. And then he stopped liking it.

"Shouldn't you be supervising this insane endeavor?" Daniel asked him.

"I am," he said, tapping his head enigmatically. "But there's not much to do at this point. The pot's on the stove and just needs to climb to the right temperature. That's a metaphor."

"Well, then by all means, let's eat before you have to go get stewed."

Daniel sat down to dine with his mother and golem: roasted peppers and mushrooms sautéed in garlic, fingerling potatoes, greens, and a cabernet, all set out on a table with a white tablecloth and a single candle. It was a small table and the distances were too intimate.

He thought Paul might abstain from food and drink to keep his system pure for the vitalization, but he took small portions of everything, even the wine. Daniel supposed a little tannin and alcohol wouldn't adversely affect a ten-ton firedrake.

Daniel poured himself a full glass and tossed it back. "You know who I wish were here? I wish Uncle Otis were here. I think I'd eat him. I know he's not osteomantically nutritious, but it'd be such a nice way of honoring what he's meant to me."

"Daniel's upset," Paul helpfully explained to their mother.

"Not at all. Let's catch up. When I last saw you, Mom, you were taking off to San Francisco with my brother, and you left me with dear Otis. He trained me as a thief and hired osteomancy tutors, and then he eventually sold me to the Hierarch and nearly got me killed. So that was my life. How've things gone for you, Mom?" He speared a potato.

"Daniel," his mother said, not with disapproval, or with hurt, but with the old edge he remembered. Daniel had never feared her. She was his protector. Right up to the moment she left. Hearing that warning tone in her voice reminded him of her steel. In Los Angeles, she was Messalina Sigilo, from Northern California, not just wife of a brilliant and well-placed osteomancer, but a mystery unto herself. No one ever quite knew what to make of her, but they sensed it was smart to fear her. To others, that tone of voice was a threat. To him, it was strangely comforting. It made him even sadder about everything.

"I guess we can catch up later, after Paul's dived into the soup. But first, I should probably expand on that comment about me being a saboteur." He refilled his glass. "What I meant by that is I came here to kill the dragon."

His mother neatly excised a potato with her fork and knife and chewed it thoroughly, her eyes searching Daniel's.

"We can't be angry with Daniel for wanting to destroy our project," Paul said, being a good brother. "He had no way of knowing we're involved with this. As far as he was aware, this entire thing was conceived and managed by Otis and the Los Angeles osteomancers. If that were the case, I can't say I'd blame him. In fact, once the project's complete, you'd be doing us all a favor if you burned Otis alive."

"I'm starting to like you, Paul." He checked his watch. "How are we doing for time? Can I ask a few questions before you have to . . . you know, do stuff?"

"I have some time."

"This one's for you, Mom. I just want to make sure I've got this straight: You're trading Paul's life in exchange for a living dragon?"

She took a small sip of wine. "I'm not trading anything. This is Paul's project. He's been working on it for his entire adult life."

"But you're still letting him jump off a cliff in an act of lunatic self-immolation." He turned to Paul. "That's a metaphor."

Paul raised his glass.

"Daniel," his mother asked patiently, "what did your dad teach you was the highest form of osteomancy?"

It'd been a long time since lessons with Sebastian Blackland. He recited the answer: "The purest expression of osteomancy isn't using magic, it's *being* magic. Not consuming the remains of an osteomantic creature, but becoming an osteomantic creature. I'd like to ask the rest of the questions. I don't feel like being quizzed."

"Paul isn't sacrificing himself. He's *becoming* himself. He'll still be with us, on this earth. I'll be able to see him, to talk to him, to love him. But he'll be different. He'll be elevated."

"That's a pretty twisted version of the lessons my father taught me."

"Sweetheart, no. It's really not. It's what he wanted for you. It's what we both did."

"You wanted me to self-immolate?"

"We wanted you to achieve the greatest osteomancy you were capable of."

"What if I wanted to be a professional baseball player?"

"Then we would have found you the best coaches and bought you a really good mitt. Did you ever want to be a professional baseball player?"

"Naw. I got hit in the eye with a ball once and set it on fire."

"That's an osteomancer's approach to things," she said, as if capping a well-constructed argument.

His mother and father had been united in their desire to make Daniel strong, to give him gifts of magic, to fulfill his father's ambitions, to serve his mother's mysterious agenda. This had the ring of truth, and Daniel felt the tug of the lure. He had her here, now, talking. Finally, all his questions would be answered. He'd understand why she fled to San Francisco. Why they'd never been reunited. Why she abandoned him to Otis. He'd learn the purpose of his pain.

He drained his glass again and refilled it.

There was something he'd been taught a long time ago.

If you had to do a thing, a thing you didn't have the nerve for, a thing that could result in disaster, but something you had to do, then you didn't hesitate. If you loved someone, you told them. You didn't worry about their response. If you were at war and you had a weapon that could defeat the enemy in a single attack, you didn't fret about the aftermath. You just dropped your bomb.

He'd learned this from Otis.

Daniel reached for the saltshaker and knocked over his wineglass.

"Oh, shit." He stood and reached across the table with his napkin to stop the flood of red from reaching his mother and golem. Hidden in the napkin was his jar of poison. "Sorry, sorry, sorry." As he clumsily mopped up and made drunken apologies, he used the napkin for cover and poured three drops of the poison into Paul's wineglass.

"You can tell us apart because I'm the clumsy one," he said to his mother.

Laughter was a rare thing for Messalina Blackland Sigilo, but she actually laughed at this. "Isn't that a liability for a thief?"

It was a good-natured jibe, and some of the tension left her shoulders and jaw, and she looked even more like the mother he remembered.

"Sorry, Paul," Daniel said.

Paul stood. "It didn't even touch me. But it's time Mother and I got to the hangar. Daniel, I'm so sorry we didn't have longer. And I truly wish I could have you there to witness this. But I'll have to keep you away until after the vitalization."

Daniel righted his glass and poured himself the last drops from the bottle. "A quick toast first. For, I don't know—not success, because I still think this is a perverse idea and I don't want Otis Roth within a thousand miles of a weapon of mass destruction. But we have to toast. You pick something, Paul."

"To reunions." Paul lifted his glass of cabernet and Mother Cauldron's poison. "To the one we just had, and to a better one in the future."

They all brought their glasses together. Daniel thought of stopping Paul from drinking. Was Paul his brother? Of course he was. And he was, without question, his mother's son. How could Daniel murder him, even to prevent him from becoming a monster?

Just short of touching his glass to his lips, Paul threw his wine in Daniel's face.

He turned to his mother. "Daniel was going to poison me," he said simply.

Venom burning his face, Daniel fell.

EIGHTEEN

The magic smelled strong and delicious in the space beneath the hangar. Sam wanted to drink it into his cells. He wanted the magic to mine its way into his bones, to settle in his marrow and simmer. This was a good place for him.

He and Em and Moth crouched among the thick concrete pillars supporting the hangar floor. There was little room to maneuver, almost all the space crammed with machinery. Seawater roared through massive pipes, into copper onion-dome boilers. Hundreds of smaller tubes rose to the ceiling, like the pipes of a great, steaming organ.

Moth wiped away sweat. "So, the dragon's cooking above us, and we're in the oven?"

"I think so," Sam whispered. "Argent's plans weren't specific about the dragon-vitalization machinery, but most osteomancy requires a heat source and a medium."

"I don't like it," Em said. "Where're all the cooks?"

It was a good question. The real osteomancy—precisely controlling the soup of magical essences around and inside the dragon—was likely happening upstairs. But there should at least be some engineers monitoring the machinery. Not to mention guards.

Moth removed one of the rukh eggs and a length of fuse wire from his bag. "I say we blow this shit up and burn the soufflé now, while we have a chance."

"It's not that easy," Em said. "If the soufflé's already made, then it's practically indestructible. We have to get closer to it so we can use the toxin."

"What makes you so sure?"

"I'm not sure, but that's what Cassandra Morales told us."

"Cassie said that? Okay, then." Moth seemed disappointed, but he wasn't going to argue with his old friend's counsel. "So, out of the oven, into the fire."

They continued on ahead, deeper into the metal forest, looking for a route up to the hangar.

"Someone's here," Em said.

Too late, Sam smelled bone.

In a flash, Moth snatched Em's bayonet from her hands and nudged the point against the small of her back. "Hands behind you," he snarled.

Em clasped her hands behind her, and Sam followed suit. A man and a woman stepped out from behind one of the onion-dome boilers. The man wore a white lab coat and carried a clipboard. The woman wore armor of bone. Her helmet was fashioned from the upper jaw of some kind of reptile, its spiky teeth curving around her face. A large scapula formed a breastplate, and interlocking vertebrae ran down her arms and legs. She unsheathed her sword, brandishing a blade of yellow bone. Outfitted like this, she had to be *praesidentum,* one of Sister Tooth's elite troops.

Sam put the picture together: a technician and his security escort.

"Am I ever glad I ran into you," Moth said. "I caught these two sneaking around. I think they're saboteurs."

The *praesidentum* took in Sam and Em and looked Moth up and down, inscrutable behind the teeth of her faceguard.

"I usually don't see uniforms down here."

"I know I'm not authorized," Moth said, "but I saw them enter the ventilation tunnels and followed them in here."

"You did the right thing. We'll take them to holding."

She wasn't buying it, Sam realized.

Moth realized it, too.

"Duck," he said. Sam and Em lowered their heads and Moth swung Em's bayonet into the *praesidentum*'s faceguard. The skull helmet fractured into several pieces, and when Moth pulled back the bayonet for another blow, it was obviously unnecessary. The *praesidentum* lay on the floor. Her head was dented in.

Moth handed Em's bayonet back to her, the barrel clotted with blood and hair. He took the *praesidentum*'s sword.

"Help us out, and you won't get hurt," Sam said to the technician.

The technician turned his head and vomited. He wiped his mouth with his sleeve. "Anything you want," he said.

He led them up a ladder to the hangar above, a space large enough to generate its own weather. The walls and the closed hangar doors seemed very far away through a veil of haze. A concrete tank large enough to house a blue whale dominated the building, its walls latticed by a web of cables and pipes. A few small portholes allowed a view of cascading bubbles inside.

Technicians worked at banks of blinking lights and gauges and dials. A lot of the lights seemed to be red. The techs flipped switches, checked their instruments, flipped more switches. There was a lot of running around and tense conversation. Nobody took any notice of Sam and his crew.

Their hostage peered at the workstations from a distance, frowning.

"Something wrong?" Sam asked him.

"I can't tell from here, but . . . yes, I think so."

"But the dragon's inside the tank?"

He nodded absently, looking like he wanted to run over to his colleagues and help them with whatever they were struggling with.

"How do we introduce something into the tank?" Sam pressed.

"Up there," said the tech, pointing far above at a grid-iron beam spanning the width of the tank. The beam supported a crane, from which hung a bucket the size of a trash dumpster.

"Lead on," Em told him.

"There's no way you're getting up there," the tech said. "I can't talk you past the guards."

Moth took hold of the tech's right hand. He caressed the tech's pinky with his thumb.

"I'm going to break one finger every ten seconds unless you figure out a way to get us up there. That's a ruined hand in less than a minute."

"Let him go," Sam said.

"Don't worry, kid. I think he's going to find himself being very clever by the time I get to his fuck finger."

"I said let him go."

They locked eyes, and Sam counted his own heartbeats. Moth released the tech. "You're the boss," he said.

Some shouts came from the workstations, and a few of the technicians left their positions, running not just with urgency, but with panic. Sam was about to question his hostage again when a sharp horn blared.

"That's the evacuation alarm," said the tech, more to himself than to Sam. "The controlling agent must have failed."

Hangar doors began to open, slowly parting with low mechanical groans. Technicians sprinted for them.

Liquid magic spilled over the side of the tank, splashing and sizzling on the concrete floor.

"Tell me exactly what's happening," Sam demanded of their hostage.

"The controlling agent . . . it's the essence of an osteomancer. Not just any osteomancer. There're maybe four or five in both Californias powerful enough. Maybe ours wasn't. Or maybe he got delayed . . ."

"Who? Who was the osteomancer supposed to be?"

"Paul Sigilo," the technician said as people dashed past

them—more technicians, laborers, even uniformed security and *praesidentum*.

Sigilo. Sam knew that name. Daniel's golem.

"Who is Paul Sigilo?" Em asked.

The tech's eyes fixed longingly on the hangar doors. "He's the son of Messalina Sigilo, the intelligence chief of the Northern Kingdom. Please, let me go. There's a chance I can get to one of the boats . . ."

Sam wasn't done with him. "What happens without the controlling agent?"

"The firedrake is unstable."

"It'll explode?"

"That would be great," Moth said with enthusiasm.

"It means the dragon will do whatever it does," the tech said. "Maybe it'll dive to the bottom of the sea and sleep for a thousand years. Maybe it'll annihilate the island and the mainland. It's not our dragon anymore."

A great shriek of moist, hot wind blasted through the hangar, reeking of molten rock cracking through ocean floor. Spider cracks appeared in the sides of the tank.

The tech shoved Sam away from him. "I'm leaving. Kill me if you want."

Sam let him go.

"Fold or raise?" Moth asked.

"Raise," Em said.

"Raise," Sam said. "Maybe it's not too late."

"I hate democracy," Moth said. He began to say something else, but screamed and stumbled.

Grimacing, he reached behind his back and pulled something from his shoulder blade: a knife. The blood-smeared blade was shaped like a griffin's tooth.

Behind him strode Sister Tooth, in a gleaming, black version of *praesidentum* armor. Her helmet, made from the skull of a minor dragon, was crowned by a ring of sharpened scales. Across her breastplate, a bandolier held an array of throwing knives. She gripped a talon-sword in her right hand and a dragon-scale shield on her left arm.

Sister Tooth was one of the old Hierarch's lieutenants, and she remained one of the great osteomancers of Los Angeles. She'd kept Sam constantly on the run, scurrying from motel room to motel room, robbing him of so many things. Daniel had taught Sam to fear her, and he did. And he wanted to test himself against her.

Moth smeared blood from his hand across his face like war paint. "Don't worry about what happens down here. I'll handle Lady Bicuspid. Get up on that bridge and slay that motherfucking dragon. Got me?"

Sister Tooth flung another knife. The blade penetrated deep into Moth's thigh. His scream became laughter, and he withdrew the knife and hurled it back. It clanged off her shield.

Sam searched his bones for dragon flame, and he began to feel the air in his lungs just beginning to warm when Sister Tooth surged forward and drove her blade into Moth's chest. His mouth stretched in a scream that became a gurgle of blood, and he dropped his own sword. Em took aim at the osteomancer and fired four shots at close range, the sounds hammering an echo in the hangar. Her bullets made tiny pits in Sister Tooth's armor. She barely seemed to register them.

Moth turned his head to Sam. Blood gushed from his mouth. He made eye contact with Sam and winked.

Still impaled on Sister Tooth's sword, he let out a great wail of agony and twisted his torso around, yanking the sword from Sister Tooth's hand. She reached to recover it, and he grabbed her wrist and snapped it like a broom-stick.

Through her howl of pain, he collapsed to his knees, coughing out blood.

Sam rushed toward him, but Moth shot out his hand. "Go," he rasped. "Go, or you're wasting my life."

Sister Tooth reached for another of her knives. Tendrils of smoke snaked from her lips.

Em took Sam's hand, and they raced for the access stairway to the bridge.

NINETEEN

The poison stole its way into Daniel's body. It unlocked the windows and doors of his defenses, snuck through his blood vessels, probed his cells, tested his osteomancy.

The sensations were familiar: the gripping cold, and the tons of weight settling on his chest. The craving to sink beneath black waves. This is what dying of tsuchigumo felt like.

He was dimly aware of the world around him. There were shadowed forms hovering over him, and he thought of the men who leaned over his father's dying body, butchering him.

"Don't touch him, Mother," someone said. "It works through contact as well as ingestion. Please come away."

"Help him." Her voice was paradoxically distant but cutting.

"I don't even know what it is. It has tsuchigumo shape-changing properties, but I'm not familiar with this variety. I'm sorry."

The concerns of butchers.

"You can't let him die."

Daniel pieced together where he was. The little dining room, with his mother and golem. He'd tried to kill Paul, but Paul had done him back.

Daniel tried to see. He couldn't tell if his eyes were open or not. A shadow hovered in front of him.

"I'm sorry, Daniel. I wanted to be your brother. I wish we had more time. I could have made you understand. We should have been brothers."

Daniel lashed out and grabbed the shadow with both hands. He tried to pull it toward him. He would spit and bite and spread the poison. He would kill the dragon. His vision cleared a little, and he saw Paul's face.

Daniel hardened his hand with monocerus hide and punched Paul's monocerus-hardened face. Paul took the blow and returned it with the force of a car crash. There was no pain, just a sense of drifting through gauze, and Daniel knew he was very close to death. He exuded contact venom, but the venom couldn't get past Paul's hardened skin. Paul raked his hand across Daniel's face, and Daniel screamed, losing ribbons of flesh to Paul's fingers.

Through the shocking pain, he heard his mother screaming. It must be very upsetting to see her boys squabble.

Paul drove his fist into Daniel's face. White flashes filled his vision. He hit him again, and Daniel's teeth shattered.

More screaming from his mother. Telling Paul to stop, or telling him to finish it. Daniel wasn't sure.

He heaved for breath. Blood ran down the back of his throat, and he choked on bits of broken teeth.

He'd been through worse.

He'd fought worse.

Paul couldn't beat him. He didn't have a chance. He was an academic, an architect, an artist, a builder. Just like Daniel's father.

Daniel was more like his mother: a thief and a murderer.

Beads of milky fluid condensed on Daniel's skin. It was the poison, forced out by his body's magic.

He reached out and raked monocerus hide from Paul's face and then, more gently, brushed his fingers across Paul's forehead. Paul gasped, and his skin turned gray.

Daniel gasped, too, but in surprise. He looked down on himself, separated from his body. The hydra and eocorn in his cells were already repairing the damage Paul had done to him. There was already new skin forming where Paul had gouged away flesh. Jagged nuggets of bone fell free from his gums, pushed out by the nubs of pristine new teeth.

He saw himself through Paul's eyes. Maybe it was because Paul came from Daniel's flesh and osteomantic essence. Maybe it was an echo of the connection Daniel established when he'd eaten lamassu a decade ago. Maybe it was Paul lashing out with some ability of his own.

No, Daniel decided he was in Paul's thoughts because they were brothers.

Daniel was Paul now.

He was confused and broken. He'd only been alive a little while, and he was so young. His head hurt from having a bullet tear through it in the strawberry field.

And now he was in a little shop in Chinatown, sitting on a hard wooden chair. The shelves were packed with little jars and paper envelopes and little cloth sacks, all redolent with osteomancy, but nothing Daniel recognized. This wasn't Los Angeles. This was San Francisco; the magics were alien to him. His mother was there, young again, in her full strength and ferocity. She demanded the man behind the counter give her and Paul a place to stay. She knew things about the man. She was a spy from this land, and she knew many secrets.

There were basements with operating tables. He was strapped down, and there were cold metal instruments digging into his brain. He didn't understand why he hurt, and he fought.

Then, later, more dark rooms, more tables, but greater understanding of what was happening. They were fixing him, the parts not built right, and the parts damaged by the gunshot in the strawberry field. He fought less.

His mother in a room of marble and emerald and bone, kneeling before a woman in a green dress and a crown of teeth: the wizard queen of the Northern Kingdom, the person whom, in Los Angeles, they called the San Francisco Hierarch. Paul was seventeen, and his mother was presenting him as a candidate for court osteomancer.

There were experiences without context. Books and scrolls by candlelight. Feverish toiling in workshops. Service for the wizard queen. The thrill of discovery, but not much fun.

And he looked at his scarred face in the mirror and saw more than one face staring back. He knew of Daniel, his lost brother in Los Angeles. They'd never met, but Paul loved him.

He saw Paul through his own eyes again. And now, at this moment, Daniel loved him back.

Paul looked up at him, silently pleading for his life.

Daniel kissed Paul's forehead and killed his brother.

He rose to his feet and stood over Paul's corpse.

"Heal him," his mother said. Her voice was frighteningly calm, like a still mountain in the moment before an avalanche.

"I can't."

"You're an osteomancer. You have eocorn. You have hydra. You healed yourself. Heal him."

"He's dead. I killed your son."

She rushed at him, grabbed his face with both hands, dug her nails into his skin. "Heal him," she roared.

"I'm sorry," Daniel said. Streaks of blood ran down his face and his mother's fingers. "There's nothing I can do. I killed your son."

Her grip loosened. She took her hands away.

"He was your brother."

There was so much dishonesty in her declaration. But also some truth.

Paul's tissues were breaking down. His skin looked like gray foam.

She turned to go to Paul's body, but Daniel took her wrist.

"Don't, Mom. It's not safe."

She regarded Daniel's hand and looked back up at him. He thought she would attack him again, and he would let her. But she closed her eyes and took a breath, and when she opened them again, he saw a little of what the Los Angeles powers feared in her.

"You thought killing Paul meant the dragon couldn't be vitalized. That the dragon couldn't be brought to life. Kill the vitalization force, and the dragon dies. Was that it? What that your theory?"

"Yes."

"Well, my son. You were ignorant. Vitalization doesn't provide life. It doesn't provide animation. It just provides control."

The osteomancer's craft was drawing magic from bones. Capturing it and storing it, and using the creatures' power. But always guided by human intelligence.

Daniel realized his error.

"You were worried about Otis having a bomb," she went on, sounding like she was pronouncing sentence on a condemned man. "But you helped create a living bomb without sentience. Without Paul's consciousness, there's nothing to control it. If we're lucky, it'll just destroy the island. More likely? It'll burn half the kingdom."

"Otis told you that, Mom. To convince you Paul had to die. Because he saw him as a threat."

"No, Daniel. I helped design the dragon. Just like I helped design Paul."

Ah. A nice sword thrust there.

He turned his back on her.

"Where are you going? We have to evacuate."

"Without Paul, the dragon has no consciousness," Daniel said. "It's even more dangerous. Isn't that what you just said?"

"Daniel . . . no. Come with me off the island."

"Who on this island can replace Paul's osteomancy?"

"I just lost one son. I won't lose another." She fell apart now, shuddering as Paul's body dissolved before her eyes, as Daniel prepared himself to die. Her face red, her voice ragged, the smell of stress hormones and grief radiating from her, she was still the traitor and spy and manipulator, and the woman who'd given up Daniel and kept her secrets. But she was also his mother, and she was in pain, and she could still break Daniel's heart.

"You have a way off the island, Mom?"

She managed a nod.

"Use it. I love you." Before he reached the door, he turned back to her for the last time. "You know what happens when you use people, Mom? They get used up."

TWENTY

Sam and Em climbed the ladder to the bridge, and Sam became horribly annoyed with whoever thought it was a good idea to call it a "bridge," because it was little more than a beam, maybe a foot wide, with no guardrails.

"You okay with heights?" Em asked him.

"They make me feel very tall. You?"

"I have no quip," she said. "I detest heights."

Sam stepped out on the beam, holding his arms out for balance. Em let him get a few feet out before following.

The Pacific firedrake lay below them in the tank, a hundred feet long from the sharp blade of its nose to the tip of its flukes. Its outspread wings spanned an even greater distance. Wing membranes undulated hypnotically in the roiling tank, like the canopy of some great jellyfish, all kaleidoscopic whorls of blue and green and purple. Fronds grew down the dragon's spine, anemone tendrils seeking fish to eat, and from its nostrils came bubbling gusts of super-heated water. Alive, the beast stirred, pulling against the heavy chains weighing it down and at the spaghetti of hoses pumping magic into its arteries.

The firedrake sang out to the magic in Sam's bones. His skeleton vibrated, as if it wanted to burst through his flesh and fly. The Hierarch had eaten the bones of dragons and wyverns and inferior firedrakes, and he passed these magical essences to Sam. The essences in him recognized the Pacific firedrake as their king.

The dragon's tail lashed out, breaking the surface of the fluid, and came down with the thud of a breaching whale. Waves washed over the sides of the tank. The concrete walls fissured and began to crumble. Arching its neck, the dragon raised its head out of the water and exhaled a storm of flame, billowing masses of orange and red edged with purple and black. The heat collided with Sam, blowing back his hair. He screamed, simultaneously terrified and exulted, and wobbled. Em reached out and grabbed his bicep, and they teetered together. Sam felt more than the tug of earth's gravity. He also felt the dragon's.

In that tiny slice of a moment, he was transformed. Sam was a magical creature, created from osteomantic cells, not unlike the dragon, and the last few days had brought him closer to new magics, and to his own power. He'd found himself wanting to test it, and surrender to it, and become it. He didn't simply want to be an osteomancer. He wanted to be osteomancy.

But there was Em, gripping his arm. She would not let him fall.

"I love you," he said, regaining his balance.

"Oh, hell, shut up and kill the dragon, Sam."

He removed the bone jar of poison from his bag. The odor pushed through the seal, thick and spidery with elements of tsuchigumo. He twisted the stopper out. Even now, it tried to change its form and leap from the jar into Sam's hand.

He hurled the jar. It made more of an indentation than a splash when it hit the osteomantic medium in the tank— the stuff was more viscous than it looked. Wisps of smoke rose as the osteomancy claimed the jar, dissolving the bone into a talclike powder and releasing its contents, a tiny swirl of black ink.

It seemed impossible that such a small quantity of poison could have any effect on the monstrously large creature, and Sam despaired that the endless span of the last few days had finally come down to a failure almost too small to notice. But then the little dark blot began to move. It spread in a slick over armored scales. Inky tendrils reached out, hungry and malignant and probing. It soaked into the dragon's hide, as if its impenetrable shell were a sponge.

The dragon's brilliant colors dimmed, the pigments seeming to evaporate, and its wing membranes grew brittle and began to flake like autumn leaves. Its tail slowly sank to the bottom of the tank. Its head and neck rose slightly higher in the osteomantic medium, like the bow of a ship sinking stern-first, and then the rest of the dragon slipped below the surface of the calming waters. It lay there, no longer moving.

Sam felt relief but no joy. Something magnificent had

been lost. The life of the dragon measured against the lives of millions of people was not a difficult equation to work out, and Sam knew he'd made the right choice. But what was it Daniel always said about Otis Roth? Otis loved maneuvering people into making awful choices. This was Sam's awful choice.

Em gave his fingers a little squeeze and kissed his cheek. "We did good," she said.

But the job wasn't finished. There were Moth and Sister Tooth. There was Daniel and his golem. He turned to climb down from the bridge when bubbles exploded to the top of the tank. Black water gushed from widening cracks in the tank walls, and a dreadful moan shook the hangar. The dragon raised its head from the tank. It stretched its jaws and screamed flames to the ceiling.

Chaos could be a gift. Daniel knew how to get things done in chaos. He found the hangar in a state of chaos, klaxons blaring, people running, the stench of osteomancy. He couldn't see Sam or the Emma or Moth anywhere.

The hangar was a vast maze of equipment, including the huge tank in the middle of it. This was the firedrake's gestation tank. Osteomantic medium spilled over the sides, releasing scents of deep sea and fire and the thin, cold edge of high-altitude air.

He called Sam's name. A weak, familiar voice answered, "Over here."

He found Moth lying in a pond of blood. His clothes were in shreds, his arms and legs lashed with deep lacerations. There was a hideous gash across his throat, a sodden mess of blood on his chest. Beside him lay a bone sword, red and wet halfway up the blade.

Daniel knelt.

"Hey, buddy."

"Ugh," Moth said.

"You okay?"

"Five minutes."

Daniel could smell the hydra and eocorn essences working to repair him. Rent tissues regrew, almost fast enough to see. But that didn't mean Moth wasn't hurt, that he wasn't in pain.

Nearby lay a woman, facedown, surrounded by shards and pebbles of shattered bones.

"Is that Sister Tooth?"

"Used to be," Moth rasped. "She ain't going anywhere."

"The kids?"

"On the bridge. Tried to buy them time."

"You did, buddy. You did great. Thank you."

Moth closed his eyes. "Five more minutes."

"I'm going to get Sam and Em and send them down to you. Can you do one more thing for me?"

Moth moaned. "Do I need to write it down?"

Even now, Moth could draw a smile from Daniel. "No. Just get them out of here safe."

Moth lifted his head and rolled over, raising himself on one elbow, then sagged back down. "What about you?"

Daniel stood. "Don't worry about me. Just take care of them."

Before Moth could stop him, he ran off toward the bridge.

"Wait," Moth shouted in a strained voice. "Five more minutes."

Moth had given Daniel his friendship and life, but Daniel couldn't give him five minutes.

Craning his neck, he spotted the small figures of Sam and the Emma near the ceiling. He almost wept with relief. For ten years, he'd had one goal—keep Sam from becoming plundered treasure. He couldn't say he'd given Sam a good life. But he'd kept Sam alive. At least he'd done that.

There was just one final task to perform, and then he'd be satisfied.

He was only three rungs up the ladder when the firedrake awoke.

Sam and Em clasped hands to keep from falling off the bridge. Flaming cable insulation rained down from the ceiling. Below, the firedrake thrashed and bellowed in a storm of foaming ostoemantic solution. Chunks of metal flew apart as the last of the chains holding down the dragon's neck shattered.

"We didn't kill it," Sam said, rather unnecessarily.

Em tugged his hand, trying to draw him back to the

ladder. He looked at her, and knowing what he had to do now, he grew angry. He wished he could solve high school mysteries with her, and make love to her, and get through a breakfast without being hunted. He wished he could visit Fernando Bautista and tell him what his wife, and Mayra and Ana and Miguel's mother, had died trying to prevent. He wished he could tell Daniel everything was okay. It didn't even matter whether or not Daniel knew he'd been consuming Sam's magic. Daniel had saved his life, and then he'd given Sam ten years of his own. He would give Daniel all his magic.

But he could do none of these things.

"Em, get to the floor."

"Not without you."

Sam didn't say anything. Not that he didn't want to tell her everything, but he couldn't find his voice. He was scared.

"Don't," Em said. "Don't you dare." She tightened her grip on him.

"You don't even know what I'm going to do."

"You're going to do something that you're afraid to tell me about, which means I'm not going to let you do it."

"I have to." He heard the pleading in his own voice. Was he asking her to let him go? Or was he asking her to give him another option so he wouldn't have to leap into the soup, let it dissolve him, break down his magic and life?

"Don't you dare!" she screamed.

The dragon's tail smashed into the side of the tank, and

a section of the concrete wall collapsed. Osteomantic solution flooded out.

"Believe me, I don't want to," Sam said. "You have another way?"

She didn't. There was no other way. She only pulled harder with both arms. He tried to plant himself on the twelve-inch-wide beam, but she was stronger than he was, and he couldn't resist her without plunging both of them into the solution.

"I have another way."

At the top of the ladder, stepping out onto the beam, was Daniel. How long since Sam had last seen him? An hour? Less? But he looked different. More weathered, with new scars.

Another way, he'd said.

He knew what Daniel meant. And he wouldn't let Daniel do it.

"Thanks," Sam began. "Just . . . thanks. Thanks for rescuing me, that first time at the Hierarch's castle. And all the other times." The words were hard to find, and hard to speak, as if he had to gouge them out of steel. "I'm sorry I ever doubted you."

The dragon writhed and broke the last of the chains. Daniel came sprinting down the beam, mindless of how narrow it was.

Em still held fast to Sam's hand. She would not let him go.

Sam knew all the osteomancy he possessed, and he needed it now, just a small bit, used with control. He sum-

moned the kraken energy lodged in his vertebrae. It trav-
eled up his spinal column, into his scapula and clavicle. It
shot down the length of his humerus and radius, into his
carpals and metacarpals, and, finally, through the bones
of his index finger. The energy was powerful enough to kill
a man. When he touched Em, he used only enough to sting.
She didn't release her hold on him, but her grip loosened
enough for him to slip out.

He spread his arms like wings and leaped off the beam.

Sam glanced off the dragon's back and rolled into the
solution. His clothes unraveled. His flesh and muscle
sloughed away. In seconds, as he descended through the
osteomantic medium, he was nothing but the rich brown
bones of La Brea specimens, the deepest, purest magic
Daniel had ever seen. Then Sam's bones dissolved into grit,
and he was gone.

Emma grabbed Daniel and wrestled with him until he
was firmly on the bridge.

She stared blankly into open space, but her voice was
firm. "You're not going after him. We have to leave."

Sam was gone.

And Moth was still on the hangar floor.

The dragon expanded its wings, and the tank walls
burst with the low, grinding moan and clatter of boulders
tumbling in an avalanche. The last of the solution thun-
dered out, sizzling as it washed over the hangar floor.
Free, the dragon stretched its wings to their full width,

more like liquid stained glass than the gelatinous membrane of a delicate sea creature. Banks of equipment tore away from the bolts holding them to the floor. Severed cables spat sparks, and fires broke out all over the hangar. The dragon gathered itself, coiling its tail. A razor-edged, jeweled mountain rose as it hunched its back. Angry at having been caged, the monster reared up on its hind legs, rising above the bridge. A terrific wind threatened to push Daniel and Em off their perch, and they clutched each other and screamed. Atop the towering neck, its sleek fuselage of a head aimed itself at Daniel. Its eyes were white-yellow suns, blinding.

Squinting through tears, Daniel looked into those eyes. He searched for a sign of awareness, of intelligence, of Sam. He saw only the beautiful, horrific fury of a Pacific firedrake.

Legends said the Pacific firedrake was the mount of gods. What an absurd lie. If there were gods, surely the firedrake was their king.

The dragon shivered, armored plates clanking like steel slabs. Cracking the concrete floor, it shifted from foot to foot. It cocked its head from side to side, impossibly fast and birdlike for such a colossal creature.

Strangely, to Daniel, it seemed unsure.

"He's finally going to fly," Em whispered.

As fast as they could manage, Daniel and Em sped down the length of the beam and scrambled down the ladder. The moment Daniel's foot touched the hangar floor, the dragon surged forward. Its back ridge sliced though the beam, right where he and Em had stood. With groans of deformed metal and cracks of snapping cables and bolts, the bridge came down. Debris was still crashing to the floor as the firedrake cleared the hangar doors.

Reflected stars lighting the dragon's translucent wings, it glided out over the waves, and then, with three air-ripping wing beats, it took to the sky.

Left behind in the wreckage of the hangar, Daniel could only watch it go.

TWENTY-ONE

Daniel, Moth, and Em washed up on the shores of Los Angeles in a leaking boat with a nearly empty gas tank.

Em navigated them to the stone jetty at Venice Beach, and from there, they dragged themselves up the beach and caught a taxi. Morning rush-hour canal traffic crept along.

They were a conspicuous group. Em still wore her combat gear and looked straight ahead in a stone-faced mask that couldn't conceal her grief. Moth slumped in a heap, exhausted, his wounds healing but his torn clothes scabbed with blood. Daniel stared out the window and searched the sky for outspread wings.

"Where are we going?" he asked Moth. It must have been Moth or Em who gave the driver directions. Daniel hadn't been paying attention.

"West Hollywood."

That meant Cassie's place.

"She must have left town by now."

"She's still family," Moth said.

They arrived at the little pink house on the tree-lined canal, and Daniel watched the cab's wake fade into ripples. He thought of running after it and getting back in, and telling the driver to go until the canal's end, and then Daniel would pick a direction and walk away from Los Angeles, all the way to the end of the earth.

He'd just repeat what he'd done for the last ten years, only without dragging anyone with him.

But there was a little unfinished business to take care of first.

"Wake up, Blackland."

Em stood on the porch, waiting for something.

"What?"

"I picked the mechanical lock, but you're still an osteomancer, right?"

Of course. Cassie would have employed sphinx locks.

He got out his jar of sphinx oil and rubbed it over the keyhole with the sponge stopper. A crackling dry-grass voice asked the riddle: "What is the word for 'secret'?"

Despite everything, he smiled. Cassie had sealed up her house with a riddle she knew he could solve.

He answered with his mother's name. "Sigilo."

She'd left the house furnished and decorated with folk-art chickens and Día de los Muertos art, and every lamp and rug and picture on the wall was a thing Daniel had never seen. Here was the person he knew as well as he knew himself, and here was the life she'd led without him.

"There's a note," Em said, picking up an envelope from the table in the little dining nook. It wasn't addressed to anyone, but she handed it to Daniel as a matter of course.

Daniel read it to himself first, then aloud. "The fridge is stocked. Help yourself."

Moth limped to the kitchen. He came back several seconds later, dejected. "There's just food in there. That's all it said?"

"There's an address for a Chinese restaurant."

And now Moth grinned, a beam of light from a grimy face. "Restaurant code. I love it. When do we go to find her?"

"I'm going to leave her alone," Daniel said.

"What?"

"You were right to keep me away from her, Moth. I do this too much, gathering a little crew together, leading them on stupid missions that always go to shit. I'm sorry I did it to you again. And you, too, Em."

Em barely afforded him a glance. "There's a Pacific firedrake. I tried to destroy it, because someone had to. It's like I told Sam—it's not about you."

Moth looked at Daniel, sad and helpless, waiting for Daniel to give him a direction. He always needed a flame to fly into.

"What's next, then?"

"You two should go home," Daniel said. "Moth, go back to Crumville and your business and your partner. Em, go back to your sisters. Thank you for helping me. Thank you for helping Sam. With luck, the dragon will take to the ocean and sleep at the bottom for a hundred years. But I wouldn't count on luck. So get away from the cities. Especially Los Angeles. Nothing good ever happens here."

He went out to the backyard and found a garden shed. This would be the "fridge" in Cassie's note. There were good conventional locks, and another sphinx lock. This time, the riddle was "What is the osteomancer's greatest flaw?"

"Self-pity," he said, and the door opened for him.

"Thanks, Cass."

He half expected to find a duct-taped Otis inside the shed, alive or dead. Instead, he found weapons and magic and enough gear and equipment to launch a one-man war. He wasn't sure what Cassie intended him to do with it. There was no one left he cared to fight.

He returned to the house.

Gabriel Argent was sitting at the kitchen table.

"He knocked," Moth said. "I figured we should let him in. Left his hound on the steps." Em stood next to Argent, gripping a chef's knife.

Daniel dragged back a chair and sat. "Gabriel. Has it never occurred to you to hide from me?"

"Water doesn't hide," said Gabriel. "It flows inevitably to its destination. In my case, that's you. I have a feeling that one day I'm going to find myself with your foot on my neck, with lightning in your teeth and fire in your hands."

"Yes," Daniel said.

"The only question is, will it be in five years or in five minutes?"

"That is definitely a question you should be considering."

"Well. Before you make out your schedule, I wanted to

show you something." Gabriel removed a photograph from his coat pocket and laid it on the table. "This was taken from one of my dam inspection planes."

He slid it across to Daniel.

With lightning already sparking in his teeth, Daniel picked it up.

The fires were out but the cinders remained hot. Yesterday, this had been a truck stop with a gas station and convenience store. Today it was blackened rubble, burned-out shells of cars, heat-blistered concrete and slag. Daniel picked through the wreckage.

"Where've you been?" he said to the footsteps crunching behind him.

"Taco shop."

"Moth get hungry?"

"No," Em said. "Well, yeah, of course he did. We got you carne asada to go. But I found a guy who was here when this happened."

She'd been back to see her sisters since leaving Cassie's little pink house in West Hollywood. They'd gotten her cleaned up and fed her and given her a soft bed with fresh white linens, but she didn't look like she'd slept much in the past two weeks. None of them had. Daniel had just returned from the Bautistas' farm, and speaking to Fernando Bautista and his children had been enough to deny him sleep for a few years.

"What did this guy in the taco shop say?" he asked Em.

"He said fire rained down from the sky. People actually went outside to look, if you can believe that."

"I can. People are always people."

"Their lookie-loo tendencies probably saved a lot of lives. The rain got heavier, and things started to catch fire. The convenience store was the first to go. Some people gassing up drove away, other people ran for the road. Then there was a scream. The guy said if the sky itself could scream, that's what it would sound like. After that, a flood of fire, and then the gas tanks blew, and then . . . Here we are."

Daniel hadn't found any bodies in the wreckage, but that didn't mean there weren't ghosts here. A firedrake's breath could exceed 7,200 degrees Fahrenheit. People vaporized at that temperature.

"If you count the Enamel Tabernacle, and Otis's warehouses, and the San Gabriel Grand Terminal . . ." Em said.

"And now here in Mecca, where that hound tracked you. The firedrake is moving north."

And if that's where the firedrake was going, Daniel would go there, too, as surely as if he were an iron filing drawn to a magnet. North, where a different Hierarch reigned. North, where his mother was grieving her murdered son.

Moth came up with a white paper bag clutched in his paw. It smelled of roast pork. "What's next on our itinerary?"

Daniel looked at the photo Argent had given him. It was grainy, taken with a telephoto lens, and overexposed against the daylit sky: a thin S-shape, like a serpent, with the smudged suggestion of wings. It was labeled with the map coordinates where Argent's pilot had taken the photo, and the letters *PF*.

Pacific Firedrake.

Daniel scratched some of the charred dirt at his feet and smelled beneath his fingernails. He got out a pen and crossed out the *PF*.

In its place, he wrote *Sam*.

ACKNOWLEDGMENTS

First and always, profound thanks to my wife, Lisa Will, for all the things, big and little. Thanks also to my editor, Patrick Nielsen Hayden, his assistant Miriam Weinberg, Patty Garcia, Leah Withers, Theresa DeLucci, Irene Gallo, Bethany Reis, and the entire team of professionals at Tor Books for art direction, design, copyediting, proofreading, sales, marketing, promotion, publicity, and all the many, many things that transformed my manuscript into a book and helped get it into your hands. Thanks as well to my agent, Caitlin Blasdell, for representing my interests so well.

I owe a great deal to the fine folks at Mysterious Galaxy Bookstore, in particular Patrick Heffernan and Maryelizabeth Hart, for their constant support and championing of my work.

Thanks to Fred Kiesche for submarine neepery, and to Chad Collier for airplane neepery. People are really nice to me.

And a very big thank-you to Deb Coates and Jenn Reese, for friendship, camaraderie, and cheerleading. And an especially big thanks to Sarah Prineas, who sent me an e-mail refuting my claim that I'd just written the worst book ever. In the end, I found some of her arguments at least worth considering.

Finally, thanks to my officemate, Dozer. He is a dog.